EVERY WOMAN
NEEDS AN ESCAPE

*A NOVEL*

# ADDICTED

**NOW
A MAJOR
MOTION
PICTURE**

NEW YORK TIMES
BESTSELLING AUTHOR

# ZANE

"The woman does incredible, erotic things with words."
—ERIC JEROME DICKEY

# zane

# Addicted

## A NOVEL

**ATRIA** PAPERBACK
New York London Toronto Sydney New Delhi

*To my children "A" and "E"*
*Mommy loves you!*
*Thank you for coming*
*into this world through me!*

**ATRIA** PAPERBACK
*A Division of Simon and Schuster, Inc.*
*1230 Avenue of the Americas,*
*New York, NY 10020*

*This Atria Paperback edition August 2014*

**ATRIA** PAPERBACK *and colophon are trademarks of Simon & Schuster, Inc.*

*For information about special discounts for bulk purchases, please contact Simon & Schuster Special Sales at 1-866-506-1949 or business@simonandschuster.com.*

*The Simon & Schuster Speakers Bureau can bring authors to your live event. For more information or to book an event, contact the Simon & Schuster Speakers Bureau at 1-866-248-3049 or visit our website at www.simonspeakers.com.*

*Manufactured in the United States of America*

*10  9  8  7  6  5  4  3*

*ISBN 978-1-4767-4804-7*
*ISBN 978-0-7434-4657-0 (ebook)*

# Praise for *ADDICTED*

"Snatched me up from the first page and didn't let me go until the end. A great read!"

—Margaret Johnson-Hodge,
author of *Butterscotch Blues*

"Hot! Sensational! This is one you won't be able to put down!"

—Franklin White,
author of *Fed Up with the Fanny* and *Cup of Love*

"Erotic and well written, *Addicted* sizzles and satisfies. Zane has managed to pen a novel that expertly portrays both romantic and earthly love and does more than simple justice to each."

—Karen E. Quinones Miller, author of *Satin Doll*

# Praise for Zane
# and her unforgettable erotic novels

"Zane's writing warms me, heats me up, satisfies me with a passion."

—Eric Jerome Dickey

"Arguably not since the emergence of Nancy Friday has American letters produced a purveyor of erotica with such mass-market appeal."

—*The New York Times*

"A legend among her fellow authors."

—*Today's Black Woman*

"Sweaty, grab-the-back-of-his-head-and-make-him-scream sex."

—*Entertainment Weekly*

# Other works by Zane

# Edited by Zane

# acknowledgments

First off, I would like to thank God for not only everything that He has given me but also for everything that He has taken away—for without failure and a great deal of loss, one can never truly be inspired. I would also like to thank my parents for bringing me into this world, nurturing my creativity, and supporting all of my endeavors. To my children, "A" and "E," thanks for the daily motivation to make something better of myself, for the moments of laughter, and for the patience you have shown while I am writing.

Thanks to Charmaine and Carlita, my biological sisters, and my brothers-in-law, Rick and David, for their continuous support and encouragement. To my sisters-in-heart: Pamela Crockett, Esq., Shonda Cheekes, Pamela Shannon, MD, Cornelia Williams, Judy Phillips, Sharon Kendrick Johnson, Gail Kendrick, Lisa Kendrick Fox, Michelle Askew, Esq., Janet Black Allen, Karen Black, Renay Caldwell, Ronita Jones Caldwell, Martina Royal, Dee McConneaughey, and Janice Jones Murray, thanks for lending an ear when I need to vent, a shoulder when I need to cry, and a joke when I need to laugh.

To Aunt Rose, my 83-year-old aunt and biggest fan, thanks for reading everything that I send you and giving a detailed evaluation. To the rest of my extended family: Aunt Margaret, Alan, Franklin, Percy, Carl, Jr., Aunt Jennie, and the rest of you, thanks for accepting what I have decided to do with my life with such sincerity.

To my agent, Sara Camilli, thanks for entertaining the dozens of ideas I come up with, sometimes on a daily basis, and for sensing something special about them even when a lot of them are as far-fetched as my imagination tends to be. The daily pep talks are always a stress-reliever for me and they are deeply appreciated.

To Tracey Sherrod, my editor at Pocket Books, her assistant, April Reynolds, and Judith Curr, the publisher, thanks for welcoming me into the Pocket family with such ease, grace, and kindness. I look forward to a long-standing relationship.

To Eric, Wendy, and Maxwell Taylor of A & B Books, thanks for taking over for me when the daily grind of trying to ship hundreds, sometimes thousands, of books became way too much for me. After dropping that hand truck on my foot at UPS and landing in the emergency room on crutches, I needed someone to step in and help a sister out. Thanks for being there. That also goes for Learie and Gail of Culture Plus Books. I could never express my gratitude to all of you for being my backbone and getting the self-published versions of my books onto every vending stand and into every African American bookstore.

To all of the book clubs, both on- and off-line, who have read one or more of my books as their book of the month, interviewed me on their websites, or simply just given me a shout out, thanks for showing how powerful word-of-mouth advertising can truly be. A special thank you goes out to R.A.W. SISTAZ for not only providing a great forum to discuss books but the business of writing as well.

To AA-AHA (African American Authors Helping Authors), I am honored to be on the Steering Committee of such a tightly woven, groundbreaking organization that encourages unity among authors instead of division. I look forward to major things from AA-AHA and I am glad to be a part of it as well as the Prolific Writer's Association.

To my fellow authors, especially those who have reached out to me and been open to networking, I wish all of you the best because this is about all of us and not just individuality. I would like to especially thank the following authors: Carl Weber, Earl Sewell, Karen E. Quinones Miller, Brandon Massey, Gwynne Forster, Deirdre Savoy, William Fredrick Cooper, Linda Dominique Grosvenor, JD Mason, Shonell Bacon, JDaniels, V. Anthony Rivers, D.V. Bernard, Darrien Lee, Eileen Johnson, LaJoyce Brookshire, Delores Thornton, Pat O'George Walker, and Eric Jerome Dickey.

Last but definitely not least, I would like to thank the thousands of dedicated readers who have supported my efforts from day one, overloaded my e-mail boxes with notes of encouragement, and visited my two largest websites: EroticaNoir.com and BlackGentlemen.com. I would like to thank every single street vendor, librarian, bookstore owner, and every single housewife, sisterfriend, or brother that has promoted my books for me. Thanks for reading my books and passing them on to a dozen friends or calling eight or more people on the phone to talk about them or for whatever hand you have played in my success. It is impossible to thank each and every one of you individually but know that your kindness has not gone unnoticed.

Peace and Much Love,
Zane

*I love you and this is forever!*
*Always has been! Always will be!*

—Zoe Reynard,
circa 1999

# prologue

Droplets of rain cascaded down the windowpanes, and the sun was merely a figment of the imagination. The dark gray clouds held it prisoner behind their foggy mist, and the day was cold and dreary at best.

Several times I wanted to dash out of the office, mumble a fabricated excuse for leaving to the secretary as I made my way through the waiting room, seeking sanctuary in the hallway. As much as I wanted to forget about the whole therapy session, the alternative was not acceptable. I desperately needed help, and it was time for me to face my fears. When I was a little girl, my mother always told me that courage is simply fear that has said its prayers. Over the years, I have tried to live by those words, and I managed to do so until this day.

My mind began to wander as I stood by the window, looking out at the cars splashing up rainwater with their tires, their windshield wipers going back and forth like pendulums. It was early evening, not quite dusk, and the Friday work traffic was beginning to taper off in downtown Atlanta. Most people were already sitting in bumper-to-bumper traffic on the interstate, ordering a round of drinks with coworkers at happy hour, or settling down in the safety of their own homes to catch the evening news on television.

I had been lucky to get an appointment at all, since it was my first time there and I had just called pleading to see the doctor that morning. A friend of mine once mentioned Dr. Spencer in passing while I was at the salon getting my hair done. She was an avid fan of the doctor's, having used her services to get over the agony of being betrayed by her ex-husband and, ultimately, a stressful divorce. Never would I have conceived seeking her advice myself—yet there I was.

Dr. Spencer's office looked about how I had visualized it: dim lighting, expensive leather furniture, including the infamous chaise longue where troubled souls revealed their deep, dark secrets, and a big cherrywood desk with a banker's lamp in the center. Bookshelves lined the walls, and a smorgasbord of degrees, certificates, and plaques adorned the wall between the two floor-to-ceiling windows behind the desk.

I noticed that my hands were trembling, even though the office was warm and toasty, a complete contrast to the cold October weather outside. She was taking too long, and my nerves were shot. I craved for just one puff of nicotine but had no cigarettes, since I had kicked the habit several years before during my first pregnancy.

Just as I was about to take the cowardly way out, walking over to the chaise and beginning to put on my black leather gloves, Dr. Spencer entered the office, making apologies for keeping me waiting. At first, I was speechless, and the words forming in my mind could not make their way to my lips.

"Mrs. Reynard," she said, more as a statement than a question, as she reached out a finely manicured hand to greet me.

Hearing my name broke the self-induced trance. "Dr. Spencer. It's very nice to meet you." I gratefully took her hand and shook it. Just the warmth of her touch somehow comforted me. "Thank you for seeing me on such short notice."

She was making her way over to her comfortable leather desk chair as she spoke. "It's no problem, really. My secretary seemed to think your situation was quite urgent, and I'm always glad to do whatever I can." I managed a slight smile as she continued. "Please, have a seat and make yourself at home." She motioned toward one of the two leather wing chairs facing the desk opposite her own.

Once she sat down at her desk, I was able to get a better look at her. Dr. Marcella Spencer was a strikingly beautiful and classy woman. The thin lines on her face betrayed her age of about forty, yet she exuded the glow of a woman twenty years younger. Her deep chocolate, satiny skin reminded me of the fudge brownies my mother would prepare for the school bake sales to benefit the PTA, and her eyes looked like black pearls. They were hypnotic.

She wore an olive green business suit, accentuated by a sexy split up the back of the elongated skirt. The suit was even more alluring due to a cloister of overlaying matching buttons. A silk floral scarf worn around her neck added an air of class, and gold earrings gave the outfit a polished look.

"Well, Mrs. Reynard." She started searching through

her center desk drawer for something, finally retrieving a gold-plated cigarette case and matching lighter. "Shall we begin?"

"Dr. Spencer, I have a request."

"What's that?" She noticed the way my eyes were diverted to the cigarettes as she snapped open the case and pulled one of the long, slender brown cancer bandits out. "Would you like a cigarette?"

"No, thank you. Thank goodness, that's one addiction I no longer have to battle." I was trying my best to seem relaxed, but it wasn't working very well.

"Then what can I do for you, Mrs. Reynard?"

"If I'm going to be revealing all my hopes and dreams, my fears and nightmares, all the dragons I'm battling, it would make me much more comfortable if you would call me Zoe."

"Oh, that's no problem, Zoe." A slight giggle escaped from her mocha-painted lips. "The majority of my patients prefer to keep our sessions on a first-name basis. Please call me Marcella."

"Thanks, Marcella." Our eyes met. "I'll do just that."

She started reaching around in a drawer again—the right-hand top drawer instead of the center one. When she placed a pad, pen, and microcassette recorder on her desk pad, I almost catapulted out of my seat. The reality of being in a head doctor's office hit me, and I began to quiver all over again.

She obviously sensed my discomfiture. "Zoe, I'm sorry if the tape recorder makes you feel uncomfortable, but I need to tape the sessions so I can go over them later for my notes. You understand?"

The way she was talking to me reminded me of my second-grade teacher, Mrs. Zachary, the old battle-ax. It made me laugh. "Sure, I understand. It's not like I'm considering becoming a movie star or anything like that, so blackmail's out of the question." I started pulling at a loose string on the leg of my black pantsuit. "Besides, don't you doctors have to take some sort of oath or something?"

"Yes, we most definitely do, and anything you tell me is strictly between you and I. It will never leave this room unless you request me to talk to someone, your husband for example, on your behalf." She pressed the record button.

"My husband!" I uncrossed my legs, got up from the chair, and started pacing the heavily carpeted floor of her office. "Oh, God, what have I done?"

"Zoe, would you like to lie down on the chaise? You don't have to. Only if it makes you comfortable." She never lost her cool. I guess she was used to nervous people.

"No thanks." I sat back down in the chair. "I'm ready to begin. I know time is of the essence."

"Well, not exactly. You're my last client of the day, so we can talk as long as you like. You seem to be very distraught, and I would like to help you if I can." A kindness in her eyes halfway made me believe she was my best friend.

I blurted it out. "My husband, Jason, and I are having marital problems." My eyes dropped down to the floor. It was humiliating to even speak the words.

"I see. Zoe, have you and Jason sought any form of counseling for your problems?"

I began to laugh out loud then, but it was a laugh of dismay. "No, hell no! Jason doesn't even know we have any marital problems."

I couldn't even manage to look at her. I felt like a child awaiting punishment by my priest for committing a mortal sin, a sacrilege against the church. "Zoe, I don't understand you."

"Jason doesn't know about any of the things I do. He hasn't a clue and if he ever found out, I would die." A single tear fell and began to creep down my left cheek. "I could never imagine living in a world without him. That's how much I love him."

"But you don't feel you can talk to him about your problem?" She leaned forward, placed her cigarette in the ashtray, positioned her elbows on the desk, and intertwined her fingers.

"Not this problem. Not now, not ever." I zeroed in on a tiny lint ball on the carpet. It appeared to be slightly moving every time I blinked my eyes.

"Relax, Zoe. Let's try this a different way." She took another puff of her cigarette and then picked up the pen, preparing to take notes. "When you mentioned earlier that nicotine was one addiction you no longer had to battle, it gave me the impression you're addicted to something else. Are you?"

The tears started flowing. It took every ounce of self-control I could muster not to start wailing like a banshee. "Yes! I'm addicted!"

"Drugs?" I shook my head. "Alcohol?"

"No, nothing like that."

"Then what are you addicted to, Zoe?"

I looked at her finally through tear-drenched eyes and vocalized the word before my guilt forced me to suppress it. "Sex!"

The look of astonishment on her face revealed her surprise. She was probably used to dealing with people addicted to cocaine, amphetamines, booze, food, but I got the distinct impression sexual addiction was a whole new ballpark for her.

"Marcella, I don't know where to begin. I have plenty of excuses for this, but no real reasons. I'm so scared my

addiction to sex will destroy everything I have; my marriage, my relationship with my children, everything." I
darted my eyes away from hers and concentrated on the
smoke rising from the cigarette, now burned down almost
to the filter.

She pulled a tissue out of the quilted dispenser on her
desk and reached across the desk, handing it to me. I
gladly took it and dabbed my gradually swelling eyes
with it. "Well, Zoe, the best place to start is always at the
beginning, so why don't we commence there and work
our way to the present."

I retreated into the bulky wing chair, letting my
shoulders sink deep into the cushions, and crumpled the
damp tissue in my hand. "The beginning . . ."

# chapter
## <u>one</u>

      The first time I ever laid eyes on Jason, I thought he was a junior-mack-daddy-wannabe that probably sat around on a Commodore 64 computer drinking grape Kool-Aid out of a peanut butter jar while watching *Good Times*. I couldn't stand his ass.

      The feeling was mutual, though, because our first physical interaction was when he gave me the finger and then spit on my saddle shoes. We were in the fifth grade, and from the day my parents and I drove up in our Ford station wagon, I knew he was trouble.

      The movers got there about an hour after we did. I was sitting on the curb playing jacks when the big truck came flying around the corner, practically tilted on one side. I figured the driver was going to lose control of the truck for sure, and every valuable possession we owned would end up strewn all over the street.

      Being the wonderful and unselfish little girl I was, my main concern was that my black Barbie didn't lose a limb or anything in the process. Table lamps, my father's eight-track tape player, and my mother's dishes were all replaceable, but the hell if I was going to be able to replace my Barbie. She was my pride and joy. I had even painted her fingernails with glittered polish and made her a sexy dress out of the red bandannas my mother made me wear to bed so my pressed hair wouldn't frizz up. Other than that, I was worried about my Snoopy Snow Cone Machine, and that was about it.

Jason and his parents lived directly across the street. He was outside that day trying to get some mail-order rocket to soar into the heavens. What a rip-off! The whole time I was watching him, the stupid thing never made it a yard off the ground. It was after about the hundredth try, when the movers had half the truck unloaded, that I noticed his ass rolling his beady eyes at me. I was using a piece of pink chalk to draw a makeshift hopscotch diagram on the street in front of my house when he approached me. His Kangol hat and leather bomber jacket made him look like a pint-size pimp. All he needed was a couple of gold teeth.

"Girl, you better quit! I'm gonna tell my momma on you!" I glared at him, smacking on a wad of Bubblicious like a cow.

"Little man, you better go play with your cheap broken rocket and leave me the heck alone!"

He got all the way up in my face then. "Girl, don't you be ordering me around! I'll stomp your skinny behind into the concrete!"

"Oooooooh, I am *soooooooo* scared!" I rolled my eyes, chastising him.

Then, the miniature version of Shaft flipped me the finger, made a disgusting noise while he gathered saliva in his mouth, and then spit on my brand-new black-and-white saddle shoes. I beat his little ass too. We were the same age, but I had him by a good three inches in height. Milk wasn't due to start doing his body good for a couple more years.

Two of the moving men broke the fight up. I accidentally scratched one of the men on the nose because I was not about to stop fighting until the fat lady sang. That's when both our mothers came dashing out of our respective houses yelling, "Oh, my poor baby!" and things like that. It was mad funny. They took over, throwing our heads into their heavy breasts and feeling all over us to make sure there was no permanent damage. Jason and I just glared at each other like two sumo wrestlers ready for round two.

My mother helped me inside like I was handicapped. In actuality, I had never felt better in my life. I was the victorious one. Jason retreated to his house as well, and that was the end of it. My parents and I did just enough unpacking that night to get by, threw some sleeping bags on the living room floor, and munched down on some KFC. My Dad hooked up his eight-track, and I fell asleep listening to the harmonized singing of Earth, Wind and Fire. It was a Saturday.

I started school the following Monday and was anxious to get there to meet all the new kids. I rushed through a bowl of corn flakes and caught about ten minutes of *The Flintstones* before grabbing my tin lunch pail and running out the door to get to the bus stop on time.

The bus was about to pull off, and I was panting by the time I caught up to it in time to bang on the door, signaling the driver to stop. After I got on the bus, he asked me who I was. I explained I was a new student who had just moved. He snarled at me, his au naturel breath almost knocking me backward down the steps and back off the bus, "Well, you make sure your teacher gets your name put on my roster A-S-A-P 'cause I'm not supposed to be picking up no knuckleheads I don't know! Now, find a seat, sit down, and shaddup!"

I searched for an empty seat and couldn't find one in the front of the bus, so I started walking toward the back. All of the kids were checking me out, and some were even snickering. I noticed most of the seats were occupied, either by two girls or two boys, with the exception of the one in the far rear. A boy and a girl, obviously suffering from a severe case of puppy love, were seated there. He had his arm around her shoulder, and she was blushing from ear to ear.

I was ready to ask the driver if I could sit on the steps when I realized the only available seat was next to the horror film creature himself, Jason. He stopped playing with his GI Joe with the kung fu grip just long enough to smirk at me. I turned around and headed toward the front to beg the driver to ask someone to trade places with me, but he yelled at me again. "You taking too long! School starts in fifteen minutes! Now, sit your *be-hind* in a seat and shaddup!"

I scurried my ass back to the seat and noticed Jason had placed his knapsack on the vinyl seat beside him. "Could you move that, please?"

He didn't respond, nor did he look at me, so I took the bag, threw it on his lap, and sat down. He was about to be a smart aleck, but I stopped him dead in his tracks. I rolled my eyes and gave him a head-from-side-to-side-with-a-finger-snap combination. "Don't say nothing to me, or I'll give you an even bigger beatdown than I did Saturday."

A couple of the kids heard me and started giggling and taunting him. He just grabbed his knapsack, held it tight, and didn't look at me the rest of the way to school.

As if things weren't going bad enough, I get my class assignment from the principal's office, go to my homeroom, and his trick ass is the first face I see. Our homeroom teacher was Mrs. Williams, and she was *displeased* to have a student transfer into her class in the middle of the fall term. She snarled at me too. Maybe it was my cherry-flavored lip gloss that was making everyone demonic toward me. "Little Miss Zoe," she started in on me as she looked over my school records, "have a seat over there by the window and pay attention. You have a lot of making up to do in order to catch up to the rest of the class."

There was one glimmer of sunshine in my day. I didn't have to sit near Jason in homeroom. He was clear across the class, and that suited me just fine. He must have been a smart-ass with everybody because Mrs. Williams had his desk pushed right up against hers, several feet away from the rest of the class. Teachers always make the troublemakers sit up in their faces, and I remember thinking to myself, "Goodie!"

My first day at Benjamin Franklin Elementary was pretty uneventful. I made a couple of new friends, got to jump rope at recess, made a deformed clay vase in art class, and learned how to count to ten in Spanish. At lunch, I sat with this little girl named Brina that thought she was the next Diana Ross. I started to school her ass and tell her she couldn't be the next Diana Ross because I was. She would fling her hair back after every bite of her Twinkie and took special care making sure she didn't end up with a milk mustache when she rinsed it down. She spent the entire lunch period bragging about everything from her collection of ribbons for her hair to the straight A's she made on her last report card.

Jason did decide to get bold for a minute and started spitting half-frozen peas across the room at the back of my neck through a straw. He made the mistake of hitting the PE teacher, Mr. Lewis, in the cheek with one and was immediately dragged by the ear to the office.

When I got on the bus that afternoon, I was lucky enough to find a seat up front. I made sure I was one of the first ones on the bus, pushing a couple of wimpy boys out my way so I wouldn't have to sit next to Cousin It. Jason got on the bus about ten kids after I did. I stuck my tongue out at him and flipped him the bird. He tried to tell the bus driver on me, but all he got was an attitude. "Sit your *be-hind* down, little man, and shaddup!"

I was playing hopscotch about an hour later when he came out of his house, stood on the curb on his side of the street, and started talking trash. "You know what? I hate you and I hope all your hair falls out and you get red pimples all over your face!"

I stopped hopping on number six with my right foot up in the air, gave him an icy cold look, and decided to pay his ass back for the comment. "Oh, yeah? Well, I hate you too, and I hope the next time you shoot that cheap rocket of yours, it gets stuck up your behind!" As an afterthought, I added, "And I hope your itsy bitsy dang-a-lang falls off too!"

I held up my pinkie finger to emphasize the point, and he left the curb, on his way over to my side of the street to finish off the fistfight we started the Saturday before. I was about to meet him in the middle when my mother opened up the front door. "Zoe, get in here and get washed up for dinner! Now!"

Walking away, I placed my hands on my hips and strutted like Greta Garbo. I turned around and addressed him with my best voice imitation. "Next time, Big Boy!"

I left his cross between Chewbacca from *Star Wars* and Scooby Doo ass standing right there in the street with his hands balled into fists and a look of hatred on his pathetic face.

I tried to keep my distance from Jason, other than in school, but my daddy wasn't making it easy for me. For some odd reason, the two of them bonded. Maybe it was because Jason's daddy was always working, or maybe it was because my daddy was good with his hands and Jason admired the way he fixed things around the house and made furniture out of wood as a hobby. Whatever it was, I didn't like or appreciate them being buddy-buddy at all.

I was up in my bedroom one Saturday morning, sorting out my record collection and singing my ass off, when my mother yelled for me to come down. I had just taken "The Best of My Love" by the Emotions off the turntable. I was about to pull my shades down and throw on "Flashlight" by Parliament Funkadelic and dance around my room, making circles on the walls and ceiling with the Maglite my daddy gave me when my mother interrupted my flow.

"Zoe, can you come down here for a second?" Her voice carried well up the stairwell, and I knew she deliberately waited for a break in the music to call for me. It was a regular routine.

"Okay, Momma. I'll be right down." I muttered under my breath while I gathered the dirty clothes out of my wicker hamper and tossed them in a laundry basket. It was laundry day, and I hadn't done a thing, so I lugged my clothes downstairs with me in order to save myself a return trip.

As soon as I turned the corner into the kitchen, my eyes lit up as I spotted the ice-cold pitcher of freshly squeezed lemonade and the cookie sheet of chocolate chip cookies with Hershey's Kisses hidden inside cooling on the stove.

"Momma, you made my favorite cookies!" I let the laundry basket drop on the floor and gave my mother a huge, elephantine hug. "You're the most spantacular, bomb-diggity, coolest mother in the whole wide world."

She let out a slight giggle and then gently pushed my hands away. "Zoe, quit before you make me spill the lemonade."

"Sorry, Momma." I licked my lips, dreaming about how delectable the cookies were going to taste hitting my throat, and decided to earn some brownie points so I could sneak a couple before dinner was ready. I retrieved my laundry basket and headed toward the basement steps. "I'm going to go ahead and put my clothes on, and then maybe I can help you with the other cleaning like vacuuming or polishing the furniture."

My mother walked over to me, wiping her hand on the bib of her apron, and placed her right palm over my forehead, checking for a fever. "Is this my child?" she asked sarcastically.

I grimaced. "Yeah, Momma. I'm just trying to do my share around here."

She gleamed at me. "Good, do me a favor before you go downstairs." She took two glasses out of the cabinet and poured some lemonade in them. Then she put four cookies on a saucer and placed everything on a wooden tray. "Take this lemonade and cookies out to the garage for your daddy and Jason."

"Jason? What the hell, I mean heck, is he doing over here?" I felt a sudden tension in the back of my neck, hotter under the collar than the pot of white potatoes my mother had simmering on the stove for dinner. "Why does he have to come over here all the time?"

"First of all, Miss Thing," my mother scolded me, "Jason isn't over here *all the time*. Your daddy's helping him build a go-cart."

"A go-cart?" That did it! "I asked Daddy to help me build a tree house like fifty million times, and he hasn't done it yet."

"You asked your daddy *once*, and he fully intends to do it, but the oak in the backyard needs some branches trimmed off it first before he can. The men are coming next weekend to cut them down, and then—" My mother glared at me, probably wondering why she was even bothering to try to explain. "Never mind all that. Just take this tray out there and then come in so you can do your laundry and vacuum."

"What about some lemonade and cookies for me?" My bottom lip was poked out more than a set of 44DDD breasts.

"After you finish your chores, you can have some."

I smacked my lips, reluctantly took the tray, and headed toward the small alcove off the kitchen leading to the garage. Why did I have to do chores while Jason got the special treatment like he was Shaka Zulu or some damn body?

As soon as I entered the garage, I was immediately jealous. There was my daddy, shooting the breeze with Jason and going over the diagrams for building the go-cart they had halfway put together on the workbench attached to the back wall. They were so busy bonding, they didn't even notice me come in at first.

"Mr. Wallace, I really appreciate you helping me out like this. My daddy's always working, and I never thought I'd have it done in time for the Cub Scout Derby next week." What an ass kisser!

My daddy patted Jason on the head like he was a

Doberman pinscher, which he kind of resembled, I might add. "Not a problem, Jason. I love working with my hands. In fact, within the next couple of weeks I'm going to start on Zoe's tree house. Maybe you could help me out and when it's done, you can hang out in there with Zoe sometimes."

"That sounds great!" I could see Jason's profile, and from the side he looked completely toothless, since he had four teeth coming in at the same time.

"Not hardly," I interjected, letting my presence be known. "Once my tree house is done, it's for me and my friends. You're not even my friend."

"Zoe, what you got there?" My daddy attempted to change the subject before I had to beat Jason's little ass again.

"Some lemonade and cookies, Daddy." I walked over and sat the tray on the hood of my daddy's silver Buick Century. "Momma told me to bring them out for you and Alf."

"Alf? I got your Alf, girl!"

Jason really wanted me to open another can of whup-ass. "Yes, Alf as in orange alien." I looked him right in his beady eyes. "Dang, boy, you look messed up with all those missing teeth." He smirked at me and rolled his eyes, so I added, "What's that on your face? A pimple or a golf ball?"

Before Jason could make a comeback effort, my daddy jumped all up in the mix, trying to protect the mongoose. "That's enough, Zoe. Don't be disrespectful to company!"

"Company? Daddy, that nucca's always over here. Why do you have to take his side every time?"

My daddy laughed. I failed to see anything humorous.

"You know, the way you two go at it reminds me of your mother and I when we were younger."

I analyzed the statement, recalling the stories of how my parents met when they were children, grew up together, and eventually married. *"Ewwwww, that's sick, Daddy!* Jason and I are nothing like you and Momma. I can't stand his ass, I mean behind."

My daddy curled his mouth up at my slip of the tongue. "Yeah, I know you meant behind." Jason grinned at me, glad to see me being chastised.

"What you looking at, fool?"

He glanced from my head to my feet and back up. "Nothing much. That's for sure."

My daddy laughed all over again. "Uh-huh, I can see it now. The two of you will probably end up married, just like your momma and I, with two or three kids and a house similar to this one."

"Daddy, I don't mean you no harm." I just had to correct him, because he was obviously hallucinating. "But before I marry that cross between a gorilla and a skunk, I will run away and become a nun."

"Hahahahahahaha." Jason chuckled like I had just said something hilarious, but I was dead serious. "Girl, you know you ain't going to join no convention!"

*"Convention?"* I pointed my finger at him. "You're so stupid. It's *convent*, dummy!" With that, I turned around and ran into the house to inform my mother about Jason's stupidity quotient. "Momma, guess what the stupid nucca just said!" That's how I first met Jason Reynard! That's how I first met my husband!

# chapter two

*Three Years Later*
*Eighth Grade*

By the time our eighth-grade year came rolling around, milk was definitely doing a body good. Jason's body, that is. In the three years since our first meeting, or confrontation, whichever you prefer to call it, the hostility between us had continued. The only differences were physical developments. I'd changed drastically from the tall, lanky, skinny girl who moved there and now had boobs and an onion ass. You know, the kind of ass that supposedly makes men cry when they see it? I may have grown another four or five inches in height but leveled off at five-foot-four. Jason, on the other hand, shot up like a tree. He was already six feet even and still growing.

We were both thirteen, and puberty was barreling in

on us like a ton of bricks. I had a crush on this boy Mohammed, a Muslim. I used to be so mesmerized when he
would recite Islamic principles to me. In my eyes, he was
a *real* man who respected his women, even when they
were only thirteen. He was older than I was, sixteen, and
had a car. I just knew I was the bomb, and all my girlfriends were envious. My parents hated him though. They
dreaded the thought of a boy taking advantage of their
little baby girl. Little did my parents or friends know, it
was nothing like that. In fact, Mohammed respected me
*too* much; the few times I tried to French-kiss him, he
gave me a peck on my lips and sent me on my way.

Jason had himself a little hoochie mama. I'll never
forget the anorexic beanpole bitch. Her name was Chandler, and she came from an upper-class family. Just because she wore the finest clothes and got her hair done
every week at the beauty parlor, she thought she was the
end-all and be-all. When I used to talk trash about her to
Brina, who was my best friend by then, she would say,
"Oh, girl, you just jealous! You want Jason for yourself!
Just admit it, walk across the street and get that boy, because you are getting on my last nerve!"

My response was always the same. "Heck, no!"

It was a Friday afternoon in October when I realized
Brina had missed her calling as a child psychic. It was a
beautiful day for that time of year. I was out in front of my
house jumping rope with Brina, who caught the bus home
with me to spend the night, and some of the other girls from
the neighborhood. I had just jumped in between the ropes,
doing the double-Dutch, when I tripped and fell on my
knees. It wasn't lack of rope-jumping skills that made me
take a tumble. It was Jason's fine ass mowing the lawn.

He was maneuvering his daddy's brand-spanking-
new ride-on mower, and his shirt was off. I noticed he

was growing a goatee. His black, wavy hair, along with his hazel eyes, were sparkling in the sunlight.

As I got up from the ground and wiped the dirt off my knees, I couldn't take my eyes off him. All the girls noticed and started chanting,

*Zoe and Jason*
*Sitting in a tree*
*K-I-S-S-I-N-G*
*First comes love*
*Then comes marriage*
*Then comes Zoe with a*
*baby carriage*

Thank goodness he couldn't hear them over the engine of the lawn mower. I simply would have died. The strangest thing happened at that very moment and I know this is gonna be hard to believe. Looking at Jason and his muscles and his face and his *everything* made my panties wet. When I went inside, half-scared because nothing like that had ever happened before, I went to the bathroom and discovered I was bleeding. Somehow, my newly discovered puppy love for Jason brought about my first menstrual cycle. Ain't that a bitch?

Later that evening, Brina and I went to a birthday party at our friend Eugene's house. Brina was spending the night with me so my mother could drop us both off and pick us up. Her mother was a single parent and had to work late that night.

The party was cool. However, I was depressed because Mohammed couldn't make it, and Jason was there with his *thing*. We didn't dance much because Eugene's parents were kind of old-fashioned and didn't want a whole lot of touchy-feely going on. They made one vital mistake though: they bought Eugene the game Twister for his big day.

Somebody spiked the punch with grain alcohol and set the party off. I don't quite remember how it happened because I was tore up, but some time between watching *Beach Blanket Bingo* on TV and playing charades, Jason and I ended up on the Twister mat together. Boy, was Chandler upset! I think she was a bit psychic as well, aware of something I wasn't. She knew Jason liked me just as much as I liked him.

I did figure it out during the game, though. Jason had to put a hand on red, I had to put a foot on blue, and his pelvic area ended up pressed against my behind. Before the hand on the spinner landed on the next color, his dick was hard, and the gigantic, elephantine sanitary napkin my mother made me wear was twice as soaked as before the game. It wasn't soaked with blood, however, but with my pussy juice.

I jumped up off the mat in the middle of the game— not because I didn't enjoy the way his hard dick was feeling, but for fear he would somehow catch wind of the sanitary napkin. The damn thing was so big, I thought for sure he would discover it, and I was so embarrassed.

My mother couldn't get there fast enough to pick us up, and when she finally did, I flew out the house like a bat out of hell, wanting to put the whole episode behind me. We went back to my house, and Brina was brushing my long, light brown hair that reached my bra strap. "Zoe, what's the matter with you?"

"What makes you think there's anything wrong with me?" I snapped at her and immediately regretted my tone. Even though Brina was my best friend in the whole world, I was ashamed to tell her what had happened.

"You've been acting weird, is all!" She pinned my

hair up with a giant hair clip. "Is it because you started your period? Don't sweat that. I've been having them for almost two years now, and they're not so bad."

I got up from the padded bench of my vanity table, cut off the lamp on my nightstand, and got into my double canopy bed. "It's nothing, really. Let's just get some rest."

Brina got in the bed and instantly fell asleep, since she was tipsier than I was. Girlfriend put a hurting on that punch. For me, sleep would not come easy, and an hour later, I was sitting in the window seat and looking up at the moon and stars. I began to imagine Jason looking at the same moon and same stars from his bedroom window, but for all I knew, he was out necking with Chandler. The mere thought of him touching her was devastating. It was hard to imagine falling for my archenemy. That's exactly what happened, though, and I made a promise to myself that somehow, some way, I would win his heart and make him mine. The sun was coming up when I snuck back in the bed with Brina, pretending to have been there the entire time.

The very next day, I forgot all that nonsense about winning Jason's heart. I think it had something to do with the way he was sucking his teeth and smirking at me when I came out of the house and started down the street to the corner market a few blocks away.

I ignored him and kept walking. I winced when I heard him approaching fast behind me on his skateboard, yet another item my father had helped him make.

"Zoe, wait up, girl!"

I rolled my eyes for my benefit alone, since my back was still facing him. "I'm in a hurry, Jason!"

I could hear him speeding up even faster then. "I said hold up, girl!"

I swung around and glared at him. Damn, he was fine! "Whatchu want, nucca?"

He caught up to me and used his heel to kick his skateboard up into his hand, placing it underneath his arm. The sunlight hitting up against his eyes was nothing short of mesmerizing. I wanted him, and at the same time I couldn't stand his ass. I was mad *confuzzled*.

"Can I ask you a question?"

"You just did, dummy," I hissed at him and folded my arms, repeating the eye roll so he could see it this time.

He sighed in frustration. "Aight, damn, can I ask you another question then?"

"You just did, dummy," I reiterated, giggling at the ingenuity of my comment.

He glared at me like he wanted to slap me. "You're a trip, girl!"

I looked down at the red-and-yellow Swatch watch I was sporting because it matched the red stirrup pants and yellow baby-doll shirt I had on perfectly. "Are you going to ask this question sometime today? Because I have things to do."

"Where you headed? Over Brina's?"

"Brina's? Brina lives like fifty million blocks away. I'm not walking all the way over there. Nucca, please!"

"So where you headed?"

For the first time, I noticed how deep Jason's voice had gotten. Boy, was I getting overheated! "To the store to get sumptin' I need." Jason laughed like I had just told an Eddie Murphy joke. "What's so damn funny?"

"Nothing," he chuckled. "I was just wondering if this *thing* you need from the store has to do with last night and what happened at the party."

"Say what?" I wondered what the hell he was talking about, so I asked him, "What the hell you talking 'bout?"

He glanced down at the sidewalk, breaking eye contact. "I couldn't help but notice while we were playing Twister."

"Notice what?" I was getting pissed off because I realized my worst fears were coming true.

He looked back up at me and blurted it out. "Didn't you have on one of those sanitation napkins last night?"

That did it! I slapped his ass right across his skank face and started walking again. "First of all, nonaya damn business, and secondly, it's sanitary napkin, not sanitation napkin, dummy!"

"Why you hit me?" I could hear the tremor in his voice, but his ass deserved it. "You always hittin' some damn body, Zoe!"

I turned around and flipped him the finger. "Why you worried about what I have between my legs?" I immediately regretted that statement the moment it left my lips. It sounded so, so, so sexual.

He grinned. "Now that you mention it, I do have another question for you."

"Aw hell, what now?"

He hopped back on his skateboard to catch up to me. "Can I ask it?"

"You just did, dummy!"

He grabbed a hold of my right elbow, and I got weak in the knees. "Look at me, Zoe."

I looked. Damn, damn, damn, he was fine! "Yes?"

"You wanna go with me?"

"Go witchu where?" Aw dayummmmmmm, he was actually asking me to be his girl, his woman, his hoochie.

"You know what I mean, Zoe." His frustration with my antics was obvious. "So do you or don't you?"

"You have a woman already, and I have a man." He

started looking down at the sidewalk again, muttering something I couldn't quite make out. "Besides, you talking about us kissing and all that stuff?"

He gave me a quick peck on the lips but never made eye contact. I was likely to faint. "Yeah, kissing and going places together and you know?"

He raised his eyebrows at me and I knew he meant the wild thang. "Ewwwwwww, hell no! Hell no, I don't want to go with you!"

I stormed off, mad. Not because he asked me, and not because I didn't want to. I was mad because it seemed apparent he and Chandler had been going at it. The mere thought of it made my stomach turn.

I heard him yell behind me. "Whatever, Zoe! I was just kidding with your skeeger ass anyway!"

I turned around and laughed in his face. "It's *skeezer*, dummy! Learn how to talk, why don't you!"

I picked up my pace and rubbed the edge of my training bra through my shirt to make sure the $3.00 my mother had given me to buy some more of those elephantine sanitary napkins hadn't fallen out.

# chapter three

Have you ever been so utterly embarrassed and ashamed that you wanted to crawl up in a hole and die?

That's exactly how I felt the following Monday at George Washington Carver Middle School. Even though it was a Monday, I affectionately renamed it Hellday.

Hell! That's what Jason tried to put my ass through that day. He went to school, obviously still feeling the sting from my refusal to go with his ass, and told everyone he could get to listen that I was on my period.

Looking back, I realize it wasn't such a horrible insult. After all, periods are periods, and all women have them just like all women have coochies in the first place. Periods are a fact of life.

I couldn't relate to that philosophy in the eighth grade, though. For me, it was a traumatic experience to have all the boys pointing at me while I walked down the crowded hallways between classes.

The girls weren't any better, giggling and snickering behind my back like they didn't already have them on a monthly basis or, for the late bloomers, weren't ever planning on getting them. The nerve of the heifers!

By the time lunch period rolled around, I was doing battle with a migraine and contemplating taking Jason out in the parking lot so I could whup his ass in front of the entire student body.

I got my tray of slop. That's exactly what school lunches were—slop. One of the local network news stations did an investigative report about school lunches and discovered that most prisoners in the United States ate more nutritious meals than schoolchildren. That's a damn shame, but I deemed it a true statement, even though I had never seen the inside of a penitentiary.

Usually, I sat right smack in the center of the cafeteria, but not that day. I took my ass over to an empty table in the far corner, hoping I would become invisible to my peers.

After taking a bite of the cheeseburger I had selected over the pepperoni pizza and egg salad sandwich, I spit it back out in a napkin. I couldn't even deal: it tasted more like a rat than a cow. I wondered if the city of Atlanta had devised a sneaky, underhanded method to get rid of the rodent overpopulation.

I glanced over toward the serving station and noticed Brina standing there, surveying the room in an effort to locate me. We didn't have any morning classes together that semester, but we always ate lunch together come hell or high water. I stood up just long enough to flail my arms in the air. Once I saw her acknowledge my presence with a nod, I quickly sat back down.

She came over and plopped her tray down across from me, throwing her legs over the bench one at a time to sit down.

"Zoe, why are you sitting all the way over here?" she asked, confused. "Everyone else is at our regular table."

"Haven't you heard?" I whispered, diverting my eyes from hers and trying to hold back a tear.

"Heard what?"

"Jason's trick ass has been going around school telling everyone I'm on my period and that I had on a sanitary napkin at the party Friday night," I blurted out, ashamed to even speak the words.

Brina started falling out laughing. She laughed so hard, she had to take a swig of her iced tea to prevent herself from hyperventilating.

"This shit's not even funny, Brina," I hissed, ready to smack her ass for betraying me. If I was upset, she damn well better be too.

"I'm sorry," she stated adamantly, holding her stomach and sucking in air in an effort to calm down. "But it's not like you're the only girl in school with a period. Like I told you the other night, I've been having them for two years now."

"That's you," I said, smacking my gums and crossing my arms over my chest. "Besides, when you started your periods, you didn't have a knucklehead running around school telling *every damn body!*"

"You're right! My bad! Jason should be ashamed of himself for doing this to you! I'm going to tell him off when I see him."

"No, that's okay! That's my job! I'm going to fix his ass but good!" A look of worry overshadowed Brina's face. "What's wrong with you, Brina?"

"Nothing."

"I hate it when people tell me nothing. Now tell me what you're thinking about?"

"It's just that when I started my period, I was big-time embarrassed too. That's why I never mentioned it, even to you. The only person I ever told was my mother so I could get some napkins from her. She didn't care though. She was drunk that night. She just threw a bag of Stayfree at me and slammed her bedroom door."

I was speechless. I had become suspicious about Brina's mother and alcohol about a year before but never asked any questions. This was the first time Brina had come straight out and admitted it.

I reached over the table and took her hand. "You want to talk about it?"

"No," she replied abruptly, tearing the plastic wrapper off her utensil packet. "There's nothing to talk about!"

I decided to leave well enough alone. I sat there pretending to be enthralled in my side dish selection of succotash, but I was really trying to think of another subject. I wanted to discuss anything except Jason, and Brina wanted to discuss anything except her mother.

"Zoe, what's up, gal?" I whiffed the air and knew who it was without even looking over my shoulder. Could the day get any worse? Hell yeah! It just did! "Umph, umph, umph, you're just lookin' too fine for words, baby!"

Lyle Harris was by far the ugliest boy in school. We'd never taken a vote on the issue, but trust me; his ass was ugmo. He was skinny, short, high yella with red zits all over his face, and thought he was an extra for the movie *House Party* with the high-top fade he was trying to sport. On top of all that, he stank big-time. You could smell his ass coming a mile away. He was in my geometry class, and the teacher, Mr. Wilson, always had to crack a window during sixth period to try to air out some of Lyle's au naturel body fumes.

I didn't even give him the courtesy of an obligatory glance. "What you want, Lyle?"

He sat down beside me on the bench, and I almost passed the hell out. Brina started holding her nose. I wanted to puke.

"Listen here, Zoe," he said, rubbing his grubby fingers up and down my right arm. "I heard you a woman now. A *real* woman."

I knocked his hand away. "Keep your paws off of me, Rin Tin Tin!"

Brina giggled. So did I.

He threw his hands out, and the central air-conditioning system got a hold of his underarm stench, redirecting it my way.

"Aight, you wanna play me like that huh?"

I igged him.

"I just wanted to holla at you. I was wondering if you wanted to go to a movie or sumptin' this weekend. That new *Lethal Weapon* joint is coming out, and I figured you might want to check it out."

I glared at him then, though that was a task. "You can't be serious? Besides, your armpits are already hollering at me. Those bad boys are screaming!"

"I'm dead serious." He grinned at me, and I almost lost my stomach contents for real. His gums were jet black. "I want to get to know you better wit' your fine ass!"

Brina fell out laughing.

"Lyle, why do you have to pick today of all days to get up in my face?" I snapped at him. "I'm not even in the mood for your drama."

"Like I said, I heard you a woman now. I figured by this weekend you might be off those pads, and we can do a little sumptin' sumptin'."

That did it! He obviously didn't know who he was messing with. I picked up my tray and threw the whole thing at his ugly-ass face.

"What the hell you go and do that shit for?"

"I warned you to leave me alone!" I got up from the table. "Come on, Brina! Let's jet! The air is mighty foul around here!"

We walked away from him. People were teasing his ass with no mercy. I felt no remorse. He asked for it.

We were halfway out of the cafeteria when I spotted Jason and Chandler sitting at a table with their clique.

"Hold up, Brina," I said, yanking Brina backward by the elbow. "I have something to take care of!"

"Aw hell, Zoe!" Brina tried to drag me in the opposite direction. "Just drop it already. Jason has had his fun, and the day is halfway over. By tomorrow, everyone will forget all about it."

As we approached their table, I heard Chandler bragging about trying out for the cheerleading squad later that week. She was positive not only that she would make it but that she would be the captain.

"I'm so pretty, I know Miss Weeden will pick me as the captain," she boasted. A couple of the other girls at the table looked away, probably wanting to slap the hell out of her. I felt the same way. She was the most uppity Miss Thang in the school. Most tolerated her, but very few truly liked her. She leaned over and pecked Jason on the lips. "Baby, will you come to the tryouts and cheer me on? I know you'll make the captain of the basketball team again this year. We'll be the top couple in the school."

"Oh, I dunno," Jason replied. "I really need to get some things done around the house Wednesday afternoon. My mom's been after me to sandpaper and repaint the shutters for months now."

"Why can't your daddy do it?" Chandler pouted, hoping to win Jason over.

"You know my daddy always works late," Jason replied. "Besides, I like doing things with my hands. Zoe's daddy has taught me a lot about building things."

Chandler smacked her lips and rolled her eyes. "Zoe?"

"Yes," I replied. Everyone noticed my arrival at the same time. All eyes were on me, but my eyes were drilling a hole through Jason's skank ass.

Brina made one last attempt to bring me back to my senses. "Come on, Zoe," she insisted, yanking on my arm. "This isn't even worth it. You might get in serious trouble. Lyle's already fuming. You and Jason can settle this at home."

Jason stood up, trying to strike an intimidating pose, and inquired, "You have a problem with me, Zoe?"

I wanted to call him every name in the book. I wanted to cuss his ass out, but when he looked at me, all I could think about was how luscious his lips looked. I slapped him clear across them.

Chandler jumped up. "Oh, no, you didn't just hit my man!"

Jason held his hand over his mouth. "Zoe, I'm sick of you and your damn hitting! What did I tell you Saturday?"

I saw a window of opportunity and decided to take it. "Yeah, what did you tell me Saturday?"

"Saturday? You saw her on Saturday?" Chandler asked, a perplexed expression on her face.

"Yeah, we live right across the street from each other. Remember?" He darted his eyes back and forth from me to her, probably trying to decide which one to deal with first. Then he stared me down with those sexy-ass eyes of his. "I told you to stop hitting all up on me Saturday."

"Was this before or after you asked me to be your girlfriend? I don't quite recall."

Jason's mouth dropped open. He was busted. Chandler looked like she was struggling for her next breath, and her stylish girlfriends didn't have a clue what to say. I had embarrassed her ass but good.

Brina intervened. "Jason asked you to go with him?" She started blushing from ear to ear, like he had asked her. "You didn't tell me that, *gurlllllllllllll!*"

Cordell, Jason's best friend, decided to throw his two cents in. "You asked that gurl to go with you, man?" He looked at Chandler, who still looked lost, like a whore in church, and guffawed. "*Awwwww snap*, he played you big-time, Chandler."

I was anticipating Jason would deny the whole thing so I could recite the conversation word for word and truly humiliate him. Much to my amazement, he did no such thing.

"I *did* ask you to go with me, and you turned me down, right?"

Jason and I just gaped at each other while Cordell kept jonnin' Chandler. "Dang, I always knew those two liked each other!"

I debated about what to say. I wanted to tell him I did long to be his hoochie, partially because I wanted to teach Chandler a lesson, but mostly because I was feenin' for his touch.

The words left my mouth before I thought them through clearly. "Of course I told your skank ass no!"

He stared down at the floor, obviously hurt. I wanted to reach out and caress his cheek so badly, but I remembered Lyle and his "I hear you a woman now" speech.

"I told you no, and you decided to go spread my business all over the school," I persisted. "That was very childish, even for you, Jason."

"I'm sorry, Zoe," he pleaded, unable to look me in the face. "You're right. I shouldn't have done it. I was just furious is all."

To this very day, I don't know where they came from, but the next second tears were gushing down both of my cheeks.

"I hate you, Jason. Just stay the hell away from me!" I started to back away from him, almost tripping over someone's backpack on the floor by the table. "Stay away from me! Stay away from my house and stay away from my daddy! I hate your guts!"

I ran out of the cafeteria with Brina fast on my heels. I sought refuge in the girls' bathroom, standing over one of the sinks crying while Brina rubbed the small of my back.

Neither one of us said anything for a few moments.

"Zoe, I realize you're upset, but you know and I know that Jason wants to be with you. It doesn't take a genius to figure out that you feel the same way, so why not stop all this foolishness and get together *finally?*"

I looked at her reflection in the mirror through tear-drenched eyes. "Jason goes with Chandler!"

"Yeah, but he made it painfully obvious just now that he would dump her in a heartbeat for you. She's probably out there going off right now on his ass."

I couldn't help but laugh, picturing it in my mind. I hoped she was getting him good in front of everyone. He deserved it after what he did to me.

"Brina, have you forgotten that I go with Mohammed?" I asked, realizing I almost forgot about him my damn self.

"I didn't forget, but you and Jason belong together. Drop that zero and get yourself a hero!"

I laughed. No, she wasn't using that played-out line on me.

"Look, I'm not feeling too good right now," I confessed, turning to face Brina. "I think I'm going to go see
the school nurse and tell her I need to go home."

Brina brushed the strand of hair back that was dangling in my face. "Are you okay?"

"Yeah, just stomach cramps," I replied. "After all, I'm
on my period."

We both fell out laughing. I felt much better by the
time Brina headed to her afternoon classes, but I went to
the nurse and faked sick anyway. I'd endured enough
drama for one day.

My mother picked me up out front, a look of worry
shadowing her face. "You okay, baby?" she inquired,
rubbing my arm after I got in the car. "You want to go see
Dr. Hill?"

"Momma, it's not that big of a deal! Just cramps from
my period."

The worry lines on her forehead dissipated a little. "Oh,
all right. Let's get you home so you can go straight to bed.
I'll fix you some hot soup and a pot of tea with lemon."

"Thanks, Momma!" I turned up the radio, pushing
the preset buttons until I found some decent music, as op-
posed to that classical crap my mother always listened to
in the car.

"No problem, baby." She patted my knee as she
pulled out from the parking lot. "It's not every day my
baby gets her first period. This is a big event."

I thought about Jason's big-ass mouth broadcasting it
and muttered, "If you only knew."

Later that evening, my daddy brought up a dinner
tray with roast beef, potatoes, carrots, and greens. "Hey,
princess!"

"Hey, Daddy!" I was so happy to see him. He always
enhanced my mood. "How was your day?"

"Just fine," he replied, setting the tray down on my nightstand. "We're having a bit of trouble getting the beams situated for the top floor, but we'll get it straight in the morning."

"That's cool!" I looked over at the tray and noticed a bunch of small daffodils crammed beside the plate. "Oh, Daddy, you picked me flowers!"

He chuckled, flashing his cinematic smile at me. "Actually, those are from Jason."

*"Jason! That trick ass!"* I covered my mouth, realizing my slip.

"Zoe, what did I tell you about using profanity?"

"I'm sorry, Daddy," I pouted. "Jason just makes me plain ole sick sometimes. You have no idea what he did to me today!"

"Yes, I do. He told me *everything.*"

"He did?"

My daddy nodded, trying to suppress a smile, and I was *tooooooooo* through. My first period was becoming the event of the freakin' century. I didn't even want my daddy to know I had one.

"Uh-huh, sounds like another lover's spat to me."

I popped him gently on the arm. "I hate him, Daddy!"

"Hate is a very strong word." He picked up the flowers and held them out to me. "Besides, he can't be all that bad. He sent me up here with these flowers and his apology."

*"Apology?"*

"Indeed! Jason's extremely sorry about spreading your private business all over the school."

"Well, I don't even want to hear all that," I hissed. "He can just forget about me ever speaking to him again."

"Is that so?"

"No question!"

My daddy pulled a crumpled piece of notebook paper out of his shirt pocket and set it down on the blanket beside me. "He must be a mind reader then, because he wrote you a letter."

I didn't say another word. I couldn't find any words to say. Part of me was dying to read the note in hopes it would declare his love for me. The other part was afraid it would be disappointing.

My daddy kissed me on the cheek and headed toward the door. "Goodnight, sweetheart!"

"Goodnight, Daddy!"

He hesitated once he got out into the hallway. "By the way, if you *should* decide to talk to Jason, he and I will be down in the garage for the next couple of hours."

I almost jumped out of my skin. *"He's over here? Now? In this house?"*

"Yep, he sure is. We're working on that china cabinet I promised your mother for the dining room."

With that, he closed the door, and I heard his footsteps going down the stairs.

I sat there for a few moments, trying to drown myself in the episode of *Miami Vice* that was on.

As fine as Phillip Michael Thomas was back in those days, it was no use. I had to know what was in the note. I slowly unfolded the paper, smoothing out the creases as I went along.

*Zoe,*
*I know you're pissed at me. I was wrong to do what I did. Please forgive me. It's just that I like you so much, and you hurt my feelings the other day. You probably don't care, since you've hated*

*me since you moved here. Chandler was mad at me today. I told her the truth though. I told her I wanted to go with you. She said I should stay with her because you would never date me anyway. Is that true? Are you still seeing that Mohammed dude? The Muslim with the raggedy car? If so, I'll leave you alone. Either way, please accept my apology. I'll see you at school tomorrow, and maybe we can go roller-skating or to a movie this weekend. I can ask my mother to drive us and pick us up.*

*Love Always, Jason*

Now, you might find this hard to believe, but I swear I didn't take a breath for at least five minutes. Jason and I were going to be together. Fugg a Mohammed! Fugg a Chandler! I was going to accept his apology and tell him I wanted to go with him the very next day, or there wasn't a dog in the entire state of Georgia.

# chapter four

All of the dogs must have gone farther south with the birds, because I never got the opportunity to accept Jason's apology. I fully intended to. I put on the most provocative, hoochified outfit I could find in my thirteen-year-old closet. It was a tight pink leotard with some form-fitting black capri pants. I went to school the next day on a mission to get my man, Chandler or no Chandler.

I planned to pull Jason aside at lunchtime and tell him I did want to go with him, wherever the hell it was he wanted to go when he'd asked me to go with him. I sprayed on some cotton-candy-scented body spray, put on some cherry-flavored lip gloss, and pinned my hair up so I would look older and sexier. I even folded my white bobby socks down as far as they would go so I could show off a little leg.

I was on my way to the cafeteria to put my plan into action when the guidance counselor, Mr. Turner, grabbed me gently by the wrist and asked me to follow him to his office. I couldn't imagine what he wanted to talk to me about. Then I narrowed it down to throwing the tray of food in Lyle's stinky face the day before. I was all set to defend myself, but I froze when we walked into his office and my mother was sitting in one of the brown metal chairs, crying her eyes out.

I only half-listened while she explained my father's death to me. I remember hearing the words *steel beam* and *construction site* and *accidental release*. It didn't seem real. After all, my father had brought a tray of food up to my room just the night before, teasing me about Jason and delivering his note. I remembered his smile, what he had on, what he smelled like, everything. Yet in the blink of an eye he was gone, and my life would never be the same.

Ironically, the death of my father is what finally bridged the gap between Jason and I. Jason had become extremely attached to my father during the years he got to know him and was crushed when he heard the news. He came over to our house that evening, and while all the adults tried to comfort my mother, he comforted me. We sat out on the front stoop, and he held me for what seemed like hours. We both shed tears all over each other and talked about the happy memories we had of my father. Jason said he was determined to finish the china cabinet he and my father had been building together. He kept his word a month later, and my mother still cherishes it to this very day.

The day of my father's funeral was rainy and dreary. Several of his friends and family members came from near and far. It was all a blur to me. I barely made it through the service, especially when his brother, my uncle Winslow, a minister from Houston, gave the eulogy. He talked extensively about their childhood antics. Hearing things about my father that I never knew saddened me to the point of complete withdrawal. Jason held one of my hands at the graveside, and Brina held the other one. When it was time to leave in the limousine with my mother and the rest of my father's immediate family members, I let go of their hands and never looked back. I just wanted to be alone in my misery.

For months I kept to myself whenever possible. I would come straight home from school; I dropped out of all of my extracurricular activities and instructed my mother to tell Brina, Jason, and whoever else I was busy when they called. It was Jason who was the persistent one, though. He wouldn't take no for an answer. He often came over to visit me, and we were actually civilized to one another. It was a great feeling. He was the only person my age I remotely felt like being around—probably because I was head over heels in love with him.

My mother was now a single parent, just like Brina's mother, and had to take on a second job to make ends meet. I felt so bad about it, but I wasn't old enough to get a real job. I baby-sat whenever I could for people in the neighborhood. Being around infants and toddlers was cool because they didn't ask me a lot of questions. I made yet another promise to myself. I swore one day I would take care of my mother and make sure money and comfort were always present in her life.

Summer came, and I was sitting on the front porch steps one night. It was a clear night, and the stars were so beautiful. I was always fascinated with stars, and my eyes were so affixed on them that night, I didn't see Jason approaching me until he was less than ten feet away from me.

"What are you doing, Zoe?" He sat down on the step below the one I was sitting on and leaned his elbow beside my thigh.

"Looking at the stars." I moved over on the step a little, away from his hand, because even a slight touch from him made me yearn for him. "Sometimes I close my eyes and imagine myself floating up among the stars. I feel weightless, and it's such a weird feeling. Yet, it makes me feel so relaxed. It's incredible!"

I darted my eyes down to his, and noticed he was looking at me like I had lost my fucking mind. "Sorry, Jason. I know I must sound plum foolish."

"No, not at all. Tell me more about them, Zoe." He sensed my hesitation. "Please, I really want to learn astronomy."

For the next ten or fifteen minutes I pointed out every constellation I could recognize to Jason, including the Little Dipper, Big Dipper, and Ursa Minor. I was surprised he actually seemed to be interested in them.

"You see that bright star over there? The North Star?" I pointed as if my fingertip could land directly upon it.

"Yes, I see it. It's beautiful. Just like you." I started blushing and placed my hands between my thighs, clamped them shut, and pretended to look down the street at an approaching car.

"I wonder if that's my mother." I knew it wasn't but was trying to change the subject. I wasn't even prepared for the "beautiful" comment. Once the car passed, I continued, "No, that's not her. Anyway, I renamed the star after my father, Peter."

"That's too cool!"

"Thanks." Jason eased up and sat on the same step as me, pressing his leg against mine. I instantly started shaking, and my knee started going back and forth. Years later, as I began to understand my sexuality better, I realized I was deliberately causing friction on my clit because I was horny. "One day, I'm gonna have a little boy and name him Peter."

"Maybe we can make him together." He reached over and started rubbing his fingers up and down my leg. I tried to jump up, but he stopped me and put his arm around me. "Don't run away from me, Zoe. Let's talk."

"About what?" I was frozen like a Popsicle. I couldn't move right at that moment if my life depended on it.

"Which one of those stars is ours?"

"Ours?"

"Yes, ours. Let's pick a star and make it our own special star. For always!" I looked him in his sexy hazel eyes and wanted to kiss him so bad but didn't have the nerve. "How about that one over there? You see it?"

I had no idea which one he meant, 'cause I was too busy looking at him. "Yes!"

"Cool! So that'll be our star. Jason and Zoe's star."

The kiss began so fast, it took me off guard. It was the first French kiss of my life, and I will never forget it. His tongue was thick and soft and penetrated my mouth after practically having to pry it open. Once I was able to relax, it was great, outstanding, miraculous, the bomb diggity.

"Wanna go inside your house?" Jason stopped kissing me abruptly after a few moments and made the suggestion. I just sat there with my mouth hanging open and his sweet saliva all over my lips. He stood up, took me by the hand, and starting pulling me up to my feet. "Come on, let's go inside awhile."

We were standing in the doorway, tonguing the hell out of each other, with my arms over his shoulders and his around my hips, inching me farther into the house, his hard dick pressing up against my wet pussy through our jeans, when my mother pulled into the driveway.

We tried our best to play it off. Jason put his hands in his back pockets, and I crossed my arms in front of me, trying to pretend like we were just standing there having a casual conversation. "I'll talk to you later, Zoe," Jason blurted out as he began to walk away. He waved to my mother as she was getting out of the car and managed a soft, "Hey!"

"Hey Mom! Have a good day at work?" I moved out of the doorway so she could get in with the bag of groceries she was carrying. "Let me take that to the kitchen."

"Sure!" She handed me the bag, and I started making my way toward the kitchen. I almost made it too without getting busted. "By the way, Zoe, I saw that!"

I turned around, getting ready to try to fabricate a story, but she wasn't even looking at me. She was flipping through the mail from that day, so I left well enough alone.

While I was putting away the groceries, I started wondering what would have happened between Jason and me if my mother hadn't shown up right then. I wondered if he was *experienced*, and hoped like all hell he wasn't. I wanted to be his first.

After I went to bed and made sure my mother was fast asleep, I masturbated for the first time. I didn't know what to do exactly, and to this day, I'm not sure whether or not I actually came. All I know is thinking about Jason and feeling on myself at the same time made me feel damn good.

• • •

Well, I finally got my man, and Chandler got pushed to the curb. Jason told her the truth, that he and I were an item. She took it hard, but I didn't care. That summer was the greatest one of my entire life. Jason and I spent almost every day together. We never did the nasty though. As it turned out, he was still a virgin and was not completely ready to do it, so we didn't. We used to hold hands and hug and neck heavily. He wouldn't let it go any farther, so I began to masturbate on a regular basis.

I assumed masturbating at such a young age was probably strange but had no idea there were underlying reasons for it. What I did not know then but realize all too well now is that my battle with sexual addiction had already begun.

# chapter five

Things were going great between Jason and me. Just think! My soulmate had been staring me in the face all those years without me even suspecting it.

I was still completely devastated over my father's death—Lawd knows no one and nothing could ever take his place. Jason helped me through it, though. We spent every second we could spare together. After school, we did our homework together unless Jason had practice. If he did, I would sit in the bleachers and wait for him.

Chandler couldn't stand me being there. As far as I was concerned, that was her personal problem. I'm surprised her eyes didn't end up permanently crossed from rolling them back and forth in her head at me so damn much. A couple of times, she almost fell flat on her ass during cheerleading practice because she was so busy trying to diss me.

Meanwhile, Mohammed was still trying. I have to give

it to the brotha. He didn't give up on love easily. I tried to hook him up with Brina, but she wasn't even having it. She'd developed this massive crush on Cordell. I used to beg Jason to sweat him about asking her out.

On occasion, we would all hang out together at the mall or the ice-skating rink in the Omni International Hotel. I hate the fact they closed the rink down some years ago. I would love for Jason and me to take the kids there and reminisce about the good old days.

Cordell and Brina did eventually hit it off, thank goodness—she was getting on my last nerve worrying about who else he might possibly like.

I hated it when Jason traveled to away games, because I didn't have any way to tag along. I thought about pleading my way onto the cheerleading squad, even though I had no interest in it, just so I could be with him.

I wanted to take things further, but Jason was content with kissing and grinding with our clothes on. That night on the porch, I just knew he was *experienced.* He fooled my ass but good. Part of me was elated because that meant Chandler couldn't throw having sex with him up in my face.

I was growing more and more frustrated. The more Jason refused my sexual advances, the more obsessed I became with getting him to go all the way. He would let the kissing get hot and heavy, and then just get up and leave me panting despondently on the couch.

I began to wonder if something was wrong with me. Most boys his age were all about trying to get some so they could brag about it to their friends—but not Jason. He wasn't having any part of climbing up inside my sugary walls.

I was willing to deal with it, yearning coochie and all, until Brina called me up on the phone after 1 A.M. one Saturday night.

"Brina, why are you calling me so late?" I whispered into the handset, trying not to rouse my mother. "My mother will have a fit if she wakes up."

"That's what you have your own phone line for, doofus!"

She laughed, but I didn't see a damn thing funny. "Brina, what is it? Is something wrong, Sis? Is it your mother?"

"No, she isn't even here," Brina replied sarcastically. "She's probably sitting on a barstool somewhere rapping to one of those ugly-ass men she keeps bringing up in here."

I didn't know what to say about that one, so I changed the subject. "Well, what's wrong, then?"

"Nothing's wrong, Zoe," she chuckled. "In fact, everything is just spantacular."

I sat up and turned on the lamp on my nightstand. "Okay, now that I'm completely lost, care to enlighten me?"

"*We did it!*" she screamed in my ear.

"Did what, dammit?"

"Cordell and I did the nasty! The wild thing! The hoochie-coochie!"

"Uh-uh, you're lying!" I yelled out, no longer caring about waking my mother up. "Tell me you're lying! Confess!"

"Sheit, I'm not lying," she giggled. "We did it, and it was *gooooooooood!*"

"You and Cordell had sex?" I was finding this shit hard to comprehend. Jason and I had been together for months and had never even gotten naked. Here this chica was calling me up braggin' on dick, and they had only been dating a couple of weeks.

"Boy, did we!"

"I have to go, Brina!" I can't describe my feelings, but I was hurt and didn't feel like talking anymore.

"Zoe, wait! I want to tell you all the details! Blow by blow, or should I say lick by lick!"

That did it! "Brina, I'll call you tomorrow! Later!"

With that, I hung up the phone. I knew I was wrong for that. There she was excited, wanting to share her first sexual experience with me, and I totally dissed her. I couldn't help myself. I cried myself to sleep, light on and all, wondering why in the world Brina could get some loving and I couldn't.

The next day I went outside and sat on the stoop sporting a pair of dark sunglasses, a black turtleneck, and black jeans like I was in mourning. I even had on black socks.

Jason came out his front door a few minutes later and headed across the street to join me. He was eating a Hostess Chocolate Cupcake and offered me half of it before he sat down.

"No, thanks," I mumbled under my breath, not even wanting to acknowledge him.

He sat down on the stoop beside me, inquiring, "What's wrong with you? You love chocolate cupcakes."

"I'm not hungry right now, is all," I replied, looking down at his feet and noticing he had a new pair of white Pumas.

"Aww, I get it now. It's that time of the month, huh?"

I pulled my sunglasses down slightly so I could snarl at him and roll my eyes. "What do you care if it's that time of the month? It's not like we do anything!"

Jason cleared his throat and starting fidgeting. He polished off the rest of the cupcake and pretended to be enthralled in a squirrel climbing the oak tree in my front yard.

"You know about Cordell and Brina having sex last night, don't you?" he asked, finally breaking the silence.

Damn, Brina was telling the truth! "Cordell told you?"

"Yeah, he called me early this morning to brag about it."

"How dare him spread Brina's business around like that?" I barked, automatically going into my protective mode. "Damn, he's almost as bad as you."

"Hold up now! Didn't Brina call and tell you? You don't seem too surprised about it."

I tried to hold back a smile, realizing I was in essence calling the kettle black. "Maybe she did. What of it?"

"How can you be mad at Cordell for telling me when Brina told you? Hell, she probably called you the second he left her place to spill the beans. At least he waited until this morning to call me."

Wow, Jason read Brina's ass like a book! I looped my arm around his. "Baby, when are we going to do it?"

He pulled his arm away from mine. "Zoe, I told you I'm not ready to go all the way. I want us to wait."

"Wait how long? Till we're fifty years old?"

I could tell he was pissed. He started huffing and biting his fingernails. "Don't be ridiculous! Are you such a freak that you can't wait until the time is right?"

"Freak?" I started to slap him but caught myself. I was trying to make a sincere effort to lay off the violence. "How can I be a freak if I don't do anything freaky?"

"Well, maybe you should call Mohammed's ass up!"

Oh no, he didn't even go there! "Well, maybe I should. He's a *real man*. He wants my body, unlike you," I said, telling a bold-faced lie. Mohammed wouldn't even give me the tongue, rather less the dick.

Jason stood up, probably just so he could look down his nose at me. "You don't know what the hell I want, Zoe! You don't know a damn thing about me!"

"And Chandler does, huh?"

"Chandler didn't ever ride my back like you're doing! That's for sure!"

I was hyperventilating, trembling, and on the verge of an explosion. "Just get the hell out of my face, Jason!" He stood there and stood there and . . . stood there. "I thought I told you to get out of my face. Did I stutter?"

"So what are you saying, Zoe?" Hell, I had no clue what I was saying! How dare he ask me that? "Are you breaking up with me?"

That was when I made the stupidest move I've ever made in my entire life. I said, "Yes, I am."

He walked away from me and left me sitting there, feeling dumb. The next day he got back with Chandler; the following week I got back with Mohammed out of retaliation, and the farce continued for two years.


I made feeble attempts to get Jason back, but he wasn't even going for it. I even broke down, gave him a heartfelt apology and asked if we could at least be friends. He told me to go be friendly with Mohammed. I never did *anything* sexual with Mohammed. He was still frontin' on the dick. I wasn't too upset because I was in love with Jason Reynard, and there were no two bones about it. I just dated Mohammed to try to make Jason jealous.

Brina and some of the other girls discovered a hole in the wall of the locker room, and they used to peek through it to get dang-a-lang sightings. I couldn't have cared less until one day Brina yelled out that she could see Jason's ass. I knocked her on the floor like I was a linebacker for the Atlanta Falcons. I peeked through the hole and started salivating, praying he would turn around so I could see his *other part*. Our gym teacher, Ms. Price, interrupted me though and delivered a serious tongue-lashing when she discovered what I was up to. Now, fifty-eleven girls had been looking through that hole for weeks, and no one got caught. As soon as I take a glance, I get cold busted. Ain't that a bitch?

# chapter six

Springtime rolled around, and it was time for the annual School Fair at Central. I was reluctant to go because Mohammed had been showing out and seemed more worried about talking my ears off about the Nation of Islam than taking my pants off. Like I said before, that was cool with me. It had gotten to the point where even being around him irritated the hell out of me. The Friday night before the fair, I called him up and succinctly told him all bets were off.

"Why don't you want me to take you?" He sounded so pitiful when he realized I was on the brink of kicking his ass to the curb. "You asked me months ago to go with you to the fair at your school, and now you're backing out at the last minute? I was supposed to be filling in for Brother Jabrail at the rally tomorrow afternoon, but I changed my schedule around and *everything* just so I could go hang out with you."

The guilt trip was not even working. It became dis-

turbingly clear to me that Mohammed had been nothing
more than a big waste of time. I listened to him drone on
and on and finally resorted to holding the phone away
from my ear while I became pleasantly immersed in another thought. I was sitting on the living room sofa when
some headlights suddenly blinded me through the cur-
tains. I moved one of the sheer curtain panels to the side
slightly and peeked outside to see if it was Momma getting off work early; I was anxious to tell her about the A I
received on my calculus exam. It wasn't Momma but I
caught the taillights of Jason's Camaro just as they turned
off. When he got out of the car, he looked like an Adonis,
a god even. He was sporting this Negro League baseball
jacket and some Levis' that were so tight, I wanted to
reach out and spank that tight ass of his. It brought on a
delightful set of ambiguous memories, including the
glimpse I got of his butterball naked ass through the hole
in the girls' locker room. Things could've been so different if I hadn't gone too far and dumped him that day. It
had been almost two years, and he still gave me nothing
but cynical remarks, dispassionate glares, and malevolent
treatment.

"Zoe, are you there?" Damn, why couldn't he just
shut up and stop whining? I was busy daydreaming about
a real man. "Zoe? Oh, so now you just gonna igg me and
thangs? That's cool!"

I watched Jason use his foot to nudge the car door
shut because his arms were full of some Kroger bags he
retrieved from the backseat. I knew I had about thirty
seconds to hit the pavement, or he would be inside and
out of my reach. My mother had mentioned that Jason's
parents were going out of town for the weekend and
asked her to keep an eye on him, so I knew he was alone.
It was time to make my move.

"Umm, Mohammed, I have to go." I shifted through the repertoire of excuses I frequently used to get off the phone with him, trying to make sure the one I was about to blurt out hadn't been abused. "My mother will be home in a few, and I need to clean up the kitchen before she gets here. Call me next week. Peace."

"But, Zoe, what about tomorrow?"

Click. Enough of all that. I jumped up off the worn and tattered sofa and quickly adjusted the dolman sleeves of the white blouse I had on with some black velveteen leggings and black leather platform shoes. I made a bee-line for the front door, pausing half a second to smile in the mirror and make sure none of the meatloaf from dinner was stuck in my front teeth.

I was determined to make a classic statement of subtlety and poise, pretending like I just happened to be stepping outside for some fresh air or something. Once I saw Jason's key hitting the lock and the lights go on in his foyer when he hit the switch on the wall, I quickly discarded that option.

"Jason, hold up just a minute!" I heard my voice and realized I was screaming, panicking even, so I toned it down a bit and then reiterated, "Hang on a second."

Even from across the street, I could see his eyes crinkle at the sides. He was probably under the automatic assumption I only wanted to say something sarcastic to him. To be honest, I had no idea what I was going to say, but I knew I needed Jason. I wanted Jason. I had to have Jason, or I might as well have slit my wrists with a plastic knife from KFC or taken an overdose of Ex-Lax or something.

"Zoe, what do you want?" He tossed the bags down on the tile floor in the entryway.

"Why do you think I want something?" I replied,

moving tentatively toward him. "Maybe I just wanted to say hey."

He gave me a sanguine smile, and I was a bit relieved. Normally, he would just snarl at me. "Well, hey."

I was at his doorway by then, and I immediately got lost in his eyes, wondering how in the hell the little nucca I used to scrape in the street with grew up to be so damn fine.

"Anything else?" he asked, beginning to press on the backside of the door like he was on alert to slam it in my face if my evil twin raised her ugly head. He knew I wanted him though. I could tell. He was just basking in the glory of knowing he had control over my conflicted heart.

I hesitated and bit on my bottom lip, contemplating what to say next. He blushed and leaned against the doorframe, and it dawned on me how tall he was. I had three-inch platforms on my five-foot, six-inch frame, and he looked like the Jolly Green Giant standing in front of me. "How tall are you?"

He grinned and let out a slight chuckle. "Is that what you came over here to ask me at this time of night? How tall I am?"

"No, but I was just wondering. I didn't realize you were so gigantic."

He rolled his eyes, but I could tell my interest in his height was flattering to him. "If you must know, gurl, I'm about six-five."

"Six-five? Damn!" For some reason, I had to look at his feet. I glanced down, and he had on the biggest-ass pair of Nikes I'd ever seen. Brina and the other gurls used to always talk about how a boy's feet were directly related to penis size. I had never bought into that, since penis size was never a fascination for me—that is, until the day I prayed like all hell Jason would turn around in the gym shower. On my way back up to look at his face again, I made a pit stop at the crotch of his jeans. My eyes ballooned when I spotted it behind the denim fabric. Not only was it big, much bigger than it had been a couple years before when we used to grind up against each other, but he either had a coconut in his pocket or he was damn sure happy to see me.

"Well, look, I'm about to go cook me some hot dogs. Aight?" I must've made him feel uneasy because he turned on me, and his grin changed to a pout. I wondered if he knew I was peeping his dang-a-lang.

"Okay, cool." I started to turn around when a lightbulb went off in my head. "You mind if I grab one of your hot dogs, Jason? Momma's working late again, and I'm *starved.*" I rubbed my belly to drive the point home. "We don't have a thing in the fridge, and I don't have a car like you, so I can't go to Kroger or grab some fast food."

I was lying my ass off, knowing good and damn well that less than an hour earlier I had munched down on the mouthwatering meatloaf and mashed potatoes with gravy Momma fixed before she left for work.

Jason glared at me, like he was registering the thought of actually letting me in the house when his parents weren't home. "Aight, come on in," he said, stepping aside. He must've wondered if I would go psycho on his ass and stab him with a butcher knife, because he emphatically added, "But as soon as we eat, you need to bounce, because I have a lot to do before the fair tomorrow."

"Whatchu gotta do for the fair?" I quizzed, attempting to throw a little slang in there so I appeared cool.

He picked up the bags and headed to the kitchen. I closed the front door and followed him. "The basketball team is sponsoring some of the activities this year, and since I'm the captain, I have to help out."

"Oh yeah? What type of activities?" He laid the bags on the counter, and I became enthralled with the tightness of his ass again. It looked ten times better up close than it did from the hole in the locker room.

He didn't notice me staring because he was busy putting some eggs, bacon, and milk in the fridge. "We got this kissing booth going on, for one thang. I'm not really trying to do it, but you know how it is?"

"Kissing booth? Word?"

"Yeah, you didn't know?"

"Nope."

Jason gave me a puzzled look. "Hmm, I'm surprised, because Chandler and some of the other cheerleaders are doing it along with us."

The mere mention of Chandler's name made me cringe. Damn, why couldn't that anorexic beanpole bitch move the hell on? I had even resorted to becoming a cheerleader to get next to Jason, but it just made him laugh. The other girls on the team were all buddy-buddy with Chandler and left me out of the loop except for the required activities. "No one said a thing to me. Then again, I'm not surprised, considering the fact Chandler hates my guts."

Jason put some tap water in an aluminum saucepan and then turned on a gas burner. "Chandler doesn't hate you. You're trippin'. What makes you think that?"

He acted like it was some sort of revelation. Jason knew good and damn well Chandler couldn't stand my ass. I don't even know why he was trying to fake the funk. "Whatever, Jason," I hissed. "So, are you and her still hanging out?"

He cut open the pack of Oscar Mayer hot dogs, dropped them in the boiling water, and then sat down across from me at the white drop-leaf table with floral place mats adorning it. "Why you wanna know? In fact, what's up with all these questions tonight? You writing a book or sumptin'?"

I looked at him contritely. "No, I ain't writing no damn book. I was just wondering because—"

"Because what?" He waylaid the rest of my sentence and it was just as well. I was about to do something dumb and ask him to go with me like he did me years before. I could hear his smart-aleck reply in my head: Go with you where?

"Never mind." I decided to change the subject. "So how long are your parents gonna be out of town, and where did they go anyway?"

"See, another freakin' question." That fool laughed at me in my face, and it finally pissed me off. My evil twin came out.

"Geesh, if I can't even ask a damn question, I might as well take my ass back on across the street!" I jumped up from the kitchen table and started stomping toward the front door in my platforms.

Jason was right on my tail. "Hold up, Zoe. I'm sorry. My parents are in North Carolina visiting some relatives, aight? Just chill, Boo."

Dang, he called my ass "Boo." A word of affection. Everyone knew "Boo" was more than just a word Casper the Friendly Ghost whispered to unsuspecting children. Maybe not before the eighties, but Boo was a certified synonym for "Baby," "Sweetie," and "Snookums" by the time the word left Jason's sexy-ass lips. I was a Boo. Aww, dayum!

"Yes, Jason?" I spun around and batted my eyelashes at him, trying to keep myself from blushing, but I realized it was a lost cause.

"What about your hot dog? What you gonna eat for dinner?"

I was appalled. How dare he build up my emotions and then start talking about some damn hot dogs, even if they weren't cheap-ass chicken franks? I sucked my teeth. "I'll just eat some Vienna sausages and some saltines instead."

I swung the door open and headed out, muttering expletives under my breath.

"Wait—why did you ask about me and Chandler for real, though?"

I didn't even look back at him. "I gotta go. I need to go condition my hair and get ready for the fair."

"So you're going then?"

"Yeah, I'm going." I didn't want to tell him that Ms. Rankin, the principal, had asked Brina and me to be clowns. Chandler and her other hussy friends were going to kiss boys all day long, and I had to be a freakin' clown.

Jason was still saying something to me when I slammed the door closed, but I couldn't have cared less. I was crushed, humiliated, fired up even. I kicked off my shoes, ran into the living room, and buried my head in a toss pillow to catch my tears.

Momma shook me awake a couple of hours later. "What's wrong, baby? Why are you lying on the sofa in the dark?"

I looked up at my mother and wanted to spill it all, but she had enough problems, including but not limited to working two jobs to support me. "I'm okay, Momma. I was just dog-tired when I got home from school today."

"You sure, sweetie?" She rubbed my back, and I sought comfort in her touch.

I got up, kissed her gently on the cheek, and took a whiff of the rose water she always dabbed behind her ears. She always smelled so feminine, even after a long day. "I'm going to bed now. Goodnight."

I was halfway up the steps when she drilled me. "What time is Mohammed picking you up for the fair tomorrow? I wanna make sure you get up on time."

I hesitated, thinking of a logical excuse why he wasn't coming. Then I remembered him mentioning the rally. "Ummm, he's not coming. He has to do a Muslim rally tomorrow, so I'm going with Brina."

My mother sounded slightly disappointed. "Oh, okay. Goodnight, Zoe."

I went in my room, left a message on Brina's answering machine telling her to come get me the next day, fell on my canopy bed, and started wailing all over again until I was fast asleep.

I woke up the next morning about eight, still devastated and confused about my feelings toward Jason and his feelings toward me. When I got down to the kitchen, Momma was cooking some ham and cheese omelets. The aroma was kicking and I was either starved or ready to see if eating till I exploded would make me forget about my troubled, nonexistent love life.

"You feel better this morning, sweetie?" Momma ran her fingers through my shoulder-length hair while I threw down on the omelet like Wilbur from *Charlotte's Web* slopping up some grub.

I wiped my mouth with a napkin and gulped down an ounce of orange juice along with some egg so food remnants didn't come flying out my mouth when I answered her. "I'm fine, Momma. I was just tired last night because it was a long week at school."

She sat down beside me and blew lightly into her coffee mug. The steam amusingly fogged up her glasses, and I remembered how it used to make me fall out laughing every time that happened in my younger years.

"Yes, I know Ms. Rankin had you and Brina working

hard on the fair." She took a sip of her Maxwell House and grinned when her legal drug started to kick in. "Did you girls get all the posters made?"

"Yes, they look great too." I slapped my forehead, looking dumbfounded. "I meant to tell you last night. Guess what?"

"What, sweetie?"

"I got an A on my calculus exam! No, scratch that. Your baby girl got an *A-plus!*"

I gleamed while she took it all in. She reached over and rubbed my shoulder. "That's fantastic, Zoe! Having Jason tutor you has really paid off!"

I frowned. It figured she would give him all the glory. I had asked Jason to tutor me in calculus one damn time, and my mother made it sound like he single-handedly resurrected my brain cells. It was all just a ploy to get him to pay attention to me in the first place. His math skills weren't all that. "I did it all by myself. Jason didn't take the test for me."

She caught my drift. "I know, baby. I didn't mean for it to come out that way. I was just—"

I jumped up and headed back upstairs. "I have to go get ready. Brina's picking me up in a few."

I heard Momma calling after me. "I didn't mean anything, Zoe! I really didn't!"

Brina picked me up in her hoopty twenty minutes later, and I was not even halfway dressed. I took a quick shower, and then lingered over every feature of my body in the foggy mirror on the back of the bathroom door. I had to admit that I was lacking a bit in the tit department, but my ass was good. All good!

Most boys at school seemed to be into girls with nice asses, but Jason obviously wasn't, because Momma could have fried those ham and cheese omelets on Chandler's flat ass.

I wasn't one hundred percent sure they were still dating because his slick behind had avoided my question the night before. I was hell-bent on finding out that day, though, one way or another. By the time the sun went down that night, I was either going to be as happy as a fag in Dickland or as depressed as a whore in church.

I never got around to conditioning my hair the night before, and it was frizzed up like I was going to audition for the role of Kizzy Kunte in the sequel to *Roots*. Luckily, once I got to school, I could put on the dreaded clown suit and cover my naps with a multicolor wig.

Brina was laying on the horn thick, so I threw on some white walking shorts. Okay, they were more like Daisy Dukes. I flung all of my T-shirts out of my top dresser drawer until I came across the red one that had *G.A.G.* imprinted on the front and the phrase "Get A Grip" in small lettering at the bottom. I had a predilection for bragging on my tits even though I didn't have much of anything. I slipped my dogs into some red patent leather slides and flip-flopped my way down the steps.

"Gurl, hurry your slow ass up!" Brina was fussing as soon as I stepped out the door into the unrelenting sunlight. It was a beautiful day for a school fair. Ms. Rankin did everything except Indian tribal dancing and casting a voodoo spell to make sure it didn't rain, and it paid off. There wasn't a storm cloud in sight.

"I'm coming, damn! You're always rushing some damn body!"

I got into the hoopty and gave Brina a brief once-over. No matter how hoochie I tried to be, she out-hoochied me every single time. She had on a skin-can't-get-no-tighter-unless-you-embed-the-clothes-in-your-ass-tight black sundress and some black leather pumps. Plus, her hair looked good as all hell. I was immediately jealous. I knew

I should have slapped some conditioner in my nappy head and thrown a plastic cap on before I went to bed. I looked like one of those ugly-ass troll dolls sitting next to Cinder-fuckin'-rella rolling with her.

"What on earth do you have on, gurl? We're going to a fair, not clubbing."

Brina rolled her eyes and flipped me the bird. I turned the radio up, even though there was more static in it than a woman's nylon half slip straight out the clothes dryer, and started bopping my head to Cheryl Lynn schooling nuccas about how they "Got to Be Real." "Dang, that's my song," I proclaimed.

"*E-ve-ry* cool song that comes on is your dang song." Brina chuckled. She was right too, 'cause on any given day, I had at least twenty favorite songs but rarely knew the words to them. Ironically, the only songs I could ever manage to memorize were the ones I hated. Ain't that a bitch?

Brina started bopping her head in unison with my naps while she did one last lipstick check in her rearview mirror before pulling off. We rode all the way to school with the bass controller on the system turned as far to the right as humanly possible without one of us breaking a nail. It made the car shake from side to side at every stop-light while we gyrated our hips to the beat.

I spotted Jason's Camaro the second we pulled up in the parking lot. I wondered if he was somewhere arm-in-arm with Chandler, and if he'd picked her up that morning. His car was already gone when I got up. I checked.

Brina threw something on my face, blocking my vision. I yanked it off and realized it was a navy blue bathing suit. I held it up, looking at her quizzically. "What's this for?"

"Oops, I meant to tell you. Ms. Rankin caught me on

the way out of class yesterday and asked if you and I could sit in the dunking booth today, so I brought an extra suit for you from home."

I threw my hands on my hips and clucked my tongue. *"Dunking booth!* What the hell happened to being clowns?"

Brina cut off the ignition and opened up her door. I followed her out of the car. "She still wants us to be clowns too, but we can take turns doing both. She was going to do the dunking booth herself, but she has a cold."

I raised my hands to my hair. "I can't do the dunking booth. My hair is messed-da-hell-up, and I was counting on wearing that stupid clown wig to hide my naps."

We started walking toward the football field where the fair was being held. "Zoe, your hair's not looking bad at all. In fact, it looks real cute."

I crossed my arms and paused briefly, tapping my right foot on the gravel parking lot, to inhale her bullshit. "Yeah, right! You know my hair is *tooooooooo* through."

"You just think that, but it's straight. You know how it is?" She stopped and turned around to face me. "Whenever your hair is filthy dirty, thicker than a ton of bricks, and pinned up, that's when peeps come out of the woodwork with compliments."

I had to give it to her, 'cause she did have a point. That always seemed to happen.

"It's when you spend eight damn hours at a beauty shop under a hot-ass dryer listening to old-ass women complain to each other about men, kids, and other women that you have to almost beat a hair compliment out of some damn body."

I laughed because she was right on the money. "Aight, whatever, but I want to do the dunking booth first. I have something I need to do a little later."

Brina's eyes bulged. "Something like what?"

I looked down at the gravel, kicking a few pebbles around and blushing. "Just something."

"Does this something have a name that begins with a J?" I giggled. "By the way, what happened to Mohammed? I thought he was coming. I was surprised when I got your message about coming to get you this morning."

I grabbed her by the arm and started pulling her toward the field. I was suddenly in a hurry to get the whole sordid business over with, one way or another. I had no clue how I was going to approach the situation, but it had to be done. "Come on, Brina. I'll explain it all to you later."

Ten seconds after I sat down on the two-by-four doubling as a bench in the dunking booth, I was regretting letting Brina talk me into the shit. First came the comment from this high-yella, snaggletoothed nucca with a lopsided high-top fade and freckles. "Damn, Youngen, look at her hair!" His little sidekicks, none of them out of the eighth grade, pointed and laughed at me. I just waved them off, hoping they would go try their luck at a cap toss game or something else at one of the other booths. No such luck.

Five minutes later, I was the one laughing at their asses. They couldn't hit the metal bull's-eye on the dunking booth if their lives depended on it. They all took turns, wasting some of the ten bucks apiece their mommas probably gave them to get rid of them for the day.

"Damn, Youngen, you didn't even come close to her!" Snaggletooth was guffawing and hitting his boy on the back after the sorry excuse for a pygmy missed the target by a good two feet, and the baseball ended up in a trash can.

"Shit, not like you did any better," he retorted, trying to swallow his pride.

I started getting in on it. "Personally, I think all of you need to go home and lift some weights because you all look like skinny midgets from up here where I'm sitting!"

They didn't know how to react when a *girl* came at them like that. They looked at each other dumbfounded, and finally decided to go waste some money on something else. "Come on, Youngen. This shit's boring!"

An hour later, I was kind of hoping to get dunked, but to no avail. At least fifty peeps had tried, and only three or four of them even hit the edges of the target, much less the bull's-eye.

It was hot as hell out there. Add in the sun beaming on me through the glass surrounding the top of the booth, and it was ten times worse. I felt like I was sitting in a sauna. Thoughts of an old movie where a boy used a magnifying glass and sunlight to set a cricket on fire flitted through my head.

Just when I was convinced my dry nappy hair was going to catch on fire any second like a pile of bushweed and leave me looking like the victim of a witch hunt in Salem, Jason, Chandler, and the rest of their clique walked up to the booth. She had her arms around his waist. How dare she?

Chandler taunted me. "Look who it is! It figures they would put her in there instead of Ms. Rankin. Half the school would love to dunk her."

Jason looked from Chandler to me. I got sarcastic with him. "She doesn't hate me, huh, Jason?"

"Chandler, cut that out," he demanded, systematically removing her arms from around his waist.

She got dramatic. "What's wrong with you? After

what she did to you, you're taking her side over mine? I don't freakin' believe this shit!"

Jason looked guilt-stricken. After all, he probably did need to save some face at that point, with all his boys looking on and all. "No, not at all," he proclaimed. "In fact, check me out while I dunk her ass real quick."

They all laughed, and Chandler smirked, looking at me like she had just hit the lottery. Jason paid for his three baseballs and threw the first one before I even had a chance to brace myself. It hit the bottom of the target, but I didn't fall. Damn, I just knew that was my ass, as big and strong as he was, but he missed!

"Ah-ha, Jason!" I taunted him. "I forgot you were blind in one eye and can't see jack shit out the other one."

His boys started howling. "Damn, man, she told you!"

Jason's eyes narrowed with malice, a look I knew all too well, and he threw the second one. He missed by a mile.

I gave an exaggerated yawn. "Wow, I'm so impressed. Now I know I did the right thing when I dropped you like the plague. Sorry ass!"

Chandler yelled out, *"BITCH!"*

"Takes one to know one, trick ass," I replied with a grin.

"Hold up, all of you step back. I got this," Jason stated avidly. I was positive he would miss by a mile yet again.

Next thing I knew, my ass hit the cold water. I could hear them all falling out laughing before I even came up for air. Jason had his fists thrown up in the air and was prancing around like he had just put Ali down for the ten count. His boys gave him high fives and slapped him on the back while Chandler gave him a big fat hug.

"Forget you, Jason!" I was ashamed, upset, and hopelessly in love with the fool but scared to admit it.

"Forget you, too," he bellowed while their posse moved away.

Snaggletooth and his buddies came walking past the booth while I was struggling to get back on the bench. Their hands were filled with everything from cotton candy to stuffed animals to corn dogs.

"HAAAAA! HAAAAA! He got your ass good, Youngen!"

I just ignored it and let them enjoy their laugh. I got back up on the bench, hunched my shoulders, covered my eyes with the palms of my hands, and listened to the annoying-ass carnival music.

A couple of hours later, Brina traded places with me. I never thought I would be so elated to put on a clown suit—anything but that damn dunking booth. After Jason dunked me, a chain reaction ensued, and I hit the cold water at least twenty more times before I lost count.

Ms. Rankin, who didn't have the sniffles or any other vague symptom of a cold, gave me a quick lesson on making poodles and other cute characters out of oblong latex balloons and sent me on my way. I had a ball walking around and entertaining the little kids, who were strongly representing that day.

I had on a red, white, blue, and yellow suit with a white, red, blue, and purple wig, white powder makeup with red lipstick surrounding my lips, and huge red clown shoes. I was doing just fine until . . .

. . . I spotted the kissing booth. To say I was severely rattled to see all the hoochies lined up to kiss Jason would be the understatement of the year. There were just as many nuccas in line to kiss Chandler's skank ass, for some unknown reason. Apparently the cheerleaders and the players were taking turns at the booth. Jason and Chandler were up at bat.

I was immediately jealous, even though I could see from my vantage point some thirty yards away that he was only giving up quick pecks. Some of the shy, problematic-as-in-uglematic girls looked like they were about to faint when his fine ass kissed them on the cheek.

My heart dropped. I contemplated going inside the school to call Mohammed from the pay phone and telling him to come get me, but I knew getting with him on the rebound wouldn't suffice. It didn't work the first time, and it wouldn't work the second. Something had to be done. Desperate times called for desperate measures.

I bought a ticket for the kissing booth and got in the line behind all the other girls waiting to kiss Jason. What the hell! It made as much sense as anything else I had been doing lately. When my turn finally came, Chandler recognized me under the wig and makeup and grabbed for her man. "Come on, Jason. It's Lisa and Deon's turn now."

Jason's attention quickened when he realized it was me. Then he grinned from ear to ear. "You want me to kiss you?"

Chandler tried to pull him away by the arm, but he brushed her off, anxiously awaiting my reply. "Jason, let's go. Now!"

He glared at her. "Chandler, let's get something straight. You don't own me, aight?" He gazed back at me. "I asked Zoe a question, and I'd like an answer."

I cracked a mischievous smile and held my ticket up. "I bought a ticket, didn't I?"

"Jason, you better not kiss that ho." Chandler was near hysterics, and all her backup hussies were ready to pounce at a second's notice.

"Back off," he replied sourly. He looked deep into my

eyes and bit his lower lip to suppress yet another smile. "So kiss me then."

They had a card table separating the kissers and the kissees, probably Ms. Rankin's idea to deter any feel-ups if someone got carried away. I couldn't reach him without him leaning over it, and since he wasn't budging, I climbed up on top of it on my knees and grabbed him by the collar of his jersey.

He gave me a peck. A freakin' peck on the forehead like my grandmother used to give me. I had my eyes closed in anticipation of a deep, passionate kiss and opened them full of disappointment.

He grinned. "Okay, there's your kiss. Now beat it."

I let go of his collar, and they all guffawed at me. I was about to get down off the table and sulk away, but something came over me. I grabbed his collar again, pulled his face to mine, and slipped him the tongue. He refused it.

"Kiss me, Jason!" I pleaded with my eyes, and then I saw it. A flicker in his eyes that told me everything I needed to know to let the rest of the words escape from my lips. "I'm so sorry for the way I treated you. I want you back. I want *us* back, and I promise things will be different from now on."

Chandler panicked and tried to pry my hands off him, but he knocked her hands away. "Jason, what is this shit? After the way she treated you, you're just gonna take her back like that?"

Chandler must have been a psychic, because I was still waiting for a final decision on the matter.

Jason's eyes and voice softened. "What makes you think things could be different?"

I took the plunge. Right there in front of the whole world. I took a quick survey and noticed all eyes were on me. Even Ms. Rankin was standing over against one of the other booths, smiling at me and raising her eyebrows in encouragement.

I took a short, restorative breath and blurted it out. "Because I love you, Jason. I always have. I want to marry you and make a son named Peter and look at *our* star every night while I lie in your arms." I couldn't gauge the expression on his face, but I had to get it all out. "I've always loved you, even when we acted like we hated each other. I'm sorry for all the things I've done, but nobody's perfect. I don't know what else to say. I just—"

He put his finger on my lips and whispered, "Shhhh, it's okay, Boo. I never expected you to be perfect. I never expected you to be anything but you, because it's you, the real Zoe, that I'm so in love with."

He grabbed the back of my head and started kissing me, *really* kissing me, and I thought I had died and gone to heaven. I could hear people applauding and cheering and Chandler cussing and stomping off, but none of that mattered. Jason was showing me some affection, and I knew everything would be perfect from that moment on.

# chapter seven

Our senior year in high school rolled around, and still no sex. Jason and I had been boyfriend and girlfriend for over three years, and it was killing me. We did a lot of making out; kissing, caressing, and things like that. He sucked my breasts and fingered me quite often, but refused to stick it in. He kept saying he wanted to wait until we were married. We planned to get married as soon as we graduated, attend the same university, and live happily ever after.

All my friends were jealous, thinking I was getting my freak on all the time, but truth be known, I was jealous as hell of them. They were getting sexed better than me. Brina was still knocking boots with Cordell. Hell, even my mother was getting some. She had a new man, Aubrey, that I had mixed feelings about. I missed my daddy terribly. No one and nothing could ever replace him but at the same time, my mother deserved to be happy, so I accepted it.

Looking back, all the signs of sexual incompatibility between Jason and I were there from day one. I just couldn't see the forest for the trees. Love is indeed blind, and it makes you imagine qualities in a person that don't exist. I used to tell myself that things would change in time. I convinced myself once we became sexually active, our sex life would be the bomb. I was more than ready to spring into action, reading any book or manual about pleasing a man sexually I could find.

Part of me wonders whether marrying Jason was the right thing. Then I think about how much fun he and I had together, how loving he was to me when my father died, how romantic he was during the years we dated, and it makes it all seem worthwhile. Besides, my love for him is real and it was the night of our senior prom when I realized that love would never die.

I was all decked out in a sexy, strapless red gown with a split going all the way up the back, showing off my well-defined legs. Jason looked too sexy for words in his black tux. My mother had taken some pictures of the two of us in our living room before she rushed off to work.

"I have something for you!" Jason handed me a long round tube, capped at both ends. Color me stupid, but I was expecting a wrist corsage or some typical gift like that. Instead, I got a tube.

"What's this, baby?" I tried to hide my dismay. He saw right through me.

"Let's sit down for a sec, Zoe." He took my hand, led me to the big, fluffy armchair my daddy used to read to me in as a child, sat down, and then pulled me down onto his lap. "Now, Boo, open it and see what you got."

I popped the cap off the end of the long cardboard tube,

becoming more curious by the second. I reached in and pulled out several sheets of paper. It took me a moment to realize they were blueprints. Jason had taken quite an interest in architecture and planned to major in it.

"Blueprints, baby?"

He put his arm around my waist, pulled me closer into him and lightly kissed me on my bare shoulder. "Not just any blueprints. Spread them open." He helped me to open them up and added, "I wanted to do something very special for you."

"For me? Ooooh, the plot thickens!" I slipped my tongue into his mouth and gave him a long, passionate kiss. "Baby, I didn't realize you actually knew how to draw blueprints already."

"Well, they're not perfect, nor totally to scale, but yes, I know how to."

"What are they plans of?" I could make out the basic shapes and rooms but understood blueprints at the time about as much as I understood Japanese.

"Zoe, these are the plans for our dream house."

"Word?" My smile was hanging so wide open, I looked like I had more teeth than a set of triplets.

"Word, Boo. One day, after we're married, I'm going to build you this house we can raise Peter in it and live happily ever after." I threw my arms around his shoulders and hugged him with all the strength I could muster. He started pointing out certain things to me on the blueprints. "These are all skylights. Practically the whole house will have a glass ceiling, so we can see the stars from every room. So we can see *our* star."

That was it! The moment I knew it was forever. Three significant things happened after that. We never made it to the restaurant to meet our friends for dinner; we never made it to the prom; and we made love for the very first time. The plans we had for waiting until after marriage became nothing more than a memory.

I was so overwhelmed by the blueprints, my heart started jumping out my chest. It was the single most romantic thing in the world to me. The mere fact Jason had spent so many hours designing the place where he wanted to build a life together made my love and admiration for him even stronger, made my desire to do something just as special for him flourish, made my pussy wet.

"Jason—" I started tugging at his bow tie, trying to get it unfastened.

"Yes, Boo?" He grabbed hold of my wrist, trying to get me to stop. "What are you doing? We have to meet Brina, Cordell, and the others at the restaurant in twenty minutes."

I got up off his lap and stood in between his legs, carefully placing the blueprints on the coffee table. "Fuck them." After grabbing both his hands and pulling him up off the chair, I added, "Better yet, fuck me."

Jason took a double take at me, trying to come up with a response. "Zoe, you're trippin'." He slightly pushed me aside with his chest so he could make a path to the door. "Come on, baby. Let's go! We're going to be mad late!"

"I'm not going anywhere." I finally got up the nerve to stand my ground. "I'm not leaving this house until you make love to me."

He turned to face me, a perplexed look on his face. "Zoe, why are you doing this? We agreed we would wait until after we got married to make love."

I walked over to him, reached my hands into the opened jacket of his tux, and placed them around his waist so I was pressed as close against him as I could possibly get. His body was so incredibly warm, and I craved to feel him inside me. "Don't you want me, Jason?"

I didn't look at him, afraid I might see a look of rejection in his eyes. Instead, I rested my head against his chest, taking special care not to get lipstick on his crisp white shirt. "Baby, you know I want you. Don't be ridiculous."

As I began to run my fingertips up and down his spine, I lowered my voice to almost a whisper for no other reason than it seemed appropriate at that moment. "Then why can't we make love right here? Right now? We've waited so long. It's driving me crazy."

"I know, Boo, but it won't be that much longer. We graduate in a few months."

I felt his dick growing in his pants and started hoping he was fighting a losing battle. I still didn't look at him. I could feel his cool breath on the nape of my neck and was just glad he was holding me back. "I think about being with you all the time, Jason. I can't concentrate on anything else."

"I tell you what. Why don't we go to dinner and to the prom and see what happens after that? Your mother won't be home until morning, so it gives us plenty of time to be together."

That's when I looked him dead in the eyes. "You promise we'll make love later tonight?"

Then the dreaded words escaped his lips. "We'll see, Boo."

I hate the words *we'll see:* they almost always mean no. My parents spoke those words to me as a child when I asked for a new, extravagant toy or dress. They said them when I asked to do something we all knew I had no business doing. Thus, when Jason said them, they cut like a knife.

I started crying, and the tears were far from fake. My fragile and oversensitive nature, which had always been

present but tripled after the death of my father, came out.
I let go of Jason and used my hands to gather up the bottom of my tight dress so I could run up the stairs faster in
my high heels. I ran into my bedroom, slammed the door,
and flung myself on the bedspread, burying my head into
a pillow to catch the tears. He was right behind me. I
could hear his footsteps coming down the hall.

Jason opened the door, and I could feel my mattress
sink farther as he sat down on the bed beside me, seconds
before he began caressing my back with his strong, warm
hands. "Baby, look, if it really means that much to you
and you don't want to wait, then sure we can make love.
We can make love right now. I don't want to see you upset
like this. It breaks my heart."

I turned my head away from him, letting my lipstick
smear all over my pillow when I changed positions.
"Jason, you just don't get it. I shouldn't have to beg you
to make love to me. This is supposed to be something we
both want."

He started running his fingertips through my hair.
"We do both want this. I was just trying to do right by
you and wait, but make no mistake about it, I do want
you. I'm not even going to fake the funk about that."

After that, we were both silent for what seemed like
an eternity. He was running his hands from my hair down
to the small of my back, and I was trying to control my
sobs, which were eventually replaced with shallow
breathing. "Zoe, are you okay?"

"Yes, I'm fine." I turned over onto my back so I could
look at him. He took the tip of his thumb and cleared the
smudged mascara away from my eyes. All of my lipstick
had been transferred to my pillowcase. "You ready to go
to the prom?"

He didn't answer but got up and walked over to my

bookcase instead, putting on a cassette of slow jams that he'd made for me to remember him by when his parents once took him out of town for a week. He was always such a romantic—making me tapes of love songs, carving our names inside a heart on every tree in his yard and mine, calling me late at night so he could hear me breathe after falling asleep on the phone, letting me wear his varsity basketball jacket.

At six-five, he'd finally stopped growing and was the captain of the basketball team, taking them all the way to the state finals two years in a row. He had the smoothest skin for a man, and he still does to this very day. My husband has always been fine, but he's never been finer than the night we first made love.

"Dance with me, Zoe." He reached out his hand for me, looking so sexy and debonair, as the first song started playing. I took it and let him pull me up off the bed into his arms. We danced, our bodies swaying back and forth slowly in the moonlight invading my bedroom through the windows.

Before the first song concluded, Jason traced the contour of my lips with his fingertips, and then our kiss began. We had kissed hundreds of times before, but this one was different. It was as if there was an exchange of souls. We became one entity as our tongues intertwined in a dance of their own.

Jason scooped me up into his arms, carried me over to the bed, and laid me down gently. He climbed on top of me, and I pushed his jacket down over his shoulders and off. "I love you, Jason."

"I love you too, Zoe." He took my hand and kissed my palm while I turned on my side so he could easily unzip my dress and slide it over the curves of my body until it was completely removed.

The way he undressed me was so provocative. He was so gentle and took so much care with me, like I was a newborn baby. When he was done, I returned the favor. Once we were both nude, we sat on my bed face to face and placed a hand over each other's hearts, feeling the rhythm of our heartbeats coincide. It was the most intense, arousing experience.

We started kissing again as he laid on top of me, and for the first time our private parts brushed up against one another with no clothes in between them. The warmth of his body made my heart flutter and my skin tingle.

The anticipation of making love for hours on end was overwhelming. I had waited so long for the moment to arrive and had envisioned it thousands of times—no, make that millions of times—in my mind. I was expecting us to explore every inch of one another with our hands and tongues, make love in every position known to man, and pass out from pure exhaustion.

What happened instead was a complete catastrophe. First, Jason got nervous because we didn't have a condom. "Zoe, what about protection?"

"It'll be okay. Just pull out real quick when you feel like you're about to cum." I was tracing the curvature of his chest with my tongue, knowing my womanhood would finally be endorsed at any moment.

"Ummm, I don't know about this, Zoe. Maybe we should wait until we have some protection." He was trying to push me off him, but at the same time not putting up much resistance to my advances.

"Jason, do you want me to beg you? Is that it?"

"No! Hell no!" I started moving my hand up and down the shaft of his thick, long dick and rubbing the precum escaping from the head around with my thumb. "I'll make sure I pull out in time."

He stuck it in, and it hurt like all hell when my hymen broke. Two minutes and about thirty pumps later, he pulled it out, and I wanted to scream. I lay there, thinking to myself, "Is this all I get?"

Jason told me he loved me, and I reciprocated. Then we just laid there, in dead silence, with his head on my left breast. A whole hour passed, and neither of us mentioned the prom, or anything else for that matter. I was depressed and Jason was . . . I have no idea what Jason was. I got up and searched through my purse for a cigarette. Smoking was a habit I'd picked up when my daddy died as a method for relieving stress. I was damn sure stressed after my first sexual experience—stressed, disappointed, humiliated, and depressed.

Before he drifted off to sleep, he expressed his concern. "Geesh, Zoe, I hope I didn't get you pregnant."

"Don't be silly, Jason. No way am I pregnant! Never that!"

# chapter eight

What can I say? Never say never!

Whoever said you can't get pregnant by having sex just one time lied like all hell, 'cause my ass sure got knocked the hell up. Ain't that a bitch?

In one sense, it really didn't matter all that much since Jason and I were planning to get married in a few months anyway. On the other hand, all the plans Jason and I had precisely worked out for the future went out the freakin' window. Everything, except the marriage itself, had to be reconsidered.

I just knew my mother was going to hit the roof when she found out, but much to my surprise, she informed us that she knew it was gonna happen all along. Jason's parents had pretty much the same reaction. I guess none of them were astonished because they all assumed we had been sexing each other for years and had just been lucky I didn't get knocked up sooner. Our friends all took it in stride as well. From the looks of it, everybody in the world except Jason and I was predicting my impregnation.

Instead of having an elaborate wedding, we opted for a small ceremony in my mother's backyard the weekend after our graduation from Central High School. I was three months and not showing yet. Brina was my maid of honor, and Cordell was Jason's best man. That was the last time I saw the two of them together, because they broke up while Jason and I were on our honeymoon. To this day, neither one of them will discuss what happened.

It was a quaint, romantic, and intimate ceremony attended by our families and close friends. Our parents chipped in together and sent us on a week-long trip to the Bahamas as a combination wedding and graduation gift.

Our honeymoon turned out to be a culmination of fun-filled days and sexually repressed nights. After prom night, Jason and I never had sex again until after the wedding. To be honest, as much as I craved to be close to him in every way, I wasn't looking forward to another sexual disappointment. On my honeymoon, that's exactly what I got—a series of sexual disappointments, in fact. It is such a strange feeling to love someone more than you love your next breath and yet be appalled when they touch you. Don't get me wrong: Jason never turned me off. He just never turned me on either. Not the way I needed to be turned on.

While they say a mind is a terrible thing to waste, they neglect to mention that a body is a terrible thing to waste also. Especially when it's a body like Jason's. My husband's past gorgeous and way past fine. In fact, I can't even think of a word that would do him justice. He's a far cry from the little knucklehead I got in a fistfight with the day we met. To make matters worse, he has a scrumptious dick. He just doesn't know how to use it.

I had been working after school part-time at a fast food joint, and Jason worked with the county recreation department. We both had plans to attend college, and one of us did—Jason. I chose to pursue full-time employment as an administrative assistant and worked for a dentist's office all the way through my pregnancy.

Jason had a full basketball scholarship to State, and we stuck with that plan. His major was architecture, of course. The times he was out of town at away games were dismal, but Brina and my mother tried their best to keep me in good spirits. As horrible as our sex life was, the little bit of satisfaction I was garnishing from being close to Jason was unavailable when he was away.

In fact, the further I got into my pregnancy, the more sexually repressed I became, and desperation set in. Simple masturbation was no longer good enough, so I began to play with toys. You name it, and I had it hidden away in a box on a closet shelf where Jason couldn't find it—everything from a dildo to a vibrator to Ben Wa balls. My fascination with sex was quickly turning into an obsession.

"Jason!"

"Yes, Boo?" He was holding my hand, caressing it gently and using his other hand to dab the sweat away from my forehead with a moistened towel.

"Jason!"

"Yes, Zoe?"

"I fucking hate you!" I pushed his hands away from me and tried to get up off the hospital bed so I could kick his ass, but the next contraction set in and kicked my ass from the inside out instead.

"Zoe, just calm down and do the breathing exercises they taught us in Lamaze class!" He came toward me

with all the pampering nonsense again and started taking
short, quick breaths, as if a demonstration was going to
make the pain go away.

"Jason, I hate you and I hate the fucking doctor and I
hate all the fucking nurses!" I paused just long enough to
clench my teeth and push. The pain was excruciating, ten
million times worse than I ever imagined it would be. I
leaned up a little off the pillow, looking like a whale trying to do a sit-up, so I could look my doctor in the eye
while he sat between my legs messing with my coochie-
coo. "Dr. Henry, I fucking hate you!"

They all laughed at me, even Jason. The nerve of the
bitches! Everyone, including my mother, had warned me
about labor. They warned me it is the closest to death a
woman could ever come. If they weren't speaking the
Gospel, then there isn't a dog in the entire state of Georgia.

The Lamaze teacher had cautioned all the fathers
that their wives or girlfriends might be a bit angry at
them during labor. Poor Jason had to feel my wrath, because I was past angry. I was ready to kill his ass for putting something so big in me, I was going to have to rip my
ass open to push it out.

The Lamaze teacher also told the women to bring a
stuffed animal or some other comforting item in the delivery room to soothe their thoughts during labor. Jason
bought me a huge, stuffed brown teddy and named him
Casanova Brown.

Jason retrieved it from a chair in the corner and
brought it over to me. "Look, baby, Casanova wants to
keep you company."

He started moving the bear around, like it was dancing the jig. Trying to focus on the damn thing made me
nauseous. I grabbed the stupid-ass bear from Jason and
threw it so hard, it hit a nurse in the head who was walk-

ing into the room. Then I slapped Jason upside his fucking head.

The rest of the delivery went about like that. I repetitively cussed everyone out and didn't care what they thought about it. It's amazing that even the shyest woman doesn't care how many people are staring at her pussy like a bull's-eye on a target during labor. At least a dozen people were in and out the delivery room, and I didn't give a rat's ass.

Seven hours and fifty-six stitches later, unto us a son was born—Peter Jason Reynard, given the first name of my father, just like Jason and I had always planned. Once I heard all the stats—6 lb. 11 oz., 21 inches long, 10 fingers, 10 toes, and healthy—I was satisfied and passed out.

I woke up in the recovery room with Jason rubbing my tummy, probably glad as hell my shape was back 'cause making love to a blue whale, even for only two minutes at a time, must've been kind of frustrating.

"I love you, Jason!" I caressed the side of his face, the same side I had slapped the shit out of during labor, with my right hand. "I'm so sorry I said I hated you and even more sorry I hit you!"

He started laughing. "I know you love me, Boo, and this is forever."

"Always has been! Always will be!" We kissed for a few moments, and then he climbed beside me on the bed, since we could both fit on that bad boy, and fell asleep in my arms. The nurse woke us up a while later so she could check my vitals.

After the birth of our son, several landmark events took place in our lives, some very good and some very bad, but together, we always came out on top.

The first emotional upset came about when Jason's mother found out she had breast cancer. His father retired from his state government job, using the early-out option, and they moved to North Carolina, where they're both originally from.

Then, my mother turned around and married Aubrey. I was devastated but had no choice except to live with it. I didn't have a clue things between them were that serious and was totally shocked when she showed up at my apartment sporting a ring.

No sooner had I recovered from that quandary when my Boo got hurt in a game and tore the ligaments of his knee to shreds. Instead of having one baby to take care of, I had two, one little and one big. Both of them as cute as they could be. I used to take pictures of Jason and Peter while they were sleeping, the baby lying comfortably on his daddy's chest, their heartbeats as if synchronized. Watching the two of them on the bed together gave me the idea of starting Shades.

Shades is my corporation. It started out on a wing and a prayer but grossed me over half a million dollars last year. Watching my son fast asleep on his father gave me the idea to make my own calendar celebrating the role of the African-American father. So many African-American women are raising their children alone, it's a blessing to see a man living up to his responsibility.

I borrowed some money from my new stepfather, who has a small contracting company, found some people willing to pose for a small stipend, and made a calendar for the following year. The cover had a photo of Jason and Peter with bare chests and sporting Atlanta Braves baseball caps. Using the computer Jason's parents bought him for his college studies, I began to advertise them on the Internet, and the most miraculous thing happened. They sold like hotcakes.

I didn't make a fortune the first year, but I made enough for us to get by between the calendar and my job at the dentist's office. Jason was able to keep his scholarship, even though his career as a ballplayer was over, and the high school we attended, Central, hired him as their head basketball coach. It worked out very well because he could attend college in the morning and coach once school let out in the afternoon.

The second year I put out three calendars: one with African-American fathers and children, one with African-American families, and an African-American swimsuit calendar featuring some coeds from the university. Business really picked up then. I started my business at a time when calendars that portrayed beautiful African-American women were few and far between. It was like selling bottles of ice-cold spring water to people stranded in 110-degree desert heat.

To make a long story short, every year Peter grew, so did our bank account. We moved out of our apartment and rented a three-bedroom house so I could use one room as a home office. The following year Jason graduated summa cum laude and got a great job with the top architectural design firm in the city.

When Peter was five, Jason kept the promise he made on our prom night and built my dream house. It's a 4,500-square-foot, five-bedroom, four-bath cul-de-sac in a new development and it has over two dozen skylights in it so I can see all the stars.

We were still decorating when I got pregnant again. When Dr. Henry said the word *twins*, I wanted to faint but had to maintain my composure long enough to hold Jason up when he practically passed the hell out. The shock wore off, and the excitement took over. We turned

one of the guest bedrooms into a nursery and began shopping for two of everything.

Of course, when I went into labor, I was ready to kick
everyone's ass again. This time Jason was prepared for
battle and wore a baseball umpire's mask, more as a joke
than for protection. I must admit the mask was mad
funny and helped keep my mind off the horrific pain. He
also brought in reinforcements the second time around,
begging my mother to stay in the delivery room and be
his tag-team partner.

Somehow, I managed to push Kyle Michael and Kayla
Michelle out, instantly making our family unit expand
from three to five. After a brief recuperation period, I got
back to business and decided to market more than just
calendars on the Net. I became an African-American arts
dealer, marketing all types of artwork from up and coming artists who had the vision but lacked the sales ability.

Now my art is sold not only on the Net but in department stores nationwide. Jason is quickly becoming one of
the most sought-after architects in this city and recently
made a 5 percent commission on a $2.1 million office
complex. Financially, we couldn't possibly be doing any
better, considering we thought all our hopes and dreams
were destroyed because of failing to use a condom the
first night we made love.

# chapter nine

I glanced at my watch, noticed it was almost 8 P.M. and started to panic all over again. "Marcella, it's getting really late. Jason's going to be worried sick."

She glanced at the small crystal clock on her desk. "You're right, Zoe. It is a bit late. We've talked a good three hours."

"Yes, I can't wait to see the bill," I chuckled. "Whatever it is, it's well worth it."

I gathered my purse, coat, and gloves and extended my hand to shake hers. "Thanks so much for seeing me, and I'll call your secretary to set up an appointment sometime next week."

"You're very welcome, and make sure you do that." We shook hands, and I started toward the door. "We didn't get a chance to discuss the foundation of your addiction. Or did we?"

"Not at all. You have yet to hear the truly sickening

part. I wanted to make sure you understood my love for Jason, how much he means to me and why he's my entire life." I lowered my eyes and started fidgeting with my gloves, trying to put them on, but I got the shakes. "Now I have to go home and make up yet another lie to tell my husband. Lie on top of lie on top of lie. That's all I seem to do these days."

"I realize you have to go, but can I ask one question before you leave?"

"Sure!"

"What exactly do you lie to your husband about?" Her eyes widened, and she seemed to be waiting to exhale until I answered. I guess the whole thing did seem a bit strange, considering I hadn't actually told her what made me an official sex addict.

"Well, did I touch upon the fact Jason's not a very passionate or experimental lover?" I asked rhetorically.

"Yes, I did get that impression. Can't you just try to work on it? It's obvious to me that you love your husband very much."

"I love Jason more than my next breath."

She grinned at me, trying to make me feel at ease. "Zoe, just because your husband can't make you see fireworks in bed and you feel your sex life is lacking something doesn't constitute sexual addiction."

I opened the door to her office, took a few steps into the waiting room, and turned to face her. For the first time, I was going to be honest with someone about what I had done. For the first time, I was going to divulge my deepest and darkest secret, one some people knew bits and pieces of, but no one understood the true spectrum of the way I did. If there were even the slightest chance Dr. Marcella Spencer could help me, I had to go for it no matter what the consequences. The alternative was to continue on the destructive path I was on, heading straight to hell in a handbasket. The words were barely audible because I whispered them. "Does having three lovers other than my husband constitute sexual addiction?"

The grin on her face quickly faded and was replaced by a look of astonishment. She was flustered. It took her a moment to gather her bearings while I struggled to hold back tears. We never broke our stare. "Yes, I would definitely say that makes you a sexual addict!"

"I figured as much." I diverted my eyes to the door of the waiting room, ready to get the hell out of there before I broke down for real. "Look, I really have to go. Jason's going to be climbing the walls if I don't get home soon."

She leaned on the door of her inner office, crossing her hands in front of her. "I understand, Zoe. We'll pick up from here next week."

"Kewl!" With that, I was gone. I tried to walk away nonchalantly, as if I had just told someone about the agenda for the next PTA meeting. Once I got on the elevator and pushed the button for the parking garage, I totally lost it and began wailing like a toddler throwing a temper tantrum. As the elevator descended, I kicked and hit the walls, wiping tears away with the sleeves of my suit and wishing like all hell the whole thing was a nightmare I would wake up from any minute. I knew better. It was all too real, and it was nobody's fault but my own.

While I was waiting for my black Mercedes to warm up, I repositioned my rearview mirror so I could take a good look at myself. I wanted to see what a cheating, disgusting, nasty, lying whore really looked like. "Behold, the whore!" I spoke the words aloud and started laughing. There I was with mascara smeared all over my big brown eyes and tears covering my smooth caramel skin. There I was with ruby lipstick smudged over my trembling lips. I hated myself at that very moment. I closed my eyes and prayed for someone to throw me a life rope.

"Zoe, where you been, baby?" The dreaded question, and I hadn't even made it all the way in the kitchen door yet.

I came into the kitchen, where Jason was sitting at the table with the kids eating a Chicken Supreme pizza from Pizza Hut, and threw my briefcase on the countertop of the island. "Boo, I'm sorry I'm getting home so late. I had a problem with one of my distributors and had to hold an emergency meeting."

"You couldn't call?"

All sorts of excuses and alibis started running through my mind. I took my coat off and flung it over a stool at the breakfast bar. "To be honest, Jason, I got so stressed about solving the problem, the time just got away from me, and before I knew it, it was after eight."

"Baby, you have a cell phone. You could have been considerate enough to take one moment out and call so I wouldn't be worried." He got up from the table and started clearing away the dishes, bringing them over to the sink where I was getting a glass of water. "I don't understand you sometimes. It's like you don't even care about whether I know where you are or not."

Something snapped. "Peter, take the twins up to their room and put on a cartoon movie for them, please."

I watched Peter gather his siblings up and do as I asked. Peter paused just long enough to ask a question.

"Daddy, can we watch that new movie you bought us? The one with the black Cinderella?"

"Sure, go ahead." Jason was rolling up the sleeves of his white Bali shirt, getting ready to bust some suds. Once the kids were out of earshot, I got back to the matter at hand.

"Look, Jason, I really don't need this shit from you tonight. I've had a very long day. You keep making it sound like I'm never at home, and that's simply not true." He stood there rolling his eyes, his hands on his hips, and that pissed me off even more. "Hell, if you had it your way, I would never leave the fucking house. You want me in the kitchen, barefoot, and pregnant huh?"

"See, now you're getting ridiculous." He cut the faucet off and started walking away, mumbling something under his breath, and I followed him into his drawing room. "I never implied anything like that, Zoe, and you know it!"

He went over to the compact stereo system on one of the built-in shelves and turned on a Nancy Crawford CD. He always listens to smooth music when he creates his masterpieces, designing some of the most beautiful and breathtaking buildings one could imagine. "You're crucifying me for expecting a phone call. A simple phone call letting me know what's up. If I did that same shit, you'd never let me hear the end of it!"

Jason was right, and I was ashamed. Once again, I was using my own feelings of guilt about my "alternative" lifestyle as a basis for arguing with him. Before I started cheating on him, we never fought but the little spats were becoming more frequent. The infidelity had to end. A lesser man would have left me, betrayed me, abused me. Thank goodness Jason's love for me overshadowed his frustration.

He sat down at his drafting table and began scribbling, breaking the lead tip out of a pencil by pressing down on it too hard in his anger. I walked up behind him and started massaging his shoulders. I could feel the tension in them, and it made me even more ashamed, knowing I was the cause of it all. "I'm sorry, baby! You're absolutely right. I should've called. It was totally irresponsible and inconsiderate of me not to do so."

He didn't say a word, just grabbed another pencil and started drawing again. I slowly moved my hands from his shoulders down to his chest and caressed his nipples through his shirt. He grabbed my left hand in his and kissed it. "It's okay, Zoe. I just hate it when we fight."

"I know, Boo. So do I."

Jason twirled the base of his elevated drawing chair around so he was facing me and looked into my eyes. "All I ever wanted to do is make you happy."

"And you do! You make me *very* happy." I pressed my palms against his cheeks and gave him a long, wet kiss. "I love you, and this is forever."

"Always has been! Always will be!" We smiled at each other, and then he started kissing me on my neck while I looked up through one of the skylights at the stars.

There was a long, uncomfortable pause. I was trying to decide whether or not I should even mention Marcella. I decided to hint around and see if the shit hit the fan.

"I met this cool doctor today. A sistah." I pushed back a little from him so I could survey his expression. I didn't see a damn thing except the so-what look. "Her name's Marcella Spencer."

Jason picked up another pencil and started fiddling with one of his blueprints. "That's nice, honey."

I walked over to the stereo and flipped through the CD rack, searching for nothing in particular but seeing if he had bought anything new.

"What kind of doctor is she?" Jason quizzed. "Maybe I can send her some business."

"Umm, actually she's a psychiatrist." I waited for the other shoe to drop.

"*Psychiatrist?*" Jason acted like I said she was a hooker or something. Like the word was a four-letter one instead of a twelve-letter one. "Where in the world did you meet a *psychiatrist?*"

"Through a mutual friend." That was only a halfway lie—I did hear about her through the lady at the beauty salon. "She's very nice and down-to-earth." Jason chuckled like I had said something funny. "Why are you laughing?"

"No reason. It just amazes me that people like that can even make an honest living," he stated emphatically, shaking his head.

"People like who?"

"Psychiatrists. Shrinks. Head doctors," he said with an edge of sarcasm. "I mean, really, Zoe. What kind of person pays someone to listen to their silly-ass problems?"

I was offended but not about to confront him by admitting I was paying, and willing to pay out the ass if I had to if it would help. "Lots of people need therapy for different things, Jason. I can't believe you're being so closed-minded."

"Well, thank goodness neither one of us is cuckoo for Cocoa Puffs," he chuckled, laughing at his own half-ass joke. "I would send her some clients if she was an internist or cardiologist or pediatrician or something normal, but a *psychiatrist?* No freakin' way! All my friends are sane. Stressed-out, maybe, but *definitely* sane."

I hunched my shoulders and paced to the window, debating whether to run out of the room before I started crying in despair. How was I ever going to tell him I was seeing a psychiatrist?

"Guess what, baby? I have some great news of my own!"

I took a deep, restorative breath and turned to face him. "What's that, Boo?" I asked, forcing a smile.

He got up, walked over to me and put his arms around my waist. "I got a huge contract today. The city wants me to design the new civic center."

"Really?" I was stunned. I knew my baby was the bomb-diggity all along, but he was really hitting the big time lately, having just completed the new YMCA. "That's great, baby!"

We shared a long, passionate kiss. I could feel my panties getting wet. Any show of affection from Jason always turned me on. "I have a great idea."

"What's that?" he asked me with a mischievous grin.

"Why don't you go grab a bottle of champagne while I go upstairs and slip into something more comfortable?"

"Hmmm, sounds promising!" He gave me a big, wet one right smack on the lips. "But what about the kids?"

"You know as well as I do those chaps are probably all passed out on Peter's bed." We both laughed. It was a regular Friday-night routine for the kids to all fall out from the past week as if they had worked twelve hours a day. "I just want to be with you. I want tonight to be very special."

"Every night with you is special."

I looked into his eyes, wishing things could be different between us. If only he could be more receptive to my needs. I pranced off like Little Red Riding Hood on the way to her grandmother's house, grinning from ear to ear and hoping he was about to portray the part of the Big Bad Wolf and eat me, just like the one in the story. I knew there wasn't a chance in hell of that happening, but one can always maintain a strand of hope. "I'll see you when you get upstairs."

# chapter
## ten

When I awoke the next morning, Jason had already left to play his Saturday-morning round of golf with his two partners from the architectural design firm. It was after nine. I was surprised all the kids were still asleep—a welcome treat, as normally they would be up at the break of dawn.

Rays of sunlight invaded the haven of our bedroom through the skylights in the ceiling. The sun is the only major drawback to having a house with dozens of skylights. It's beautiful but can become a nuisance sometimes. As long as I get to see my stars at night, it's all good though. When it rains, it's so sexually stimulating. Then again, most things are sexually stimulating to me.

Unfortunately, after Jason and I proclaimed our undying love for one another in his drawing room the night before, it was followed by yet another sexual disappointment. After he fell asleep, I snuck into the bathroom, sat on the countertop, and masturbated with the dildo I kept hidden behind the cleaning supplies in the lower cabinet until I came.

Lying there thinking about it was bringing on an episode of depression, so I decided to get up and get moving. I called Brina, my partner in crime, and asked if she wanted to take the kids and hang out someplace for a little while. As expected, she was wide awake and down for whatever. We decided to hook up in about an hour at her place. I took a quick shower and got dressed. I woke the kids, who had all been bathed the night before, got them ready to go, left Jason a note on the fridge, and headed for Brina's.

When we got to Brina's, her ass wasn't ready. I could hear the shower running in her apartment as I was knocking. I opted to retrieve the key she always hid on top of the emergency lamp in the building corridor rather than wait for her to finish. The loafers I had on were killing me, and I wanted to rest my feet for a while. The kids and I bumrushed into her place. I turned on some Saturday-morning cartoons for them and went into her bedroom just as she was drying off.

"Girl, hurry your ass up!"

She jumped, obviously unaware we were already inside. "Damn, Zoe, you scared the hell out of me!"

"Sorry, Sis. I didn't mean to freak you out." When she dropped the bath towel to the floor, I was staring at her body. Not because I thought she was sexy—lawd knows I'm strictly dickly—but because her arms, shoulders, and rib cage were all covered with bruises. I quickly shut the bedroom door, anticipating the highly emotional conversation we were about to have.

"Brina, are you out of your freakin' mind? You're still letting Dempsey's skank ass beat on you?"

Brina started throwing on clothes faster than a runway model changing clothes between appearances on stage. "Zoe, he doesn't mean it. Sometimes he just has a rough day at work, and shit happens, you know?"

"Yeah, shit happens, and when I catch up to his ass, he's going to find out what kind of shit happens when he messes with my best friend!"

I was fired up. I couldn't believe she was letting his limp-dick leprechaun midget ass beat on her. Dempsey was this little trick Brina met at a nightclub, which was hint number one she didn't have any business with him. Add to that the fact he was unemployed 90 percent of the time, drank more vodka alone than a Russian football team can drink altogether, and had five kids by four different women, and you have a shitty-ass excuse for a man, one of those scrubs TLC is always singing about: a Sexually repressed, Childish, Raunchy, Useless Bastard!

Brina was almost completely dressed in a black sweatsuit, comparable to the jeans and cardigan I was bumming around in for a Saturday escapade. I turned on the TV in her bedroom, hoping to drown out our voices even more so the kids wouldn't hear us. Then I got medieval on her ass.

"Brina, let me tell you something. You're too good for that trick. He's a fucking waste of oxygen."

"Zoe, look, let's not start this shit again today. Let's just go hang out like we planned."

"Hang out? We need to be hanging at the damn emergency room! Look at your ass!" I walked over to her, attempting to console her, and she flinched due to all the pain the bruises were causing. I took my index finger and pressed it against one of her ribs, and she collapsed on the bed, bent over in pain. "Sis, I think your rib is fractured."

I reached for the telephone, but she grabbed the receiver out my hand. "Who are you calling? Jason?"

"Hell naw! Jason's playing golf, and he can't help you

anyway. I'm calling an ambulance, and then I'm calling
the police so you can file charges against his trifling ass.
This shit stops right now. Today!"

Brina and I started having a tug-of-war over the
phone and I almost accidentally knocked her upside the
head with it before I wrestled it away from her. "No, Zoe!
You can't call the police! He'll kill me, Sis!"

I hesitated for a brief moment, letting the words sink
into my head, and then I replaced the receiver on the cradle. My voice suddenly went from a holler to nearly a
whisper as I sat down on the bed beside her. "Kill you?"

She started sobbing, and I got her a tissue off the
nightstand. "Brina, has he threatened to kill you?" No
reply. She blew the mucus out her nose and pretended she
didn't even hear the question. "Where is he anyway?"

"Dempsey caught the bus home to Alabama for the
weekend. It's homecoming at his alma mater."

"Oh!" I didn't know what to say. I was worried about
Brina, and at the same time I wanted to kick her ass my
damn self for being so stupid as to stay with him. Part of
me wished I knew a voodoo priestess I could call and
arrange for Dempsey to be fatally bitten by an Alabama
black snake. That would have put an end to it all.

"Zoe, gurl!" She jumped up from the bed, walked
over to the dresser, and looked in the mirror while she ap-
plied some lipstick. "Let's just get out of here and enjoy
ourselves. It's a beautiful day out, and the kids don't need
to be cooped up in here."

I picked up the phone again and started dialing.
"Zoe, I thought I asked you not to call the police. I'm
denying whatever you tell them, so it's a waste of time."

"I'm not calling the police. I'm calling Jason at the
country club and telling him to come pick up the kids so I
can take you to the hospital."

The line was busy, so I pressed down the reset button and started dialing again. "Zoe, I'm not going to the hospital either."

While it was ringing, I got pissed off for real. "Listen, Brina, you may have convinced me not to call the police, *for now*, but your ignorant behind is going to the hospital if I have to rope and gag your ass to get you there."

I had Jason paged and I was waiting outside Brina's apartment building when he pulled up in his hunter green Land Rover. After we got the kids buckled in, Jason followed me back up the walkway to the entrance so I could fill him in. He was more anxious to get his hands on Dempsey than I was, but I told him the trick had beat Brina's ass and run like all punks do.

We kissed each other good-bye, said I love you, and I watched him pull off with the kids before I went back inside to get Brina.

"So, where are Jason and the kids going? Home?" We were in my car en route to the hospital, and Brina was trying to discuss any and everything but the matter at hand.

"No, he took them to Family Adventure Fun Park, that place over in SW that has the balls to jump in, crawling tubes, arcade, and all that."

"Cool!"

The sun was irritating my eyes, even with the sun visor down, and I was nursing one hell of a migraine. "Brina, you do realize you have to end the relationship with Dempsey, right?"

She rolled her eyes, smacked her lips, and turned the radio volume up to a ridiculous level. "Can we just talk about something else, please?"

"Hell no, we're going to talk about this!" I turned the radio completely off. "That fool has got to step. He's nothing but bad news. When does this all end? When he uses you as a punching bag one time too many, fucks around, and kills your ass?"

"You're trippin' hard. You just don't understand my life, Zoe."

"Then enlighten me! *Please!*"

I almost ran a red light but was able to screech to a halt just in time. Good thing, too, because there was a police car right behind me. "You and Jason have this fairy-tale life. You always have had. Shit doesn't come easy to me like that. A good man is hard to find."

"And you think Dempsey's a good man, Brina? Chile, please!"

"He may not be perfect, but he's all mine, and he loves me."

"How can you come out of your face and say he loves you when he gives you a beatdown whenever the hell he feels like it?"

"Think what you want, Zoe. He loves me, and I love him back."

The entrance to the emergency was dead ahead, and I could see the flashing lights on an ambulance that had just pulled in. "You need help, Brina. Serious help, and I don't mean the physical kind either."

I pondered over Brina's situation as well as my own while I waited for her in the crowded waiting room in the emergency wing. It was flu season, so people were hacking and sneezing all over the place. They almost sounded like a snot chorus. It was disgusting, not to mention unhealthy.

To most people, I guess Jason and I were living a fairy tale, but they were on the outside looking in. Then again, Jason thought we were living a fairy tale too. I was the only one who could distinguish fantasy from reality.

The ironic part is, I had planned to tell Brina about everything that afternoon, asking her to help me overcome my man problems. I was going to tell her how I would leave my house pretending to go one place but end up someplace where I had no business, committing adultery I never planned on in my wildest dreams. Instead, I was waiting for the doctors to patch her ass up, administer painkillers, and ask her a bunch of questions we both knew she had no intention of answering truthfully, if at all.

I decided there was no way Brina could help me when she couldn't even help herself. So I decided against confiding in her. I would just pretend to be the happy, successful, content woman she wanted me to be. Ain't that a bitch?

"This wait is *wayyyyyyy* too long, Brina," I complained, standing near the entryway of the Cheesecake Factory on Peachtree and trying to stay out of the way of people coming in and out.

"Zoe, I just checked with the hostess a minute ago, and she said there are only two parties ahead of us. Calm down." Brina was standing so close to me, I could feel her breath on my cheek. She had that hospital ethyl alcohol/bleach smell all over her. "We rarely get to hang out anymore, just me and you. You always have the kids with you, so let's just have lunch and catch up."

"Catch up?" I couldn't believe she was putting on a front like we hadn't just left out of the emergency room. "The only thing we need to catch up on is why you're still letting that Dempsey maggot open up a can of whup-ass on you whenever he feels like it."

She darted her eyes around, embarrassed, trying to

make sure nobody heard my last statement. "Do you have to talk so loud?"

I realized I was talking pretty loud, so I toned it down a peg or two. I was still pissed, though. "Brina, I have a great idea. Let's just order carry-out and head back to your place so we can discuss this openly and honestly without any interruptions."

"We can discuss it here," she interjected. "I don't want to go back to my place right now. I'm sick of being cooped up in there every day after work. Why do you think I'm always so gung-ho about hanging out with you and the kids? My life is mad boring."

I was on the brink of insisting that we leave regardless of all that. I just didn't deem it appropriate for us to be there in light of earlier events. Before I could air my objection, they called our name and led us to a table by a window overlooking the Saturday traffic on Peachtree. Once we sat down and ordered a couple of margaritas, I decided to get all up in her business.

"Brina, why are you so bored? Doesn't Dempsey ever take you out anyplace?"

She looked astonished, as if the mere thought of a man taking a sistah out on an actual date is unheard of in Atlanta. "Take me out with what, Zoe? You know Dempsey has trouble holding down a job, and what little money he does make goes to child support."

"Yeah, child support or liquor," I replied sarcastically. "Am I missing something here? Let me see if I have all of this straight. He's a lazy alcoholic sperm bank who comes over to your place just so he can fuck you, beat the shit out of you, and then leave?"

"You just don't understand where I'm coming from," she stated brazenly. "Dempsey has a softer side to him that only I see."

I chuckled, more out of anger than anything. I couldn't believe my ears. "Brina, you deserve so much better than this, but you can't see it for some reason. You and I go way back." I reached over the table and gently took her by the hand. "We're like family. You're the closest thing to the sister I've never had, and I refuse to sit back and watch you do this to yourself one more minute."

"Do what to myself? Allow a man to love me?" Her bottom lip started trembling, and so did her hand. She tried to pull it back, but I tightened my grip. "Zoe, I'm not beautiful and successful like you. The world is at your feet. You have a bad-ass home, great kids, a mother who actually remembers you exist, and a fine husband who adores you."

I wanted to scream out that I was just as tormented as she was, but her problems were more urgent. In fact, they were bordering on life-threatening so I refrained from discussing my sexual obsession and the effect it was having on my life. I desperately needed to talk to someone. It looked like Dr. Marcella Spencer was my only choice, though; Brina was certainly in no condition to help me sort through my emotions.

"I'm barely making enough to get by," Brina continued. "My mother's always asking me for money. When I'm with Dempsey, it's the only time I truly feel safe." *No—she didn't say safe?* "It's not like I have men knocking down my door these days. I used to, though. You remember that, don't you, Sis? You remember when I was beautiful like you?"

That did it! I squeezed her hand so hard that I practically drew blood. "You listen to me! You're still beautiful! You always have been and always will be!" I calmed down a little and loosened my grip. I was so upset, I had to fight back the tears. Brina was always the confident one. People used to call her conceited in high school, but I would defend her and explain that she wasn't conceited—she was just convinced she had it going on. "That Dempsey bastard has destroyed your self-esteem, and I'm not having it. I'll do anything to help you, Brina. Anything! Jason and I both would do anything for you. Don't you know that?"

She looked me over with the tear-drenched eyes of a child. "I know you will."

"But I can't help you unless you tell me what you need." The waitress came back to the table and asked if we were ready to order our meals. I asked her to give us a few more moments. We had yet to even open up the menus. Once she walked out of earshot, I continued, "This is the first I've heard about any financial problems, Brina. Why didn't you ask me for some money?"

"I could never do that!"

"Why not? That's what friends are for, dammit!"

"I don't want you and Jason giving me handouts. I know how hard it was for the two of you to get where you are. I watched your dreams come true right before my eyes, and I could never take away from that."

I mulled it over for a moment in silence. I never realized Brina could be so damn stubborn. "Okay, fine. I won't *give* you anything. I'll make you earn it." Brina looked at me, full of confusion. "Come work for me. It's the perfect solution, and we can spend a whole lot of time together."

She started chewing on her bottom lip, lost in thought. "I don't know about this, Zoe. I don't want to mess up a good thing. I've been at my company for a while now."

"And they haven't promoted you, given you a raise, or done a damn thing for you except give you a bunch of aggravation." I smiled at her, hoping to encourage her to accept. "Besides, I pay well, and you won't have to fight with me to take vacation time or to leave early or anything."

She laughed. "That's true. My boss, Mrs. Green, can be a mean old heifer when I ask to leave even an hour early."

"So accept my offer then, dammit."

"But all I have are secretarial skills, and those aren't all that great. Do you even have an opening at your company in the first place?"

"No, but I'll make one up. I'm the owner. I can do whatever the hell I want." She still hesitated. "I don't have a personal assistant. I never have had, but now that I think about it, I could surely use one. You could go visit artists with me and hang out at galleries and art shows. Do power lunches. You would love it."

The waitress came back again, about to cop an attitude since we were taking up table space and not eating. I could understand it. Business is business and tips are tips. The Cheesecake Factory was packed since it was a Saturday afternoon. We finally put the waitress out of her misery, glanced over the menu, and ordered a couple of grilled chicken salads with blue cheese dressing, some cheese toast, and a basket of chicken tenders.

"Well?" I asked, giving Brina my undivided attention while we waited for the food. "What's your answer?"

"Let me think about it, okay?"

Now it was my time to be confused. "Think about it? Do you know how many sistahs would jump at the opportunity I just offered you?"

"Yes," she replied, giggling, but I failed to see the joke. "I'm just not sure I can deal with you as my boss. You're my best friend and all, but I know your temper tantrums better than anyone, and when we get into it, we *really* get into it. I remember how you and Jason used to go at it all the time when we were kids."

"I'm offended," I stated, even though she was right to an extent. "I'm strictly professional at work. Now as far as me getting in your ass about trifling things after work hours, that's still a free-for-all playing field."

"Like I said, let me think about it, Zoe. Either way, thanks for the offer. I wouldn't expect anything less from you. You're always there for me."

I dropped it. In fact, I dropped everything. The money issue, the work issue, the Dempsey bastard issue. We enjoyed our lunch and caught up on insignificant things. Once I dropped her back at her place, I asked to use her bathroom before I headed home. I can only imagine her surprise when she discovered the check for five thousand dollars I left on her vanity. I left her a note saying she better not even mention it, and she better cash it, or I would be mad at her ass. I also told her not to dare thank me for it because that's what friends are for, but urged her to give some serious consideration to my job offer. I was hoping she would see things my way and accept.

# chapter eleven

"It's nice to see you again, Zoe." Dr. Marcella Spencer was setting up her tape recorder when I entered her office. After she had it all hooked up and ready to catch my dirt, she came around the desk and shook my hand.

"Nice to see you again, too." It was Wednesday—five days since our initial conversation.

"How are you? Have a seat."

She motioned to the same wing chair, which was destined to become my home away from home, and I gladly sank into it. I was exhausted from being treated like a sex object during my creeping episodes and from the added stress of worrying about Brina. "I'm making it."

"Hmmm, making it doesn't sound too positive. You want something to drink? Coffee, tea, water, maybe a soft drink?"

"No thanks." She was being extraordinarily friendly,

and I began to wonder whether she had been feenin' all week, anxiously awaiting to hear about the sexual escapades of the freakazoid slut she had as a new client.

"Zoe, do you want to stay in the chair or use the chaise this time?"

"I'm fine right here, Marcella. Thanks!"

She grabbed her pen and pad, ready to jot down all my sins, but I had no intention of having another panic attack. The thing with Brina had made me realize one thing. I needed help just as much as she did, and it was time to get it.

"So, Zoe, shall we begin?" She was all ears.

"Sure." I rubbed my eyes, both of them having bags underneath them from lack of sleep. "Where should I start this time?"

"Well, I basically know about your relationship with your husband. You were quite frank regarding your lack of satisfaction sexually." There was a silence, and I waited for the other shoe to drop. It did. "When you were leaving last time, you mentioned you were having three extramarital affairs, which, I will assume, is what you need the most help with?"

I answered her sarcastically. "Ummm, yeah, you could say that fucking three other people is the heart of the problem."

I regretted the way I came off at her and immediately apologized. "I'm sorry. I didn't mean to take my frustration out on you. There's just been a lot of shit going on in my life lately."

"I understand. Believe me, I do."

"Really?"

"Yes, and whatever I don't understand, we will work on together. Trust me, Zoe! There's nothing you can tell me that will make me think any less of you. I'm here to help."

Her hands started trembling, and I got the distinct impression she was more nervous than I was. I guess a woman who fucks men like she changes panties would make anyone uneasy.

So I began. "I love Jason and my kids dearly. They're my heart and soul. I only wish they were enough to fulfill all my needs. I have three regular lovers other than my husband. Each one of them gives me something different. For months now I've tried to stop this madness, but I can't. My addiction to sex has taken me over."

"I see."

I hate it when you spill your guts out and someone says "I see." It makes me feel like they are either bored, skeptical, or appalled. I got up from the seat and walked over to one of the windows. I don't know what my fascination is with looking at the sky, but I definitely have one. Maybe I missed my true calling to become a weather forecaster. It was cloudy that day, and the sun was about halfway tucked away for the night.

"While I love Jason more than life itself and would die if he ever found out, he's never been able to sate all of my sexual desires. He's very old-fashioned and thinks a man should have total control in the bedroom. Jason believes in very little foreplay. He'll only have sex with me in the missionary position. He'll only have sex with the lights off, and he's totally against oral sex. I brought up the subject of anal sex once, and he almost had a heart attack."

"So you decided to seek fulfillment of your needs someplace else?"

I took a seat on the chaise longue and lay down in

Marcella's office for the first time. The secrets I was about to reveal to her had tormented me for so long. While it might be painful, it was going to be a great relief to get it all off my chest. "Because we fell in love so young, I'm the only lover Jason's ever had. As far as he knows, the same is true in my case. Up until a year ago, Jason was in fact the only lover I ever had. Then the madness began. . . ."

# chapter twelve

         I was attending the opening of a new public high school when I first met Quinton. It was a magnet school, specializing in the performing arts, and Quinton was the artist commissioned by the city of Atlanta to paint a mural in the cafeteria.

Quinton Matthews was renowned throughout the world, and as an arts dealer, I was very familiar with his artistic talent. I had seen his picture once, but it didn't do him justice.

When I arrived at the opening, I was late, and the mayor had already done the traditional ribbon-cutting ceremony. A business associate, Rebecca Swanson, had invited me, and before I made it ten feet into the cafeteria she greeted me with a huge smile and a glass of champagne.

Meeting Quinton Matthews was my main reason for attending. At the young age of thirty, he had already achieved legendary status as a contemporary artist. I was hoping to sweet-talk him into letting me produce some of his originals as prints and add them to my sales collection.

The mural Quinton designed on the cafeteria wall was nothing short of breathtaking. It depicted dozens of teenagers, of all ethnic groups, involved in various activities, everything from ballet to playing musical instruments to portraying Shakespeare on a stage.

As I walked along the wall, pausing to glance at each scene, I shuddered to think how many hours it must have taken to create such a masterpiece. I also wondered what kind of man had the vision and creativity to commit himself to such a task. It reminded me a lot of Jason, the time and effort he put into his architecture.

The high school wasn't the only place I had seen Quinton Matthews's work up close. His creations were all over the city. My favorite was one of the Atlanta skyline on a concrete wall in a downtown MARTA station. I used to go down to the station, just a few blocks from my office, sit on a bench, and eat lunch. The mural seemed to have a calming effect on me, and sometimes even an arousing one. I have no idea why, but I somehow equated his creative nature with sex. Then again, I equated most things with sex back then.

Maybe that's why I was such a huge fan of his, and perhaps the real reason I wanted to meet him was curiosity—not about his work, but about the man himself. Curiosity might kill most cats, but it made the cat between my legs purr.

When I got to the section of the mural depicting a group of ballerinas with their arms neatly folded over tutus, standing on the hard toes of ballet slippers, I felt someone breathing down my neck.

"You like the mural, huh?"

His voice was deep and distinguished. I didn't turn

around. I assumed he was one of the several hundred patrons who had come to the opening to see how their generous donations were spent.

"I don't *like* it! I *love* it! Quinton Matthews is a great artist, isn't he?"

"Hmm, if you say so."

I didn't like the sarcasm in his voice and quickly spun around, ready to defend my favorite artist and confront the arrogant son of a giga monster who lacked a true appreciation of his gift.

"Listen, he's—" I froze.

"Yes? He's what?"

I must have had the most ridiculous look on my face, because I was damn sure embarrassed when I realized I was face-to-face with Quinton Matthews himself.

"Mr. Matthews!" I grabbed his hand and started shaking it like a political science major who's just snatched up the opportunity to meet the president of the United States. "It's such an honor to meet you!"

He stopped shaking my hand but refused to let it go when I tried to retrieve it. Instead, he lifted it up to his mouth and kissed it. "One problem."

"What's that?"

"We haven't officially met yet, Ms.?"

"It's Mrs. Mrs. Zoe Reynard." I flashed the wedding ring on my other hand at him as if I needed to provide some form of physical evidence to support the statement. I was really trippin'. I was used to meeting men, but I was acting like a nervous teenager around Quinton Matthews.

"Damn, just my luck." I noticed he was still holding my hand and pulled it away, pretending I needed it to prevent my purse strap from falling off my shoulder. "The good ones are always taken."

I started blushing. Hell, who wouldn't blush with a man that damn fine paying them a compliment.

Like I said, I had seen his picture in the newspaper before but *dayummmmmmmmm!!!!* Quinton was about five-eleven, green eyes the color of emeralds and a clean-shaven bald head. His skin was the color of burnt sienna, smooth and flawless, and his smile perfect.

He was sporting a dark gray double-breasted suit with a crisp white shirt, unbuttoned just enough for me to see the baby-fine hair on his chest.

I was so busy checking his ass out, I didn't see Rebecca approaching. As a matter of fact, he was checking me out too, and making no bones about it.

"Zoe, I'm about to leave. Bobby's running a fever, and the school just paged me to pick him up."

Rebecca could have been calling out the winning numbers for that night's lotto, for all I cared. "Okay, Becca. Take care, girl."

She gave me a quick pat on the arm. "Alright, girl. Take care, Zoe."

I realized how rude I was being. "Hold up, Becca. Have you met Quinton Matthews, the muralist?"

"Yes, we've met." They shook hands, but nowhere near the seductive way he and I did. "Nice to see you again, Quinton. Your new mural is the bomb!"

"Thanks for the compliment!"

While he was thanking her, I was trying to sneak a peek at the bulge in his pants. I snapped back to my senses; I knew good and damn well I had no business thinking about another man's dick.

"Zoe, I really have to run!" Rebecca was already halfway to the door, bumping into a waiter and almost causing him to spill a whole tray of drinks, when she yelled out, "I'll call you tomorrow!"

I waved at her as she disappeared from our view.

"Mr. Matthews, I really have to be running along also." Suddenly, I was scared to even be near him.

"Aw, so soon?"

"Yes, my husband will be expecting dinner at a certain time, and I still have to stop at two different places to scoop up the kids and all."

"I understand. Domestic life must be hectic. Don't let me keep you." He was talking to my breasts and not my face, which made me even more uncomfortable. The black dress I was wearing didn't seem that revealing, but he made me feel like I was working the corner in the red light district.

"Well, nice meeting you, and once again, I really do love your work."

"Thanks."

I started walking away, feeling his eyes on my ass, when I remembered the business proposition I had come there to make in the first place.

When I turned around and headed back toward him, he started grinning. My lips were forming the words when he inquired, "Let me guess. You want me, don't you?"

I felt like hollering "Hell, yes!" but managed not to. "Actually, I want to talk with you about the possibility of marketing some of your work."

"Hmm, is that right?" His eyes started exploring my body again. "Well, we can definitely discuss it if it means I get to see your fine ass again."

That did it! My nipples got hard, and my pussy got wet. "Here's my card." I pulled one of my engraved business cards out and handed it to him. "Whenever you can find the time in your busy schedule, I'd appreciate it if you can call me so I can go over what I have in mind."

"Well, I already know what I have in mind." I started

blushing while he glanced at the card. "An arts dealer, huh?"

"Yes. Exclusively African-American art."

"Cool."

"Thanks, and I look forward to hearing from you soon." I zipped my purse back up. "It's no rush, though. I realize you're in high demand."

"How about tomorrow morning? Say nine o'clock? My place?"

I was shook! My lips were trembling, and his eyes held me in a trance. He dug in his pocket and handed me one of his cards. I looked at the address of his studio and made a mental note that it was within walking distance from my office. "Nine tomorrow would be great. Thanks."

"My pleasure." He took my hand and kissed it once more.

"Well, I'll let you get back to your other admirers. I didn't mean to hog your attention."

"Not a problem, Zoe. I can call you that, right?"

"Please do, Quinton." Damn, on a first-name basis already! I wondered if that meant hellified sex was right around the corner.

I was leaving, trying to get out of there before my mind went even further into the gutter than it already was, when he grabbed me around the waist from behind and spoke softly in my ear. "You cannot begin to imagine the things I want to do to you."

He took my earlobe into his mouth, small hoop earring and all, suckling on it for a brief second until I freed myself from his grasp.

I hauled ass toward the door, face flustered and heart pounding so hard in my chest, I could actually hear the echo of it ringing in my ears. I glanced back at his fine ass one last time. He was still staring at me.

He held my business card up to his well-defined lips, smelled it like it had been hand-dipped in fine perfume, and used it to blow me a kiss.

I daydreamed about him all the way to the twins' day-care center, more worried about what might not happen the next morning than what might.

I got home, threw a couple of Cornish hens in the oven, told Peter to go do his homework, popped a cartoon video into the great room VCR for the twins, and then went to my bedroom and locked the door. I laid there on the bed, fantasizing about Quinton Matthews while I masturbated and hoped I would cum before Jason got home.

I came three times in twenty minutes and would've cum at least three more if Peter hadn't knocked on the door, informing me that he'd broken the lead of his pencil and couldn't find his pencil sharpener.

# chapter thirteen

"Jason," I whispered, trying to wake him up gently by rubbing him on the shoulder.

Still half asleep, he answered. "Yes, Boo?"

"I need to talk to you."

He opened one eye, sat up just far enough to glance at the alarm clock on my side of the bed. "Zoe, it's three in the morning. Can't this wait till later?"

"No, not really."

It was storming that night. One of the worst lightning storms of the season, and the weather center had issued a flash flood warning. The lightning was coming in from all directions and appeared to be dancing on the carpet. I couldn't fall asleep if my life depended on it. I was like a bitch in heat. My pussy was feenin' for some action.

Jason took a deep breath and propped himself up on his pillow. "You wanna talk? Okay, let's talk. 'Sup, Boo?"

"I want to make love."

He sighed. "Zoe, we made love less than three hours ago. Can I just get some sleep, please?" He turned over on his stomach, his head facing away from me. "I have an early day tomorrow, baby."

What I should've done, at that moment, is tell my husband the freakin' truth. I should've told him that, even though I love him and would take a bullet for him, I needed him to be more sexually open and willing to try new things. I should've suggested we seek counseling. I should've told him I started masturbating way back in junior high school and had been doing it ever since. I should've told him about all the sex toys I had hidden all throughout the house and at my office. I should've demanded he try harder to fulfill my needs and desires. I should've forced him to listen to me for a change instead of just brushing me off whenever the conversation turned to sex. Instead, I lay there listening to the thunder, watching the rain and lightning, and praying I wouldn't get into trouble the next morning when I went to discuss business with Quinton Matthews.

I knocked even though the door was already ajar. "Mr. Matthews?"

"Come on in, Zoe!"

I entered his studio, which doubled as his apartment, at exactly nine sharp. I didn't see him, but I could hear him moving around in the loft upstairs. "Hello. Good morning. Am I too early?"

"No, right on time." He appeared at the top of the steps with nothing on but a pair of silk pajama pants. He was wiping the last of some shaving cream off his face with a towel when he came down the steps to join me. "Care for some coffee?"

"I'm fine, thanks. I have enough nervous energy already. I don't need caffeine to exacerbate it."

"You're just a little Energizer bunny, huh?"

I smiled. "Yes, but I hardly ever wear pink and I don't own a drum."

We both laughed, and then he motioned me toward the leather sofa. "Have a seat, Zoe."

I sat down, putting my briefcase on the marble coffee table in front of me. I made sure I brought enough information with me to try to sell his ass on the idea the first time around.

"Well, you may have natural energy, but I need some coffee. Be right back."

I watched him walk into the kitchen and then took a quick survey of his place. It was awesome. I assumed he was buying the space, because just about every wall had a mural on it. They were all magnificent, and he had a set of crates covered with black velvet in one corner. I figured they were used for people to sit on and pose while he spent hours on end painting their portraits.

I noticed there was a canvas on the easel and decided to be nosy. I went over, lifted up the oilcloth covering the piece, and looked at it. I was surprised to discover it was a portrait of the governor. The state must have commissioned him to do it for the state capitol building. Quinton made him appear so lifelike, it was unreal.

The studio was located on the top floor of an old department-store warehouse downtown, which had been renovated and turned into huge lofts. There was only one other tenant on his floor, located at the other end of the hall.

"Hmm, inquisitive too. I like that in a woman." I didn't notice he had returned with a steaming hot mug of coffee in his hand.

"Sorry." I replaced the cloth. "I guess I was a bit out of line. It could've been a portrait of your woman or something like that."

"Well, for future reference, I don't have a woman." He started looking me up and down again. "At least, not yet."

I turned toward the window, away from him, so he wouldn't see me grinning from ear to ear. "Oh, wow!"

"Oh wow, what?"

I walked closer to the window so I could get a better look. "The mural you painted at the MARTA station. It's right across the street."

"Yes, it is. In fact, that's how I came across this condo. They were renovating the building while I was working on the mural, and well, you know the rest."

"Cool. I didn't realize you were right across from it. I go there a lot and eat lunch, but I approach it from another direction."

He took a sip of his coffee, so close to me by that time, I could hear him gulp it down. "Why do you go there and eat lunch? I didn't know they had a restaurant over there. Unless you include the hot dog vendors on the corner."

I giggled and looked back at him. The sunlight was hitting his green eyes, and I almost fainted. "Very cute! No, they don't have a restaurant. It's just that my office is not that far away, and I love the mural, so I walk over here and eat the lunch I bring from home. Walking is good exercise."

"From where I'm sitting, you don't need any exercise."

"Well, since you're standing and not sitting, I'll take that as an almost compliment." I brushed past him, catching a whiff of his aftershave and the soap residue left over from a shower he obviously took before my arrival. "Shall we get down to business?"

I sat down on the sofa, opened my briefcase, and

started pulling out the presentation folder I had rushed to prepare that morning, since I had no idea he would agree to see me the very next day after we met.

"Hold up." He put his hand on top of mine, pushing the folder back into the briefcase. "Basically, you want to take some of my works, turn them into marketable, affordable prints, and then sell them through your arts business?"

"Yes, that's exactly what I want to do. Now, if you'll allow me to show you some figures I worked out, we can—"

"Don't worry about it. I trust you, and we can do this."

"Huh?" I was shocked. "You're agreeing to it just like that?"

"Yes. I made some phone calls last night and checked you out. It's all good. Anyway, I've been thinking of doing a venture like this for quite some time."

I was ecstatic and had to keep myself from jumping up and doing cartwheels. "Well, I don't know what to say."

"Say it's a deal, and we can work on all the figures at a later date."

I reached for his hand to shake it. "Deal!" He held true to form and kissed it instead.

"Well, I'm sure you have a lot to do today, so I'll get out of your way. Thanks so much for the opportunity to market your work for you."

I closed my briefcase and got up, headed for the door. He followed me, grabbing me by the elbow and swinging me around. "Just a sec. Why are you always running away from me?"

"I'm not running! Don't be ridiculous!" Damn shame he was so right! "I just know you have things to do." I pointed to the canvas on the easel. "Like painting the governor and awesome things like that."

"Hmm, well, you know, you're not the first person who has asked me to do this whole business thing."

I had never thought of it that way. A man as talented as he was must have received offers on a daily basis. I looked him in his sexy, mesmerizing eyes and asked, "Then why did you tell me yes?"

He started pressing up against me, and I backed up until I ran out of space and my ass was pinned against the door. "Zoe, I was hoping you would do something for me as well."

Talk about being a nervous fucking wreck! I wasn't sure whether to ask what he wanted or not. I was afraid I might like the request a little too much. "Really?"

"Yes, really."

I could feel his breath on my cheek. "What might that be?"

"Let me paint you."

For a moment, my mind registered him saying, "Let me fuck you." Wishful thinking, I suppose.

"Paint me?"

"Yes, paint you." He took his hand and removed a piece of lint off my black tweed business suit. "You're so beautiful. I want to paint you. Free of charge, of course, and I want to hang the portrait of you over my bed."

I started stuttering when his bare chest pressed up against my hard nipples through my blouse. "What, umm, I mean, why do you want to do that?"

As long as there is a breath in my body, I'll never forget the next words he spoke to me. "I want to paint you and hang it over my bed so when you are here, we can make love underneath your splendor, and when we are apart, I can behold your beauty and satisfy myself just by the mere thought of you."

My lips started trembling, and I began to feel light-headed. Maybe all of the blood rushed to my throbbing pussy like it does to a man's dick when he becomes aroused. Hell if I know. All I did know was my ass was about to be in a world of trouble. I had never thought about fucking another man before I laid eyes on Quinton, and I should've run. I should've never been there in the first place, but I was there, and he was real, and the desire to be with him was hypnotizing.

When he kissed me, I tried to push him away. Okay, I tried to push him away with just a teeny bit of effort. His kiss was soft and deep all at the same time. It reminded me of the way Jason used to kiss me way back in the beginning. He reached down, picked me up, and pressed my back against the door. I straddled my legs around his back. My pussy was so freakin' wet.

Our kisses got more profound, and I should've stopped him. Looking back, I realize there are so many things I should've done differently. I'm so ashamed about what happened next.

He carried me over to the sofa, laid me down on it, and traced a path down my body with his mouth, pausing to gently nibble on my covered nipples. He pulled on them, one at a time, with his teeth, and I could see my breasts expand through my silk blouse as he moved his head back and forth.

I sat up and tried to put my feet on the floor so I could get up. "We can't do this! I'm married!"

"Not happily. If you were happily married, you wouldn't have kissed me."

"Yes, I'm *very* happily married, and I have to go. This just isn't right."

"Nothing has ever felt so right. You know it and I know it. You want me just as much as I want you." He started rubbing my thighs and pulling off my lace-top thigh-high silk stockings. "Just lie back and relax, baby. I would never hurt you."

That was it! The moment I realized I was fighting a lost cause. My mind was saying no, but my body was saying yes, and my body won by a landslide. I lifted up my hips so he could pull my black lace panties down over my legs and off.

I made one last attempt at salvaging my cheatless marriage record by whispering, "Please."

Then I buried my head into one of the toss pillows on his sofa, drowning my moans in it while I had my pussy eaten for the very first time.

# chapter
# fourteen

Damn shame I did that! I let that man feast on me for a good hour, and unfortunately, I loved every minute of it. I had done extensive reading on cunnilingus, but of course, Jason didn't do anything but go downtown and window-shop. He never actually purchased anything.

I couldn't imagine cumming as many times back to back as I did. I lost count somewhere after twenty. Every time I tried to pull away, he would pull me back down toward him, whispering things like, "Give me my pussy!" and "Damn, you taste delicious!"

He was fingering me and pulling some of my juice out with his fingers so he could suck it off. Scared the living daylights out of me. When he finally came up for air and starting pulling down his silk pajama pants, I jumped up. I took a good look at him. His face and chest and hands were all smothered with my essence.

I started grabbing for my belongings, shoving my

stockings and panties into the side pocket of my large purse. "I really have to go!"

"Before you taste me, baby?" I looked up from the sofa, and his dick was all up in my face. I was so nervous! Lawd knows I had never sucked a dick!

I scooted down on the sofa to an available section where I could get up. "I can't do that! Sorry! I'm a married woman, and I love my husband very much! What we just did was wrong! Dead wrong!"

He followed me to the door. I could feel the sticky substance rubbing between my upper thighs as I walked. "It may have been wrong, but we both wanted to do it."

I wasn't going to try to deny it. I did want him to eat me out so there was no point in even faking the funk. I looked Quinton dead in the eyes and admitted, "Yes, I did want it, but it can never happen again."

I opened the door and walked out in the hallway, finally feeling a bit out of danger of doing something else freaky with him. His pants were still down in the front, and I didn't even notice his dick bouncing around in the air until he reached down and covered it back up. "So, when will I see you again? To talk business, of course."

"Yeah, right! Business!"

I pushed the button on the elevator, which was one of those service elevators all warehouses have, with the gate you have to pull up and down. It arrived at the floor, and he came rushing up behind me to lift it. "Let me get that for you."

"Thanks. I'll be in touch."

I got on, and he pulled the gate back down while I pushed the button for the garage level. As he was disappearing out of view headfirst, I heard him yell, "I'm sure you will be!"

Driving the few blocks to my building, I broke out in a cold sweat. I parked my car and went up to my suite, informed my secretary, Shane, to hold all my calls, and retreated to the sanctuary of my private office. Once I locked the door, I pulled the chain to close the vertical blinds. Even though I was on the tenth floor, you never know who may be watching.

I took one of the wooden African figures that a fellow arts dealer shipped me from Africa off my desk. It was a small head sitting on a wooden base, it was carved in the image of an African tribesman.

The head was round like a dildo, and I didn't hesitate to throw my leg up on my desk and stick it in my pussy headfirst. The cold, hard wood felt strange inside my pussy walls, but I figured fucking it was better than fucking Quinton, and lawd knows, I wanted to fuck him so bad right at the moment.

After I came all over my desk chair, I started thinking about the way he ate me out and how much I enjoyed it. If only Jason was open enough to experiment with sex, our love life would've been so much better.


It was after ten when Jason and I finally got all the kids bathed and put to bed. He was lying on our king-size sleigh bed watching the news when I came up from checking to make sure the stove was off and all the doors were locked.

As fine as Quinton was, he couldn't compare to my husband. Jason has always been, and will always be, the finest man in the world to me. He was wearing a pair of white cotton pajama pants, and as usual, he had left the matching shirt of the set on the bed for me. We often did that, split a pair of pajamas. I grabbed the shirt off the bed and headed toward the master bath. "I'm about to grab a quick shower, Boo. Wanna join me?"

I knew what his answer would be before he replied.

"No, baby. Go ahead. I'm going to catch the rest of the news."

Jason never wanted to shower or bathe together. It seemed like anything that would have brought us closer together physically was a taboo to him. I got in the shower. The warm water felt great hitting up against my skin. I thought about Quinton, all the things he had said and done to me. I realized no matter what, I had to avoid seeing him again at all costs, even if that meant forgetting about the business deal. It was inevitable what would happen between us, and I couldn't allow it.

As I dried off, I looked into the huge mirror that spanned the entire length of the double-sink vanity. My body had changed a lot over the years, but my breasts were still erect and firm, and my ass was nice and round. My skin was flawless, something that has more to do with genetics than anything else. So many times, I thought the sex problems with Jason and I were my fault. A lack of attraction on his part. That night, I decided to find out.

"Jason, look at me."

He ignored me and opted to catch the sports section of the news instead. I walked in front of the television and cut it off.

"Zoe, why did you do that?"

"Because I want you to look at me." I was butt naked.

He sat up on the bed and glanced at me. "Okay, I'm looking. You need to put some clothes on before you catch a cold. Remember how sick you got last year after we went on that ski trip?"

"No, I mean really look at me. After all the years we've been together, you're still uncomfortable looking at my nude body, aren't you?"

"Don't be absurd!" Jason really did look at me then, tracing the outline of my body with his eyes just like Quinton did at the school cafeteria. "You're very beautiful, Zoe, but you already know that. That's why I married your crazy ass."

I went over to the bed, pushed him on his back, and climbed on top of him. "Oh, so you married me for my looks, huh? Damn shame! All this time I thought you married me because you admired the way I beat your ass the first day we met."

We both started laughing, and he tickled me. I was laughing so hard because we were on the bed tussling about like we were kids again. "I thought I told you never to bring that shit up. Besides, you were taller than me back then."

I started laughing so hard, I was crying. "We have to make sure we tell the kids all about the day I gave you a beatdown when they get older."

He started laughing as he climbed on top of me and pinned my hands down with his own. "Fuck you, Zoe!"

I stopped laughing and looked him in his beautiful hazel eyes. "Jason, that's exactly what I want you to do. Fuck me!"

The mention of sex immediately threw him back into his shell. He climbed off me, propped up a pillow, and lay back down. Then he reached for the remote off the nightstand and turned the news back on.

"Jason," I whispered in his ear, propping myself up on the pillow beside him, "I was thinking we could, maybe and only if you want to." I was so nervous, I couldn't barely get the words out. "Maybe we could try oral sex."

"Zoe, that's disgusting! I've already told you fifty million times how I feel about that."

"How do you know it's disgusting unless you try it?" I

pulled the string on his pajama pants and was pleasantly surprised when he didn't stop me from pulling his dick out.

I moved down on the bed and rubbed his erection with my hand. I laid there for a few minutes, my head resting on his thigh, just enjoying the sight of it, the veins popping out of it and the way it was pulsating inside my palm. Jason had never let me play with him like that before, and I got excited thinking all our sexual problems were about to come to an end. I convinced myself he was finally ready to explore other horizons, be more creative in bed, give me all the things I had always read and dreamed about.

Jason set my ass straight when I tried to put my mouth on his dick. He yanked my hand off him and pulled his pants back up. "Zoe, what did I tell you? I don't want to do that! Not now! Not ever!"

"But Jason, I want to taste you so bad. Why can't I?" I was devastated.

"I know what it is!" he exclaimed, shaking his finger all up in my face. "Brina and the rest of your hussy girl-friends have been drilling their nasty sexual escapades into your head. You need to leave all those bitches the hell alone."

"*Bitches?*"

"Yes, bitches! Did I stutter or something?"

I couldn't believe I tried to suck my own husband's dick and was about to have an argument with him instead. "First of all, this has nothing to do with Brina or anybody else. This is about me and you."

"Whatever!" He turned the television off, and the lamp on the nightstand. Then he turned away from me on the pillow. "I'm going to sleep."

"Jason?"

"Zoe, I think it's best we just leave this whole subject matter alone. I don't want to argue with you."

"I don't want to argue either. I love you." I started rubbing his back. He pulled away from me.

"It's just that you sound like a straight-up ho sometimes, and you aren't a ho. You're a married woman with children and responsibilities. All of your friends are too busy hanging out seeing how many men they can bed down."

"That's not true."

"Whatever. Go to sleep."

I didn't say another word to him. He fell asleep within minutes, and I got up from the bed and went down to the kitchen to put on a pot of blackberry tea. Sitting there on our screened-in porch, drinking my tea and listening to all the birds and animals making noises somewhere out in the trees, I became enraged. I was angry about Jason and his lack of affection toward me. I knew he loved me, but he always became irate and resentful whenever I broached the subject of our sex life, or lack thereof.

I was frustrated with myself for settling for his limitations and not demanding more. I had tried to talk to him so many times but he always ended up saying I was acting like a ho. Then I thought about it. Why shouldn't I become a ho? Why shouldn't my sex life be just as exciting as Brina's and my other girlfriends'? Jason was right about that one thing. I did hear all about their sexual escapades, and it made me jealous. I was sick of hearing about great sex. I wanted to *have* great sex.

I returned to bed and stared at Jason in the dark. Then I looked up at the stars, wondering why things had to be like this. Before I fell off into a deep slumber, I had already made up my mind. If Jason wouldn't give me the love and affection I needed, I would find it in the arms of another man. I would find it in the arms of Quinton Matthews.

Contrary to all the nonsense I talked to myself that night about fooling around with Quinton, I lost my nerve. For two weeks, I didn't call him or go anywhere near him. I loved my husband, and betraying him was not going to be as easy emotionally as I thought.

I considered asking Jason to go to a marriage counselor with me, but I knew good and damn well he would get angry. I threw myself deeper into my work and started working longer hours at the office. Jason complained because he often had to change his schedule around to accommodate mine, so I did what most women do in a time of crisis. I called my mother.

After very little convincing, my mother agreed to watch her grandchildren three evenings a week so her baby girl could pursue her career. Besides, she always complained about not getting to see Peter and the twins enough, and I think Aubrey was beginning to get on her last nerve at home. So it was a done deal, and it gave me a well-deserved break from rushing home to cook dinner every night, helping with homework, breaking up fights between siblings, and on and on.

It was on one of the evenings I was working late at the office that I decided to relinquish my wedding vows and go see Quinton Matthews. It had been a very stressful day, and when I called Jason to seek comfort in his words, he told me he would have to get back with me and then hung up on me without saying 'bye.

I decided to go for a walk in the cool air to clear my

head and ended up at the MARTA station where my favorite mural was located. I sat there on the bench, thinking about the fact that Quinton was so close. His building was right across the street. I looked up at his loft and saw that the lights were on. I played out the best- and worst-case scenarios in my mind, and to be honest, none of them made me feel comfortable. Finally, I decided I wanted to know what real sex felt like, if only once.

When I got off the elevator on his floor, I noticed there was a young woman taking some garbage down to the trash chute. She was obviously the other tenant on the floor, and her door had been left ajar. I knocked on Quinton's door and got no answer, so I knocked harder.

"You looking for Quinton?"

"Yes, is he home?"

She came prancing down the hall toward me, and I noticed she was wearing a dance leotard and tights. She felt my eyes on her. "Oh, 'cuse the way I'm dressed. I'm a professional ballerina."

"That's great!"

"Yeah, my parents bought me this loft so I could have plenty of practice space. I think they kind of wanted my ass out the house anyway, you know?" She started smiling, and I returned the gesture, hoping she would not embark on telling me her whole life story.

I repeated my earlier question. "Is Quinton home?"

"Naw, I saw him leave out about ten minutes ago. You just missed him."

"Oh okay, thanks!"

I turned to get back on the elevator. "Listen, he went over to the movie theater on Spring Street to catch that new Denzel movie. If you hurry, you can get there while the previews are still showing."

"No, I don't think so. I'll just catch up to him some other time."

"It's up to you, but he went to the movies alone, and I'm sure he would appreciate the company of a beautiful woman."

I blushed, wondering why this girl would be telling me all this. "Thanks for the tip."

"You're more than welcome, Zoe."

I swung around to face her. "How do you know my name?"

"Quinton and I are real close friends, and let's just say, he's mentioned you." She started giggling. "On *numerous* occasions, I might add. He was hoping you would come back around."

I was so flattered, and I'm sure it showed all over my face. "Is that right?"

"Yes, and I must say, he described your ass to a tee. You are very beautiful."

"Thanks!" The elevator finally arrived and I pulled the gate up to get on. "Goodnight."

"Goodnight, Zoe. By the way, I'm Diamond."

I got on the elevator and pulled the gate back down. "Nice to meet you, Diamond."

I pushed the button for the garage, and the elevator started going down. "And Zoe, if you ever decide to take a walk on the wild side with another woman, I'd just love to turn your fine ass out!"

I couldn't believe she said that shit to me. All sorts of things started going through my mind. Was Quinton fucking her, or were they just friends? Did he tell her he ate my pussy? Was I about to bite off more than I could chew?

I didn't have the answers to the questions, but nevertheless, less than five minutes later I found myself parking outside the movie theater. On the way in, I decided I would pretend to just accidentally bump into him, but I knew that wouldn't work, since Quinton and Diamond obviously told each other everything. So I bought my ticket, went into the dark theater and didn't even try to hide the fact I was there looking for him. I went from aisle to aisle whispering his name until I heard him call out, "Zoe, over here!"

He was sitting on the far end of an aisle, right beside the wall, and I joined him. The theater was not crowded at all, maybe thirty people tops, and everyone was spread out. "So, what brings you here?"

"Good question." I couldn't say the real answer. I couldn't say I had come for some dick. "Diamond told me where to find you, so I decided to join you. Is that a problem?"

"No, hell no. I'm glad to see you. You had me worried I might not ever see you again." He reached over and grabbed a hold of my hand, pulled it up to his lips, and kissed it.

For the next hour or so, we sat there in silence watching *He Got Game*. We held hands, and I was shaking like a leaf. Quinton told me he was going to grab some nachos and a drink from the concession stand and asked me if I wanted anything. I told him I would take a soda, and he said, "Okay, be right back."

I was desperately horny, and as soon as he disappeared up the aisle, I started rubbing my nipples through my blouse. I knew there was something wrong with me, even back then. Thinking about sex twenty-four/seven and playing with myself day and night had to be a sign— a sign I was not willing to recognize.

Quinton came back with the nachos and drinks. I quickly returned my hands to my lap, pretending to be

Ms. Innocent. But when he sat back down next to me, something snapped.

I reached over and started caressing his dick through his jeans, and he was clearly pleased. "Now, that's what I'm talking about, Zoe. You want me to pull it out for you?"

I quickly replied, "Yes, pull it out."

He unzipped his jeans and whipped out his dick, already hard. "Now, what are you going to do with Timex now that he's come out to play?"

"Ummmm, Timex?"

"Yes, he takes a licking and keeps on ticking." We both started laughing, and I almost choked on the soda I had just sucked up through a straw.

"Well, let's see. What shall I do with him?" I was a nervous wreck, but not about to back down.

I sat my drink down on the floor, took the cup of warm cheese sauce that came with the nachos, and poured half of it all over his dick. He flinched. "Oops, my bad, let me get that for you."

I leaned over the seat and started to lick the cheese off his dick. Then I got up and moved in between his legs, kneeling down on the floor so I could get more access. I started sucking his dick like a pro. One would have thought I had years of experience, even though it was my first time. All that reading really paid off; Quinton was moaning like crazy and holding on to the armrests of his seat for dear life.

I sucked the head first, and was hooked on the taste of a man's juices from the second some of his precum hit the back of my throat. The shit was on from that point. I deep-throated that bitch and loved it. I almost gagged a few times, but I caught a rhythm and sucked the shaft and caressed his balls until he came in my mouth. He started trembling and acting like he was having a seizure.

I was hesitant to let his dick out of my mouth, even when it got soft. I wanted some more.

I sat there for a few minutes, gently licking and sucking his balls, before I got up and announced, "I have to go."

"What the hell do you mean, you have to go?"

"I have to get home. Enjoy the rest of your movie." I was gathering my coat and purse.

He started getting loud with me in the theater. "You're crazy! Always running away! You're just going to come in here, suck my dick, and leave?"

"Shhhh! Keep your voice down. Yes, that's exactly what I'm about to do. Leave."

"Forget this movie. Let's go back to my place. I want to be with you." He started feeling all over my thighs, trying to get his hand between my legs, but I wouldn't let him.

"Quinton, I have to go. It's been real, and thanks for the, ummmm, whatever you want to call it."

He sat there shaking his head as I made my way to the center aisle. I turned back toward him. "Besides, I owed you that from the last time. One good lick deserves another."

When I got in my car and started the ignition, Quinton startled me by preventing me from shutting the driver's side with his hand.

"Zoe, you can't leave me like that," he said seductively, making me weak in the knees even though I was sitting down. "Let's go back to my place and talk. Just talk."

"I can't, Quinton. I really do need to get home. It's getting late." I was determined to hold my ground until he started running his fingers through my hair and I lost it.

"Come take a ride with me," he suggested. "I want to show you something special."

"Something like what?" I inquired, full of curiosity.

"Something I'm positive you will like." He could tell I was about to give in and leaned over to cut off my engine and remove my keys. He pulled me up out of the car. "There's one little condition though."

"Which is?" I asked with a raised eyebrow.

"Let me blindfold you."

Now common sense should have told me to take my ass home, but I didn't. I followed him to his car, got in, and sat there patiently while he looked in the back for something to cover my eyes with.


"Can I *please* take this blindfold off now?" Quinton had stopped his car and walked around to open up the passenger door for me. I could feel the cool night air rush inside, in direct contrast to the heat that had warmed up the interior of the car during the ride over.

"Not yet," Quinton replied. "Give me your hand."

I reached my hand out. He pulled me up and out of the car. The first thing I realized was that we were standing on some sort of gravel. Now I knew what the noise had been when I heard something hitting up against his tires a few seconds before the car came to a halt. "Where are we, Quinton?"

"Practice some patience, my dear." He led me by the hand and pushed my hips backward so I was sitting on the hood of the car, the engine still warm underneath my bottom. "I want to make sure your first look is a perfect one."

"My first look at what?" I was getting nervous. Why, I have no idea. I had just got finished waxing his dick in a movie theater, after all. That's the one thing I was sure he wasn't planning to show me. I already had an eagle's-eye view of that bad boy. "Come on, take the blindfold off, please!"

"Just one more second." I heard him walking around, and then the driver's-side door opened. A minute later I heard "Got to Give It Up" by Marvin Gaye blaring from the car stereo. Before I knew it, Quinton kissed me gently on the nape of my neck and climbed on the hood beside me. "I used to listen to this song all the time when I was a kid, eleven years old to be exact. I would bring a little tape player out here and play it over and over again while I worked."

"Worked?" I was completely lost. "You had a job when you were eleven?"

"Sort of," he replied, untying the blindfold and letting it fall in my lap. "I was working on this."

My mouth fell open in awe at the vision before me. We were by the railroad tracks in SWATS beside an old, deteriorated and abandoned warehouse. Quinton's headlights were on, illuminating the most magnificent mural I had ever seen. I covered my mouth to keep my tongue from falling out while I climbed down off the hood to take a closer look.

"Oh, my goodness, Quinton! You did this when you were eleven years old?"

"I started it when I was eleven," he replied. "It took me almost five years to finish it, though. It's the first mural I ever painted, *and* the most special."

The mural was of an African-American family sitting around a gigantic wooden table eating dinner—everything from a big, juicy turkey to corn on the cob to collard greens. A huge fire blazed in the background, both a cat and a dog were sitting on the hearth, playing with a ball of red yarn together. The features of the people were so intense, so descriptive, right down to the wrinkles on the mother's brow. There were five people in the picture: a man, a woman, and three beautiful children. The youngest little boy resembled Quinton so much, there was no mistaking it was him.

"Is this a mural of your family, Quinton?"

"No, my family was fucked the hell up." I turned around in astonishment, not expecting such a negative response. The pain was written all over his face. "My father left my mother for a white woman when I was five. My mother let herself go after that until there was nothing left. When I was nine, she killed herself. She slit her wrists over the kitchen sink while she was washing dishes. Just decided she had endured enough bullshit from everyone, I suppose."

I rushed back over to him and drew him into my arms, letting his head rest against my shoulder. "I'm so sorry to hear that."

I kissed him on the forehead and he drew away. "Why are you sorry? You didn't have a damn thing to do with it."

An uneasy feeling began to wash over me. There was anger in his voice, bordering on hatred. I began to wonder what I was doing there in the first place. I should've been home with my husband and kids, where I belonged. "Why did you bring me here, Quinton?"

"Because I wanted you to see it," he answered in a low, husky voice. "I've never shown this to anyone before. Not ever."

"It's beautiful," I stated cautiously. "Who are the people in the picture?"

"They're the family I wished I had. They're the family I should've had. Instead, my older brother and sister and I ended up living with our grandmother. She tried the best she could, but her heart was broken after my mother's suicide. I think every time she looked at us, it reminded her of her own failures. She always blamed herself for my mother, but it wasn't her fault. It was that bitch-ass father of mine who did it." He walked over to the wall and started fingering his mother's eyes lightly. "Do you know that bastard didn't even have the decency to come to her funeral? He was off in Hawaii with that white bitch of his, lying on the fucking beach!"

"I'm so sorry, Quinton!"

"Stop saying you're sorry, dammit!" he screamed at me. I started trembling in fear. He must've recognized it, because he came over and wrapped his arms around my waist. "I didn't mean to hurt you."

"I'm okay," I replied hesitantly. "I just can't think of any other words."

He looked me deep in my eyes. "Then don't say any more words."

Our kiss began, and to this day, I'm not sure where the passion in my lips came from. All I know is it did, and it was earth-shattering. Before I knew it, we were both naked, making love on the hood of his car. We didn't say another word to each other. The whole time I kept staring into the eyes of the woman in the picture, wondering how much pain she must have been in to take her own life that way.

Quinton and I exploded in unison. I struggled to breathe because I had never had an orgasm like that before, not even when I masturbated, and trust me, I had that shit down to a science.

Quinton finally broke the silence. "Zoe, I know that this is wrong," he whispered, sucking gently on my left nipple. "I shouldn't have these feelings for another man's wife, but I do." At that point, I didn't know what my true feelings were, so I remained mute. "I just want you to know that I don't have any great expectations. I just want to be with you whenever and wherever I can."

My mind flashed back to Jason. I pictured him sitting at home in his drawing room, waiting patiently for me to come home to him. I pictured my kids tucked snugly in their beds, dreaming of faraway lands and fairy princesses. I sat up abruptly and started feeling around for my clothes so I could get dressed.

"Quinton, I don't know what to say right now. Something special just happened between us. I realize that, and just so you know, I've never cheated on my husband before."

He ran his fingers through my hair. "I know you haven't." He started sucking on my earlobe, and my body yearned to give in to his desires all over again. "I know this is confusing, but we can make this work, somehow."

I got lost in his eyes and I could have sworn my heart stopped beating for a brief second. "Can we go back to the theater to get my car now? Please?"

"Sure thing." He put on his clothes, and we rode back to the theater in silence. He rewound the Marvin Gaye tape and sang the words so low they were barely audible.

When we were pulling into the parking lot, I asked him, "What ever happened to your brother and sister, Quinton?"

"I'd really rather not discuss that right now," he replied, taking my hand and kissing my fingers one at a time. "We'll talk about it later."

I let it go. He saw me to my car and made me promise to be in touch soon. I reluctantly promised. What I should've done is told him to stay away from me. That I was no good. That we were no good together.

When I got home, everyone was asleep. I took a quick

shower to rinse away my sins and joined Jason in bed. He draped his arm and leg over me and whispered, "I love you," in my ear, halfway between being awake and being asleep. I kept my back to him and stayed awake for the remainder of the night, letting the tears trickle down my cheeks onto the pillowcase.

# chapter fifteen

Quinton and I started seeing each other on a regular basis after that, and while I felt guilty, I couldn't stop. It felt too damn good. I stayed away from him for about three days after the little movie theater/train yard episode, and then I decided to go over to his place. I must admit I knew he and I would end up fucking if I went over there. That was exactly what I wanted, and that was exactly what I got.

It was about dusk when I showed up at Quinton's loft. He answered the door wearing an apron, and the aroma of his cooking hit me as soon as I got off the elevator.

"Zoe, what a pleasant surprise! Come on in!" He moved aside so I could enter his loft.

"Did I catch you at a bad time?"

"No, not at all. In fact, your timing is perfect. Now I don't have to eat alone."

"Well, I'm not really that hungry, but I could use a glass of wine if you have one."

"Sure! Have a seat, and I'll be right back."

He went into the kitchen and returned a moment later with a bottle of red wine and two wineglasses. He poured me a glass and walked over to the sofa to hand it to me. "Zoe, take your shoes off. Make yourself at home."

"Thanks, I will." I kicked my black high-heeled pumps off and leaned back on the sofa to sip on the wine. "So, what you got cooking?"

"I decided to try this recipe for lasagna I saw on a cable cooking show earlier today."

I started giggling. "You watch cooking shows? Wow, you are full of surprises."

"Yes, I do." He starting eyeing me all over again, and for the first time, it didn't make me feel uncomfortable in the least. After sucking his dick with nacho cheese on it, among other things, shyness was no longer an option. "Let me go take it out of the oven so we can talk."

"Okay!"

I decided to be nosy again and took a peek at his easel. He had removed the portrait of the governor and replaced it with a portrait of a beautiful African-American woman. I was immediately jealous. "She's the wife of a friend. She asked me to paint her portrait as an anniversary gift for him."

"That's cool."

He walked up behind me and covered the portrait back up with the oilcloth. "Don't worry, baby. This dick's for you."

"Hmm, is that right?"

He started blowing in my ear. "Damn skippy."

He took me by the hand and started leading me up the steps. "What the hell do you think you're doing?"

"Taking you to bed. You have a problem with that?"

"As a matter of fact, I do. You're trippin', assuming I came over here to fuck you." I pulled my hand away from his, and he came closer to me, pressing his chest against mine and grabbing me around the waist.

"That is what you came over here for, isn't it?"

"Hell naw! I hate to bruise your male ego but I came over here to discuss business." He and I both knew I was full of shit.

"Yeah right, Zoe."

"Hmm, well, whatever. I should be going now because you're buggin'." I started walking over to where my shoes were so I could put them on when he picked me up and flung me over his left shoulder. My ass was all up in his face. "What the hell?"

He carried me up the steps, flung me down on his queen-size waterbed, and started undressing me. "Listen, Quinton, I didn't come here for this. *For real!*"

"Then look me in the eyes, Zoe, and tell me you don't want me." He and I gazed at each other, and I wanted to tell him I didn't want him, but the words wouldn't come. "Enough said. We already crossed the line the other night, Zoe. There's no turning back now. We need to finish the feelings."

Quinton got me totally undressed and then removed all his clothes as well. The neon sign at the hotel across the street was blinking steadily, and flashes of red outlined his body as he stood at the foot of the bed. He spread my legs open with his hands, and after that we didn't say a word to each other. We just fucked.

He ate my pussy again and then stood on the edge of the bed. I figured out he was waiting on a blow job, so I complied and loved sucking it. When he came in my mouth, I was in heaven and probably moaned louder than he did. He started fucking me, and by the time

Quinton fucked me for twenty minutes, I was a maniac. I began to think my lack of experience showed, especially when he pulled me on top of him and I froze. I had no idea how to ride a dick. I was used to the missionary position only.

I gave it a try. He helped me by guiding my hips up and down until I got the hang of it. I had remembered reading somewhere to tighten my muscles while I'm on top, and I did that. He started moaning real loud while I contracted my pussy muscles on his dick. I was so proud of myself. It may sound silly, but being sexually repressed as long as I was and finally getting fucked the right way twice in one week was one of the most stimulating events of my life.

The next six months were filled with confusion, guilt, and a newfound sexual freedom. Quinton took me to heights I had never known physically, and frankly, I became a nymphomaniac. There weren't enough hours in the day to have sex, and when I wasn't with Quinton and Jason was ignoring me as usual, I began to masturbate ten times more than usual.

I even masturbated with an umbrella once in my car. It was a rainy day, and I had to pull over because it was pouring down too hard to drive. I parked underneath an underpass and didn't make it five minutes without playing with myself. My obsession with sex was getting way out of hand, but it was beyond my control.

Quinton was just as creative sexually as he was with a paintbrush. He taught me so much about sex, including how to 72, a variation of the old 69, where three fingers are inserted into the ass for extended pleasure. He turned me on to liquid latex. We poured it over each other's bodies and let it harden before we fucked each other. The only parts that weren't covered were my nipples, my pussy, my ass, and his dick. It was a wild sensation. It felt like wearing a tight, full-body mask. I loved it.

Everything was going great. I had the husband of my dreams, who loved me and was a great father to our kids, and I had the lover of my dreams as well. Everything was perfect, or so I thought.

"Zoe, sit still."

"I'm trying to, but my back is itching." I was sitting on one of the velvet-covered crates, posing for Quinton while he painted a portrait of me. It was the second one. He had already painted one and hung it over his bed, just like he said he would. He wanted another one to hang in the studio itself.

"Okay, let me scratch it for you then." He put down his paint palette and came over to put me out my misery.

I started laughing while he scratched my bare back. "That tickles!"

I was nude from the waist up, having agreed to let Quinton paint me that way. I was becoming bolder by the day. "Zoe?"

"Yes?"

I thought he was going to say something like he wanted to fuck or wanted to go out and grab a bite to eat, but never in a million years could I have been prepared for what came out of his mouth. "I want you to leave him."

"Umm, say what?" I was frozen like a Popsicle.

"I want you to leave your husband and move in here with me. I want you to do it like yesterday."

I got up from the crate and put on Quinton's silk bathrobe I had laying nearby. "Quinton, you know I can't leave Jason! Not now! Not ever!"

"I see. Well, then, Zoe, we have a serious problem."

I started caressing his dick through his pants. "No, we don't have any problems, Boo."

"Stop it!" He pushed my hand away from his crotch and walked over to the window. "This isn't working out anymore. I need you to be here with me all night, every night. Not just when it suits you. This isn't fair to me."

"Quinton, you knew from jump I was married. Why did you get involved with me if you wanted more?"

He turned around, looked at me, and threw his hands up in the air. "Hell if I know. I just had to have you. From the moment I first laid eyes on you, I knew you were the one."

"Well, I can't be the one. Not in that way." I started up the steps to get dressed. "I'll leave and I won't ever bother you again if you don't want me to. I promise. I'm sorry, Quinton. I never expected things to turn out like this."

"No, you aren't going anywhere!" He caught up to me on the stairs, tore the robe off me, and pushed me down on one of the steps. Then he took his dick out his pants, moved my panties to the side with his fingers, and fucked me right there on the steps. "We'll do it your way. I would rather have a part of you than nothing at all."

For a brief moment I feared him. There were times when he seemed to have an evil side to him, but I could never pinpoint it. I would often try to ask him about his older brother and sister, but he would become tense and change the subject. The only halfway decent response I ever received from him was, "They're long gone!" I had no idea what that meant.

Driving home that night, I wondered whether I should break it off with Quinton for good. In my heart, I knew it was the right thing to do, and only trouble could come out of it if I continued the affair. He had laid his cards on the table and made me well aware of his wants and desires. Continuing to fuck him meant three things: trouble for him, trouble for me, and trouble for my marriage. But I couldn't stop. I was straight-up hooked. I was addicted.

# chapter sixteen

"Peter, get Kyle down off of there before he falls and busts his head open!" It was family outing day, and Jason and I had taken all the kids to the park for a picnic.

"Zoe, don't yell at them like that. Let boys be boys."

I sat back down on the blanket next to Jason, after being comfortably sure Kyle wouldn't fall off the jungle gym. "Jason, you talk that mess now, but you'll be the first one having a panic attack if one of them gets hurt."

He smiled at me. "Well, you have a point there."

Jason looked so gorgeous with the sunlight shining across his face and the breeze blowing through his curly hair. "So, how's work been going, Boo?"

"Hmm, it's okay. I'm trying to finish up the blueprints on the new civic center."

"I'm so proud of you. You're really coming into your own."

"I'm proud of you too, baby."

I started picking at the grass, pulling blades of it up and tossing it aside. I was trying to figure out a way to talk to him about sex. I was so scared. Kind of like the people on talk shows who bring their lovers halfway across the country to tell them something because they didn't have the nerve to tell them in the privacy of their own homes. "Jason, I think I have a problem."

"What problem is that, Boo?"

He was sitting there munching on some seedless grapes, intently watching me for a reply, and there was no way in hell I could come out and tell him I had been fucking another man, so I settled for a different approach. "I don't think my fascination with sex is normal. Some pretty strange things have been happening lately."

I knew immediately he would get nervous. The mere mention of sex *always* made him nervous. He started looking away from me, pretending to be spellbound by a flock of birds. "Strange things like what, Zoe?"

My big chance had finally arrived. It was time to come clean and confess everything. "Jason, I've been mastur—"

"*MOMMY!*" Jason was up off the ground before I was, rushing to see what was the matter. Kyle had indeed fallen off the jungle gym and scraped a knee. After I cleaned the wound with a towelette and put a bandage on it from the first-aid kit Jason kept in the Land Rover, Jason gave him a piggyback ride around the playground area to cheer him up.

So much for coming clean. I had the other two kids help me gather up all the picnic items and put them in the truck. On the drive home, Jason came up with what he thought was the solution to all of my problems. "Zoe, about what you were saying before, I think you're just stressed out from working too hard."

"But I never got a chance to tell you what I meant."

"I know, but we can't discuss it in front of the kids. We'll talk about it later." My heart felt like stopping. "Like I was saying, I think you've just been working too hard. Why don't you call up Brina and plan a girls' night out or something? I'll watch the kids."

Little did he know, in the past few months I had barely gotten any work done at all, since I was spending more time at Quinton's loft than at the office. "Okay, Jason, maybe I'll do that."

I decided hanging out with Brina wasn't such a bad idea. It had been ages since we spent some time alone, just the two of us, and I was hoping she would be more receptive to my problems than Jason. I needed someone to talk to, and my husband was obviously not the one.

After we got home, I called Brina and left a message on her voice mail, telling her I wanted to get together that night. She called me back while I was soaking in the tub, and Jason brought me the cordless. He acted like he was embarrassed to look at me naked and handed me the phone with his eyes averted.

Brina and I decided to meet at a club downtown about eleven. I threw on a white spandex dress with white heels and pushed my hair up in a bun. Jason kissed me good-bye and told me to have a nice time. Then I was on my way.

When I got to the club, the Zoo, it was pandemonium in its finest form. I've never seen so many people sweating to get into a club before in my life. I waited on the sidewalk, opposite the red velvet rope where people were lined up awaiting a chance to get in, and looked at every car that drove by, wishing Brina would hurry the hell up. I was going to suggest we go someplace else when she got there because I didn't think we had a prayer of getting in the place anytime soon.

She finally came strutting up the sidewalk about eleven-thirty, having parked around the block where I didn't see her pull up. Girlfriend wasn't playing either. I thought my dress was bordering on hoochie, but Brina's was straight-up slutty. Hell, I'm not even sure you could call it a dress. Less than 30 percent of her body was covered, so it was more like a rag. Girlfriend had her torso, her arms, her legs, and half her ass exposed. She was sporting that black hoochie mama shit too.

"Damn, 'bout time, Brina! I was getting ready to go home and take my ass to bed."

"Sorry, Sis." We hugged and kissed each other on the cheek. "I was trying to make sure I had everything in the right place before I left out."

"Not much to put in the right place. Your ass is half naked." She gave me a slight punch in the arm, and we both laughed.

"Zoe, shaddup, Sis!"

"Brina, look at this line. We have a better chance of getting in a Michael Jackson concert. Let's go someplace else."

"Hell, no. We're going up in this bitch right here. Follow me, Sis."

I followed her and thought she had lost her damn mind when she bypassed the entire line of people waiting and walked straight up to the bouncers instead. "Hey, Snake, 'sup, Boo?"

Damn shame she knew the man! I knew why he was nicknamed Snake right off the bat. His muscular arms were covered with snake tattoos, and to be honest, his face resembled a boa constrictor, but that's neither here nor there.

" 'Sup, Brina? You're looking mighty fly tonight!" She gave him a peck on the lips, and I wanted to hurl.

She pointed at me. "This is my best friend, Zoe. It's her first time here."

He shook my hand and held it while he gave me the once-over. "Nice to meet you, Zoe."

With that, he unhooked the rope and let us enter the club in front of all the others. "You ladies have a nice time."

I joined Brina in saying, "Thanks, Snake!"

Once we found two stools at the bar, I got all in Brina's business. "I take it you come here a lot?"

She lit a cigarette. I desperately wanted to take a pull but refused to even go there. "*Gurrrrrrrrrllllllllll*, have I got some shit to tell you!"

"Well, I could use some good news, so tell me."

The bartender came over and took our drink orders. "I started coming here about two months ago. A sistah from work turned me on to this bitch. Anyway, about the third time I fell up in here, I met this fine-ass nucca named Dempsey. We've been talking ever since."

"You go girl! I didn't know you had a new man. Tell me everything. I want all the details, and of course all the dirt."

The bartender returned with Brina's rum and coke and my banana daiquiri. For the next fifteen minutes, we sat there chatting and giggling while she told me all about her new love interest. Little did I know then that the Mr. Wonderful she was describing would end up beating her ass as a recreational sport in the near future.

I was a bit tipsy. Okay, I was tore the fuck up! I started looking around the club and decided it was a bad-ass club. They had these cages with scantily clad dancers in them, both male and female, and they had live animals such as birds, raccoons, koala bears, and even a silver-back gorilla, all locked up in cages.

They were playing mostly reggae, and the dance floor was packed to the brim. The club had wall-to-wall fine-ass men in it. My ass had no business looking, but there was one who stood out from the rest like a black man at a Ku Klux Klan meeting. He was too damn fine but was surrounded by a shitload of woman trying to get in his pants, so I ordered another drink and just admired his fineness from afar.

He was tall, *real tall*, just like my husband, give an inch or two, dark like licorice and looked just as tasty. What really attracted me to him was his pearly-white smile, his dimples, and his round, muscular ass. I imagined his ass muscles contracting while he pumped his dick in and out of me. My mind was truly in the gutter.

"Brina?"

"Yes, Sis?"

I decided to come on out with it. "I met this guy. A really famous African-American artist named Quinton Matthews."

"Cool, what kind of art? Sculpting, painting, what?"

"Painting. He's most famous for his murals, though. You know that mural we walked to from my office that time?"

"Yeah, the one at the MARTA station?"

"He did that one."

This guy came up, interrupted me, and asked me to dance. He was a true countrified bama so I said, "No thanks!" Besides, I really wanted to come clean with Brina.

"That's great. So how old is he? What does he look like? Hook a sister up, Zoe!"

She was so far off base, it was pathetic! "Brina, you just got finished telling me all about your new man like two seconds ago. Dempsey. Remember him?"

We both giggled. "Hell, yeah, I remember him, but you know us bachelorettes need to have at least one man riding the bench at all times for backup purposes."

"You're silly!"

"I'm just telling it like it is. All of us can't be lucky enough to find true love like the kind you and Jason have."

Damn, why did she have to say that! I lost my nerve. I was about to tell her I was having an affair, but how could I after she said that? Everyone on the outside looking in has always thought my life was perfect. Little did they know my life was barely satisfying at the best of times and pure agony at the worst. I was about to come on out with it anyway when this pimp daddy wannabe came up to us.

"Hey, lovely ladies. 'Sup now?"

I didn't answer, but Brina did. " 'Sup with you?"

"Chillin', love. Just chillin'." I pegged him to be one of those brothas who was chillin' twenty-four hours a day. "Wanna dance?"

Brina looked at me as if she needed my permission. "Zoe, you mind?"

I couldn't believe she would stoop that low for a dance, but I responded, "No, go for it!"

"Aight, girl. Hold my purse for me." I took her purse, and she made her way to the dance floor, after having a hell of a time even getting up off the bar stool with that damn hoochie dress on.

I was sitting there all by myself when the one I had my eye on came over and took Brina's place on the stool beside me. "Hello, beautiful!"

His voice was deep, his eyes were mesmerizing, and he looked ten times finer up close than he did from the other side of the room. "Hello."

"How are you?"

"Fine, and you?"

"Just great, beautiful." The *beautiful* thing was turning my ass on big time. "Care for a refill on your drink?"

"Sure, thanks." He waved the bartender over to order another round. I checked him out from head to toe. Everything from his black, silky hair to his freshly polished wing-tip shoes.

We got the drinks, and our conversation took off from there. He surprised me by having a civilized conversation as compared to the I-wanna-take-you-home-and-fuck-the-shit-out-of-you one. I didn't have a lot of experience with hanging out at clubs. I married so young and started having babies, there were dozens of things my friends got to experience that I missed out on.

We danced for a long time together. In fact, the club lights came up, letting us know it was almost closing time. I searched for Brina and finally located her over at a corner table, sitting on the pimpster's lap. I peeped at my watch, and it was almost three in the morning. I just knew Jason was going to have a freakin' fit. When he told me to go out, he didn't expect me to be out so late. I was positive the all-your-friends-are-sluts speech was on my agenda before I could fall asleep.

"Well, it was nice meeting you, ummm . . ." We had talked all that time but neglected to exchange names.

"Tyson. The name's Tyson."

I shook his hand. "Nice to meet you, Tyson. I'm Zoe."

"Zoe, that's a beautiful name for a beautiful woman."

I blushed as the DJ cut the music and people started to flood out the club doors on their way home to bed, with or without a partner, or headed to an all-night diner for some food to cure their munchies.

I started walking over toward Brina to tell her it was time to go. I had both our purses flung over my arm, having never tracked Brina down on the crowded dance floor to give hers back. Tyson followed me, but I was hoping he wouldn't. I didn't want to be put in the position of having the dreaded let's-exchange-numbers conversation.

"Zoe, slow down, beautiful."

"Sorry. It's just that I really need to get home. It's late, and my husband will be worried."

*"Husband? Damn!"*

"Yes, see my ring?" I held my hand up so he could get a good look. "I thought you knew."

"No, I don't know anything unless you tell me. I really wish you had said something though."

"Why is that?" I got defensive. "So you wouldn't have wasted all night talking to me when you could've picked up another woman and taken her home with you instead?"

"Naw, see now you're trippin'. Nothing like that, beautiful. I just got myself all worked up this evening, hoping we could get to know each other better."

"Well, we can't." I don't know what it was, but all of a sudden I became irate. "It was nice meeting you. I have to go."

I rushed over to Brina. "Brina, it's getting late, Sis, and the club's closing. You want to walk out together, or should I go on ahead?"

She was obviously all into the knucklehead. "Zoe, you go ahead, girl. I'll call you tomorrow."

"Okay, bye." I didn't have time for the bullshit. I got about ten feet when I realized I still had her purse, so I went back and gave it to her. When I turned around again, Tyson was nowhere in sight. I was relieved. His ass had turned me on *tooooooo* much. I was afraid he might fuck around and turn my ass out.

I got outside into the cool, crisp air and started heading toward my car when I heard some faint footsteps behind me. "Zoe, hold up, beautiful!"

I thought to myself, Oh, shit!

He increased his pace until he caught up to me, which wasn't hard, considering his legs were so much longer than mine. "Yes, what is it?"

"I just wanted to give you my number in case you want to talk sometime." He handed me a matchbook from the Zoo with his phone number written down inside of it.

"Okay, whatever, but I wouldn't hold my breath if I were you."

"Why are you being so mean, beautiful?"

"No reason. Sorry I was rude. It's just real late, and I'm dog-tired."

"I understand. I'll let you go. You take care, and I hope to hear from you. The ball's in your court."

When he walked away, I was enthralled with his ass. I began to wonder why single men go after married women but didn't ponder over it too long. I tossed the matchbook into a wire trash can on the sidewalk and continued on to my car.

I got in the car and sat there for a few moments, sucking on a breath mint and trying to get my bearings together. I wasn't drunk, but I wasn't exactly sober either. I thought about how great the conversation between Tyson and I had gone before I decided to get bitchy. Then I thought about what Brina said about always having one riding the bench as a backup.

I pulled out the parking garage, stopped by the trash can, and put my hazards on just long enough for me to jump out and dig the matchbook out with the number on it. I drove home listening to jazz and endured the infamous all-your-friends-are-sluts speech from Jason before falling fast asleep.

# chapter
## seventeen

For a while, things went on as usual. I kept creeping around with Quinton and hoping that Jason would open up to me in some form or fashion. Mostly, I was praying like all hell I didn't get cold busted.

Quinton pleaded with me dozens of times to leave Jason, but to no avail. I made it perfectly clear to him that leaving my husband was simply not an option. I admit I painted a pretty glum picture of my marriage to Quinton, but through all of our problems, I never stopped loving Jason for one second.

The little voice inside me kept telling me it would all backfire on me eventually. After all, nothing good lasts forever, and whatever you do always comes back to haunt you. I just couldn't pinpoint when, where, and how the other shoe would drop. It didn't take too long to find out.

It was a Friday night, and typically, I never visited Quinton on Fridays and Saturdays. I reserved that time for Jason and the kids. We would go out to dinner or to a movie and then cuddle up as a family and read books or play board games.

This particular Friday, I altered my routine and went to see Quinton. I had endured a rough day at the office, and I figured a round or two of hellified sex was just what the doctor ordered. My game plan was to swing by the loft, get my freak on with quickness, and head on home for a night of videos and microwave popcorn with the gang. If I'd taken my ass home from jump street, I would've saved myself a lot of humiliation, and inevitably, a hell of a lot of trouble.

When I got to the loft, the door was wide open like he was expecting me. I walked on in, but Quinton was nowhere in sight on the bottom level. I decided to tiptoe upstairs and try to surprise him. He wasn't there either.

On my way back out, having no idea what to make of the situation, I heard some slow jams coming from Diamond's loft down the hall. I sauntered on down there, hoping she could shed some light on Quinton's whereabouts. I assumed he had made a run to a carry-out or convenience store or something of that nature. He couldn't have gone too far with his place unlocked like that.

When I got within a few feet of her door, instinct told me to turn around. Curiosity made me keep walking, though. It was obvious she was throwing down with someone—I could hear the loud moans. My face flushed with anger. I almost half-convinced myself what I was thinking was wrong, but I had to find out if my suspicions were on the money.

Her door was slightly ajar. I gently pushed it open wider. Diamond was knocking boots with somebody all right, and that somebody was Quinton. He was banging the hell out of her up against the wooden bar spanning the wall of the room. The wall was covered with a mirror.

I just stood there for a few seconds, letting it all register in my mind. The tears built up in my eyes, matching the hostility that was already inside me. Droplets of sweat were trickling from their bodies. He hungrily took her left breast into his mouth while he caught a rhythm and started fucking her harder.

I was turning to leave when he glanced in the mirror and saw me standing there flabbergasted in the doorway. Before his skank ass could even yell out my name, I was down the hall, pushing erratically on the call button for the elevator. I pushed it about twenty times, even though once would have sufficed.

"Zoe!" Quinton came rushing toward me, pulling his pants up on the way. The pathetic bastard!

I started to not even acknowledge his ass, but the anger took over. "Let me guess," I stated sarcastically. "You were helping her change a lightbulb when you slipped on a ballet slipper and fell in?"

"Zoe, listen to me please!" He grabbed my arm, and I immediately yanked it away.

"Don't touch me, you, you, you . . ." I couldn't even think of a word to fit the bill.

"What just happened between Diamond and I was a mistake," he insisted. "It's never happened before, and it'll never happen again!"

He was not even fooling me! "Whatever! I don't want to hear your pack of lies!" I banged on the elevator button again. "I just wish this damn elevator would hurry up!"

Do you know what that nucca did? He had the nerve to cop a 'tude with me! "Look, it's not like you're not fuckin' married! You go home and lay up in the bed with him every night while I have to go to sleep alone!"

I held my hand up in his face so he could talk to it because I wasn't listening.

"I asked you, hell, I *begged* your ass to be with me, Zoe!"

I knew he had a valid point, but I wasn't going to allow him to turn the situation at hand around on me, so I asked him, "How long have you been fucking her?"

He just kept on his own rampage. "I wanted you to leave him and move in with me, but you treated our relationship like some sort of joke!"

I screamed it at the top of my lungs the second time around. *"How long have you been fucking her?"*

Quinton shook his head in dismay. "I just told you, this was the first and last time."

He tried to reach for me again, but I backed away from him. Diamond poked her head out of the doorway. I yelled out, "Bitch!"

Quinton darted his eyes in her direction and waved her away. She went back inside her place and slammed the door. "Zoe, let's just go in my place and talk this over," he pleaded with me.

"Talk it over? *Sheeeeeeit*, there's nothing to discuss." I pointed down the hall. "Take your skank ass back in there with your skeezer. I'm going to take the stairs. This elevator's taking too damn long."

He grabbed for me one last time and hooked a finger on the back waistline of my skirt. I slapped his hand away and headed for the stairwell. "Get your fuckin' hands off of me, Quinton! You smell like pussy and I hate you! I fuckin' hate you!"

I took the steps two at a time on the way down, hearing the echoes of him screaming out my name until I got to the garage.

I wasn't any good the rest of the weekend. On Sunday afternoon, I asked Jason to watch the kids so I could go visit Brina alone. He was down for that, since he had a bunch of buddies over to watch a college football game anyway. He was probably glad to get the Mrs. out the house so boys could be boys. For a minute, I got offended; it was almost like he wanted me to be a ghost. I started to stay home out of spite, but I really needed to get away for a few hours, so I made some deli wraps and cocktail sausages for his crew before I went on my dreary way.

When I got to Brina's place, I heard a bunch of clamor coming from inside her apartment and immediately wanted to find out what the hell was going on. I knocked on the door and as soon as she answered, I asked, "What the hell's going on?"

"Hey, Sis! 'Sup? I didn't know you were coming by."

"I decided to surprise you, but I'm the one in shock." I barged my way into her apartment, ready to kick someone's ass if need be. "Why all the yelling? I could hear you as soon as I came in the front door of the building."

"Oh, Dempsey and I were just having a *slight* disagreement. It's all cool now. He's my baby boo."

Before I could ask where the so-called romantic Dempsey I had heard so much about was, I noticed Brina had a black eye. I grabbed her by the cheek and held her head steady so I could get a better look. "What in the hell is that?"

"None of your fucking business, that's what!" His trick ass came around the corner from the bathroom, talking trash and zipping up a pair of baggy jeans.

If he was going to come at me like that, I was damn sure going to reciprocate. "Hmm, your pathetic beanpole, anorexic ass must be Dempsey."

"Who the fuck are you?" He darted his eyes at Brina. "Who the fuck is she?"

I decided to answer his question, since Brina seemed to have lost her tongue. "I'm her best friend, and the one sistah who's going to ram her foot up your ass and cut off your dick if you ever lay another hand on Brina!"

He laughed like I was playing tiddly-winks with him. He must've missed the memo, because I was not the one. "Yeah, right, you trifling bitch! I'll kick your little ass too!"

He was clearly drunk. He was staggering, not to mention reeking of alcohol. I reached into my coat pocket and pulled the switchblade I kept there for protection when I was walking from the office to Quinton's or wherever else downtown, popped the blade open, and pushed it up against his throat, forcing him back up against the wall.

I don't know what came over me, but I was prepared to open a can of whup-ass and take it to the bridge if need be. "Looka here, trick! Don't try to play with me, and if you ever touch Brina again, I'll slit your fuckin' throat! Now get your shit and get the hell out!"

"Damn, sistah, chill!" He threw his hands up in the air, not willing to find out if I was frontin' or not, and slowly moved sideways away from the blade. "I'm going! I'll leave right now!"

I put my knife away and went to hold the door open for him. "I know your ass is leaving! Get out!"

He put his cheap, bama tennis shoes on, got his coat, and left without saying another word. Brina sat in the fetal position in a corner, crying her eyes out. After he was gone, I put the double lock on the door and turned on her. "Are you crazy?"

She used the sleeve of her nightgown to wipe the mucus from her nose and tears from her eyes. "Zoe, I don't need this right now. I really don't."

"Well, you're going to get *this* right now! How in the hell are you gonna let that man beat on you like a punching bag?"

"Dempsey's been having a lot of problems at work and with his family back in Alabama." She got up from the corner and went into the kitchen to get a cold glass of water from the faucet. I followed her.

"And? I fail to see what any of that has to do with him beating up on you. Lots of people have problems. They don't beat their woman to relieve their stress."

"Look, Zoe, I love Dempsey! That mess you just pulled was wrong! Pulling a blade on him like that!" She slammed the glass down on the counter, almost breaking it.

I lowered my voice, trying not to let my true emotions show because part of me wanted to slap the shit out of her for being so damn ignorant. "Brina, I love you, but I'm leaving. I refuse to stand here and listen to you defend that ignorant bastard."

"You're so wrong! You just don't understand!"

"Whatever. You want your ass beat, so be it. Women always say people don't understand, but unless you have an awakening, he'll continue to beat up on you. I can't help you until you're ready to help your damn self." I gave her a hug and a kiss, grabbed her by the chin so I could take another look at the shiner he gave her, shook my head in disgust, and left.

I didn't feel like going back home so soon. Most of the malls were closed already, being it was Sunday, so I decided to just drive around for a while. My life had been really traumatic the past few days. First catching Quinton banging the hell out that ho and now finding out Brina was letting some bama pulverize her. I wasn't paying attention to the road and almost crashed a red light. I slammed on the brakes, and the tires screeched to a halt mere inches from the pedestrian walkway.

My glove compartment popped open. Everything in it

flew all over the front seat and floor of the car. I pulled
over to the curb, turned on the interior light because the
sun was setting, and started picking up the mess. Somewhere in between the tube of dried-up lipstick that had
probably been in there since Peter was a baby and the
car's registration certificate, I ran across the matchbook
with Tyson's number inside the cover.

I contemplated things and decided since Quinton was
fucking that hoochie, bringing my benched player into
the game might not be such a bad idea. I knew my ass
was wrong, but I pulled out my cell phone and dialed the
number anyway. He answered on the third ring, sounding
like he was half asleep. He perked up when I told him
who was calling and rushed to give me the directions to
his place before I could even dig a pen out my purse to
write them down.

I arrived at his apartment complex about twenty minutes later and realized straight off the bat I had no business driving, rather less parking, a Mercedes anywhere
near it. However, he lived on the bottom level, and I was
able to find a space right in front of his door, so I took the
risk.

Tyson answered the door after I barely tapped on it.
He was obviously looking out the peephole awaiting my
arrival. His one-bedroom apartment was cozy and
nicely decorated. I could tell he was a man who took
care of himself and his belongings. He was wet, barefoot, and in a pair of jeans only. I was flattered he had
gone through the trouble of taking a shower before I
showed up. We both knew I was making a booty call,
and I'll take a pair of fresh, clean balls over sweaty ones
any damn day.

Tyson and I kicked it for about ten minutes, just
shooting the breeze. He asked me if I wanted a drink, I

told him no thanks, and then he decided to cut the bull-shit. "Take off your dress."

"Excuse me?"

"I said take off your dress."

He was sitting on a dining room chair, and I was standing over by his entertainment center, looking at some family photos. I should've cussed his ass out and left, but I reached behind my back and unzipped my gray casual dress instead. I lowered it off of my shoulders, stepped out of it, and ended up standing there only in my black slip, panties, and black leather, low-heel pumps.

"Come over here." He spread his legs open and patted his right thigh, motioning for me to sit on it.

"Damn, aren't you the assuming one, and demanding too! Sheeesh!" I was talking junk but walking over toward him at the same time.

"I'm not assuming anything. I'm just not into playing games. We both know why you're here, woman, so come and get what you came for."

I decided if he could be off the hook, I could be off the hook too. My nymphomaniac evil twin woke up and took over. "Don't mind if I do." I sat down on his leg and started rubbing his crotch. "Ummm, damn, is he hard for me already?"

"He stays hard. Take him out and put him in your mouth."

"Hmph, I think not." I removed my hand. "You do me first."

"Oh, so it's like that, huh, Miss Zoe?"

"Damn straight. No licking, no sticking." He grinned as I got up off his leg and climbed up on the table. He stood up just long enough to turn his seat around so he was facing me.

"Ummm, okay, I'll play along with your little game."

He raised up my slip and started trying to pull my panties down, but I wouldn't lift my hips so he could get them over my ass.

I grabbed his face with my hands and slipped him the tongue. It was a brief, rough kiss, but I was in the mood for something rough for a change. When we came up for air, I instructed him, "Rip my panties off!"

As big and strong as Tyson was, he had to exert little effort tearing them bad boys off. He tossed them on the floor, stood up, and started kissing me again, pressing my back onto the table's cold metal surface. He decided to take it to the bridge and ripped the straps off my slip too, pulling the nylon material down over my ribcage so he could grab both my breasts at the same time and bite gently on my nipples.

I grabbed the back of his head, bringing his mouth closer into my breasts. He pushed them together, taking both nipples into his mouth at the same time so he could suckle on them. He licked a trail with his tongue from my nipples down the middle of my stomach to my belly button, pausing there to dip his tongue in it and then blowing on it to make his saliva dry up. Damn, that shit turned me on!

He spread my legs open and went to work on my pussy. Tyson's technique was different from Quinton's. He bit on my clit, and while it was painful, it made me cum almost immediately. I was discovering yet another part of my sexual desires I never knew existed. I discovered I liked it rough.

That fact became even more obvious when he made me sit in a chair while he held my head and plummeted his dick in and out my mouth. I thought his dick was going to knock all of my front teeth out at one point. He was working his thang in and out my mouth so fast, but I held my own and sucked him until he came. His cum had a different taste than Quinton's. It was more salty. Once I realized that every man's cum had a distinctive taste, I began to wonder what Jason's cum would taste like. The man I wanted to taste the most wouldn't let my mouth anywhere near his dick.

"I have to go!" Tyson had just exploded in my mouth, and there were still a few droplets of cum trickling out the sides onto my chin when I blurted it out.

He looked at me like I had lost my fuckin' mind. "You've got to be kidding!"

"No, I really do have to go." I got up from the chair and headed toward the door. Looking back at it now, I don't know what my issues were, but I definitely had some. It was almost as if I thought oral sex wasn't actual cheating or something. Like with what I did with Quinton in the beginning, I intended to leave it at oral sex and go home. But Tyson wasn't even going out like that.

I was standing on the backside of his couch, putting my dress back on, opting to ditch the torn panties and slip at his place, when he came up behind me and pushed me over the back of the couch so my head ended upside down and my feet were dangling off the floor. "Tyson, stop!"

"Sure, I'll stop when I'm done." I tried to get up, but he was too strong and forced me to stay bent over while he stuck his dick in my pussy from behind. He fucked the living daylights out of me, and there was no point in saying it wasn't what I really wanted. The streams of cum and pussy juice trickling down my inner thighs onto the floor told the true story.

He fucked me so hard, I could feel his balls slamming up against the back of my thighs while he pumped his dick in and out of me. When it was all over and he had busted his second nut, he let me down. I finished getting dressed, and we were both breathing like we had just crossed the finish line in a twenty-six-mile marathon. I had never been turned out in such a fashion.

After I got my shoes on, I headed for the door. "Hold up, Zoe. I know you're married and all, but do you have an office number where I can reach you? I want to see you again."

I opened the front door of his apartment and glanced back at him sitting on the couch, still trying to catch his breath. "No, I'm a housewife. I don't have an office number."

"Pager? Cell phone?"

"No, none of that." My ass was lying big-time, but keeping my anonymity was the one bright side to the whole fucked-up situation. Tyson only knew me as Zoe, and that's all his ass needed to know.

"So, will I see you again?"

"I'll be in touch!" With that, I left his place, got in my car, and drove home. Jason still had a couple of friends over when I arrived home. The game was over, but they were sitting around drinking beers and talking about various player's career statistics.

He waved at me as I came in. "Hey, baby. Have a good time with Brina?"

"Yes, we had a nice, long talk." Yet another lie! I was getting too good at fabrication. Before Jason could get up to come over and give me a kiss, I told him I was going upstairs to take a hot shower because my back was sore. I didn't want him to smell sex on me, and besides, my back and everything else was sore from being fucked so hard.

When he came to bed later that night, I was asleep, but he woke me up to have sex. I was ecstatic—he was the only man I ever truly wanted in the first place. As usual, he just used me to do his do, and when I tried to go down on him, he refused me once again.

I decided to tell him the truth about what happened with Brina. Well, kind of. I conveniently made it sound like I stayed there for hours after Dempsey left, comforting her, when that wasn't even the case. However, the black eye was pure fact, and Jason told me to stay away from the stupid bitch if she was dumb enough to let herself be beat like that. I ended up having to listen to the all-your-friends-are-sluts speech, but I fell asleep in the middle of it.

# chapter
# eighteen

"Mrs. Reynard, there's a Quinton Matthews here to see you." My secretary's voice screeched out over the speaker on my desk. I was in the middle of drinking a cup of hot tea and almost spilled it on a pile of prints, new additions to the collection. I had decided not to use Quinton's work because I knew the affair would eventually have to end, and I didn't want anything tying us together when it did. I wanted the break to be clean, and as far as I was concerned, the affair ended the day I caught him with his dick all up in Diamond's pussy.

"Send him in, please." I released the speak button on the intercom and wondered why the hell he would risk coming to my office when he could've called. I wasn't about to confront him in the outer office. All I needed was some drama getting into the hands of gossipmongers.

He stormed into my office like he owned the place and sat on the edge of my desk. "Zoe, why haven't you called me or come by?"

His ass was really trippin', so I told him, "Your ass is trippin'. Why the hell do you think I haven't?"

"You tell me!" He started getting loud on a sistah.

"Keep your voice down," I insisted. "This is a business." Once he calmed down and started breathing through his mouth again, I added, "You know why I haven't called your ass. Get real! The last time I saw you, you were fucking the hoochie down the hall."

"I told you that was an accident." He came closer to me, trying to give me a hug. "It's all about you and me, Boo. You're my girl."

"Get your fuckin' hands off me!" I started getting loud my damn self.

"See, now you're the one overreacting."

"Naw, hell naw, I'm not." I really didn't want to re-hash the dirt, and definitely not in my office. "Could you do us both a favor and just leave? I have a lot of work to do. I've fallen way behind fooling around with you."

We were both on our feet by that time, having a good old-fashioned Mexican standoff. I didn't have a damn thing to say and neither did he. We just stared at each other until he finally broke the silence. "I'm not giving up on this relationship, Zoe. That's the bottom line. If I have to camp outside in your secretary's office with a sleeping bag and a box of Twinkies, so be it."

I couldn't hold the laugh in. "Oh, so now I'm a joke, Zoe?" I laughed harder until the tears starting rolling down my cheeks and I was holding my stomach. The fact of the matter was what he said was hilarious, but the situation wasn't.

I regained my composure because he was truly getting pissed. "Quinton, I'll call you. I promise."

"When?"

I rested my ass on the edge of my desk. "Tomorrow."

"Why tomorrow? Why can't I see you this evening?"

"Because I really do have a lot of work backed up on me, and tonight Jason and I are having some friends over for dinner." The workload was true, but the dinner was a lie. I had something else in mind for that night.

"Okay, fine. I'll leave, but I better hear from you tomorrow, Zoe, or else!"

"Or else what?"

"Or else I'll come back, throw your ass over my shoulder, and carry you out of here."

We both giggled at that one. "You'll hear from me. I promise." I don't know why I forgave his ass. I guess it's hard to blame someone for going astray when you're married your damn self.

"Let's seal that promise with a kiss, and then I'll believe you." We started kissing, and one kinky thing led to another. Five minutes later, I pushed the speak button on the intercom and told my secretary to take an early lunch. Then Quinton fucked me on top of my desk, and we devoured each other for lunch.

When I left work that evening, after calling Jason and telling him I had to meet one of my distributors to talk business, I made a beeline for Tyson's apartment. I was feenin' for his ass big-time. I simply loved the way he was rough with me that first time.

He had just gotten home from the auto garage where he worked as a mechanic when I got there. He was covered with motor oil and grease and looked sexy as all hell to me. I was taking things to the extreme, having fucked Quinton on my desk earlier that day and now getting ready to fuck someone else before driving home to my husband.

Tyson was happy to see me and told me to hop in the shower with him. I stripped down to nothing and did just that. He made me prop my leg up on the edge of the tub so he could eat my pussy, and then I sucked his dick before he held me up against the wall with my legs straddled around his waist and fucked me rough just like I wanted.

We got out the shower, and I told him what had been on my mind that whole day and the reason I was really there. "Tyson."

"Yes?"

"I want to try something real freaky!"

His eyes widened; he gawked at me and said, "Word? Like what?"

"I dunno," I replied because I really didn't have a well-thought-out answer. "I was just going to leave it up to you. You seem like a man who knows how to turn a sistah out the right way."

"Hell, yeah, if that's what you want." He paced around the bed naked while I propped myself up on a pillow so I could admire the view.

Finally, he said, "Look, if you're really down for this, I have an idea."

I decided to let all my inhibitions go and threw caution to the wind. "Cool! I'm down for whatever."

Boy, why the hell did I say that? Less than five minutes Tyson had me tied to his bed butt-naked on my stomach with a blindfold on. I was just ass out and had no choice but to be down for whatever.

He lubricated my rear like a Corvette and then took it literally. Much to my surprise, the way he did it was painless. I realize now it was all in my head, and because I didn't have time to let fear build up, I took it in the ass without all the psychotic fears going on. He took his time with me, and when it was all in, he worked me just like he did with vaginal sex.

Tyson came, and we were lying there with his soft dick still inside me when there was a loud knocking at the door. "Tyson, open this damn door! You fuckin' bastard!"

"What the hell?" I turned my head toward the door but couldn't see for jack because of the blindfold. "Who is that woman banging on your door?"

All he whispered was, "Shhhhhhhhhh, she'll go away."

"Untie me right now!"

He covered up my mouth with my hand, and I was pissed. "Just be quiet, Zoe. I'm not answering the door. That ho's crazy."

"Tyson, I know your ass is in there with some bitch! Open the damn door, now!" He stayed on top of me, his dick in my ass, trying to prevent me from squirming. "You ain't nuttin' but a lying, cheating, male tramp! Just wait till your ass comes out that bitch! I got something for that ass!"

Then she left—at least, we thought she did. He got off me, removed the blindfold, and untied me. I hurriedly got dressed. I didn't need yet another lover that was fucking someone else.

"Zoe, she's my ex. I've *been* finished with her skank ass." I didn't need another lame explanation either.

"Whatever!" I got fully dressed and started looking for my keys. "She's not my problem, Tyson! She's yours!"

Wrong again! She was my problem. He walked me outside and came to find out the heifer had cut all my tires and scratched the word *BITCH* on the side panel of my car with her keys. She was long gone, and good thing she was, because I would've been going down the river for homicide that night.

People sitting out on their stoops were having a good

laugh, saying, "Oh shit!" "Damn, must be some good dick!" and "That's what your ass gets for fucking around!"

I went back into Tyson's place to call the auto club. I couldn't believe this shit was happening. How in the world was I going to cover my ass on this one? Like they say though, where there's a will . . .

I instructed the tow truck driver to haul the car to my regular service garage near my house, all the way on the other side of town. He was pissed but had no choice, since that was one of the benefits of having the gold plus plan.

After telling Tyson to kiss my black ass, I hopped into the cab of the truck with the driver, cursing under my breath the whole way to the garage.

I had to make it look good, so I called Jason from my cell phone when we were almost there and told him the car had been vandalized outside the restaurant downtown where I had met a distributor to discuss business. I told him to pick me up at the garage in ten minutes. The tow truck driver, an old countrified hick, was staring at me when I closed out the call. I gave him a glare and told him, "Mind your own fucking business!"

Jason was already there when we pulled up at the garage, talking to our mechanic. The expression on his face when he saw the car, which had to be towed on a flatbed since all four tires were flat, was definitely one for the books. After asking me fifty questions, all to which I answered, "I have no idea. It just happened," he decided he was just elated I wasn't harmed in any way.

That night, we made love more intensely than we ever had. He started out by coming in the bathroom while I was taking a bath, rolling up his sleeves, and washing my back. I almost fainted from that show of affection alone. Then he dried me off, carried me to bed, and gave me more time and attention than he ever had before. It still wasn't great sex, but it was a sign that maybe there was hope for us yet. I didn't ask him for oral sex and heaven knows anal sex was out the freakin' question. I was just glad that, for once, he made me feel like he desired me as much as I did him.

# chapter
# nineteen

In light of the way Jason made love to me the night of my brush-with-death experience (according to him), I decided to throw myself headfirst into my marriage. I had messed up big-time, but the bottom line was, I still loved my husband more than life itself, and he was the only man I ever truly wanted.

I planned the ultimate romantic evening for that Friday. I asked my mother, who had already gone far and beyond her duties as a grandmother, to stay with the kids overnight so I could kidnap Jason and attempt to turn his ass out. She agreed to stay over, and I picked up Jason at his office. We were sharing the Land Rover, since the Mercedes was still in the shop.

He thought I was picking him up just to go home and do the regular dinner with the kids, followed by watching a couple of sitcoms and the news-before-bed routine. When he saw I was headed in the opposite direction from our house, he demanded to know, "Where are we going?"

"I have a surprise for you, Boo!"

"Zoe, I'm kind of tired. I was looking forward to just chillin' out tonight." He started rubbing his temple like he had a headache.

"Jason, I spent all day planning out tonight and asked Mom to stay overnight with the kids. Please don't ruin this for me. If nothing else, do it to make me happy."

He glanced at the backseat and noticed I had a small suitcase. "Overnight, huh?"

I smiled at him, reached over, and rubbed his thigh. "Yes, Boo, overnight."

He gave me a devilish grin. "Okay, I'll go along with this. Sounds promising."

"Oh, it is. Believe me, it is." I moved my hand farther up his thigh and then started caressing his dick through his trousers. He didn't stop me, and I was in shock. Not shocked enough to stop, though. I held fast to that bad boy, which grew rock-hard, until we got where we were going.

We pulled up at a little Greek restaurant at the end of town about six, and Jason was thrown for a loop when I led him by the hand straight through the entry-level dining area and up the back stairs. When we got upstairs, all the patrons were seated on fancy floor cushions, drinking cocktails and socializing in the dim, smoke-filled room.

"Zoe, what the hell is this place?"

"You'll see," I giggled, leaning over and giving him a kiss. He didn't just peck me back for a change. He tongued my ass down just like in high school, and I savored it for as long as I could.

The music started, and the first belly dancer made her way to the center of the room and began her dance. Jason started laughing like I knew he would. It was the *old* Jason I was trying to resurrect—the one who used to talk mad shit all the time, the one who was the romantic target of every girl at school even though he was unavailable, the one who stole my heart somewhere between giving me the finger and a game of Twister.

The dancer was buck wild, and all the old, beer-bellied men were clapping and sticking money in the waistline of her sheer-leg pants. Jason and I both enjoyed the show and ordered some drinks. After the third dancer came out, I excused myself, telling him I was going to the ladies' room. I was lying, but it was a good lie this time.

When the announcer called out the name of the next act, Jason almost hurled his drink when the man said, "Zoe!"

I came out in a white sheer costume, laced with gold, and did a special belly dance just for Jason. I had been there earlier that afternoon, taking lessons from one of the real dancers, which is why I knew my way around the place so well. I danced seductively while all the other patrons watched, and Jason was blushing.

What tripped him out the most was when I shook my belly in his face and he noticed my freshly pierced belly with a silver charm stuck in it with the name *Jason* engraved on it. I finished my dance, got mad applause, and fell gracefully into his lap. He removed the veil that was covering the bottom half of my face and planted a big, wet juicy one on me. "I love you, Zoe!"

"I love you too, baby!" I kissed him again and started to get up. "Be right back. I'm going to get dressed."

He slapped me on my ass while I was walking away. "Do that, you crazy fool!"

When I came back, dressed, he assumed we would be eating there. "I'm starving. Let's go downstairs and grab a bite."

"Ummm, excuse me, Mr. Reynard, but this is *Mrs.* Reynard's night and *Mrs.* Reynard has other plans for dinner."

"Well, excuse the hell out of me!" We both laughed and held hands all the way back to the parking lot.

Our next stop was a Japanese restaurant, the kind with private dining rooms concealed behind silk-screened, sliding doors. We ordered a pot of green tea after being escorted to our little private haven. Our shoes had to be taken off upon entry to the restaurant, and once again, we got to sit on pillows. Jason commented, "You know my back is going to be screwed up after all this, right, Boo?"

I leaned over and whispered in his ear, "I'll give you a nice back rub then." He kissed me again, and I was thinking he hadn't kissed me so many times in one day since *way* back. As an afterthought, I added, "Maybe you'll let me rub something else too."

I slid the tip of my tongue in his ear and then blew in it. "Be right back, baby. I have to tinkle."

Was I lying again? Hell, yeah! Instead of the Japanese woman who had originally waited on us bringing the pot of tea in, I did it myself, dressed as a geisha with an oriental silk robe on and a big-ass black wig. "Zoe, you're too damn much! Why are you buggin'?"

"Because I love to see you smile, and tonight you're smiling a lot." He laughed. I knelt down on the floor beside him because I couldn't sit Indian-style with the long robe on. I looked him in his eyes and meant every word as I spoke them. "Jason, I would do anything to make you happy. I love you, and this is forever."

"Always has been! Always will be!"

We started tonguing the hell out of each other big-time. When the regular waitress came in with our appetizer, Jason had my robe halfway open and was about to

pop a tit out to suck on. I stayed in the robe and wig for
the rest of the dinner and fed him with chopsticks, wiping
his mouth and chin off every time a morsel of food accidentally missed its target.

"Okay, Zoe, I'm almost scared to ask what's next.
Crazy ass!"

We were standing outside the restaurant, waiting on
the valet to retrieve the Rover. I walked up close to him,
stood on my tippy-toes, and kissed him briefly. "What do
you want to be next?"

"Hmmmm, well, if I recall right I tried to take the
lead earlier this evening and was informed that this was
*Mrs.* Reynard's evening and *Mrs.* Reynard makes all the
decisions."

I pinched him gently on his arm. "Damn right, Mrs.
Reynard makes all the decisions."

He grabbed me and started tickling me. The other
people waiting on their vehicles were looking at us and
laughing. As we drove off to our next destination, I was so
happy. For the first time in ages, Jason and I were having
a genuinely romantic time together, just like when we
were younger.

It was a warm, clear night, and I was glad, because
the next stop on my agenda wouldn't have worked out
right if it hadn't been. We took a long drive out to an observatory about an hour away from Atlanta. We had
never been there, but it was one place I had always
wanted to go. We got there just in time to catch a slide
show in the planetarium, and then we went to the obser-
vation deck to look through the gigantic telescopes at the
stars. I think I loved that part of the evening more than
Jason did. Even though he listened to me rant and rave
about the heavens all the time and had kept his promise
by building me a home full of skylights so I could see the

stars whenever I wanted, his appreciation of them wasn't
nearly as profound as mine.

Before we left, I did what I really came there to do
and adopted a star. I adopted *our* star, the star Jason and
I selected together the first night we kissed on my front
stoop. The donated money went to help with the upkeep
of the observatory. They gave us a framed certificate with
the name of our star, "Ambrose," which is Greek for im-
mortal and undying just like our love, imprinted on it.
Our names were also put on the certificate along with the
words, *Always has been! Always will be!*

It was time to head to our final destination, which
was a cozy bed-and-breakfast inn in the countryside.
When we got to the Waterside Inn, we were shown to our
room, which had a balcony overlooking the small lake on
the property.

I had some chilled champagne delivered to our room
and then asked Jason to take a hot bubble bath with me. I
practically had a heart attack when he agreed. We took a
long bath together in the old-fashioned bathtub. I sat behind him with my legs straddled around his waist. We
had one of the most intimate, provocative talks of our
marriage, and I was overwhelmed at how open he was
being.

We made love on crisp, white sheets underneath a
handmade quilt and it was beautiful. We engaged in
much more foreplay than we had in a long time. Back
when we were still virgins, we would make out for hours,
but when the sex between us started, it seemed like the
intimacy went away. In one night, I was getting both the
intimacy and the sex, and I was loving every minute of it.
Everything was great until . . .

. . . I tried to perform oral sex on him. He went ballistic. "Zoe, stop that shit! DAMN!"

"Jason, what the hell is wrong with you?"

"You know I'm not into that." He jumped up from the bed and put on one of the heavy terrycloth robes provided by the hotel.

"How can you not be into something you've never tried? I don't get it." I wanted to tell him how good the shit really was and how I was a pro at deep-throating a dick, but having him file for a divorce wasn't part of my seduction plan, so I left that one alone. "Jason, come back to bed. We don't have to do that if you don't want to, baby."

He came back to bed, and we fell asleep in each other's arms. I just didn't want the whole night to be ruined. I had put too much heart into it for it to end with an argument. I was just happy we were making some sort of improvement in our sex life, even if it was a far cry from what I really needed.

Way over in the morning, something happened to me. It was as if something snapped. I woke up, started crying, and ended up in the bathroom with the door shut, crouched down on the floor between the toilet and the bathtub. I didn't want Jason to hear me wailing like a three-year-old, but I couldn't hold it in. All I ever wanted was for one man to love me, and he does love me. He has loved me all my life. Whenever Jason and I make love, it is like winning the lottery to me, but at the same time, it almost feels like he is just doing me a fuckin' favor.

chapter
twenty

"Marcella, I'm totally exhausted!" It wasn't so much exhaustion as it was stress. I'd been discussing my sex life with her for hours and still hadn't gotten to the *really* deep part. Not that I was looking forward to revealing that situation at all.

"Zoe, that's fine. I understand." I glanced up from the chaise longue at her. She was sitting in the leather wing chair beside it, scribbling away on her notepad. "We've covered quite a bit of ground today. We made a lot of progress."

"Did we?" I asked, perplexed.

"Did we what?"

"Make a lot of progress?"

"Of course! The mere fact that you were able to discuss your problems is a significant breakthrough." She smiled at me timidly, probably wondering if I was buying into her bullshit. "Like I said, we covered a lot of ground."

I sat up and rubbed my eyes. They were sore from

shedding so many tears. Half of the time I was talking, I
kept my eyes shut so I wouldn't even have to look at her. I
didn't want to see the disgust on her face. As I readjusted
my eyes to the dim lighting in her office, Dr. Marcella
Spencer didn't appear disgusted at all. I knew she had to
be hiding it below the surface. She didn't want me to pick
up on her loathing. How could anyone not hate a despica-
ble, cheating, lying, manipulative tramp like me? Even
those getting paid to pretend otherwise?

"Yes, we covered a lot of ground, but—"

"But what, Zoe?"

"Do you think you can help me? Honestly? How do I
stop this madness when it has taken total control of me?"

"Well, the first thing I should ask is, How do you feel
about Quinton and Tyson? Are you in love with either one
of them?"

I pondered her question. "I can't be in love with
Quinton or Tyson because I'm in love with Jason."

"So you don't feel it's possible to love more than one
man at a time?"

"I care about them both—Quinton more so than
Tyson—but it's not love. They give me things I need. I'll
admit that I've become accustomed to being with both of
them. I never intended to be with Tyson more than a
couple of times, but at this point, I'm with all of them
every week. This shit has got to stop. That's the bottom
line."

"I see."

Damn, not that "I see" again! "Marcella, can you just
answer my previous question? Do you feel as though you
can help me get out of this mess?"

She sat up on the edge of her chair, moving in closer
to me. "I'm going to be perfectly honest with you. Sexual
addiction isn't exactly my area of expertise." I wondered

how far not exactly. "However, there are certain things that apply to all types of addictions."

She hesitated. The last thing I needed was to be held in suspense. "Such as?"

"Well, are you aware that both alcohol and drug abuse rehabilitation programs work on a multi-step matrix?"

"Excuse me?" I inquired, realizing all hope for a speedy recovery was fading fast. "Are you telling me I need to stop on a gradual basis?"

"Something of that nature, but listen!" She raised her voice an octave, sensing my irritation. She was damn right too. I was mad irritated. "Just like any addiction, it's extremely hard to go cold turkey on—"

"Umm, hold up a second! Are you telling me I should keep fucking these other people and lying to my husband?"

"Zoe, calm down." She headed to her desk to get a cigarette. "You just have to relax and hear me out."

"Calm down, my ass!" I jumped up and started putting on my overcoat. "I can't freakin' believe this shit! I finally get the nerve to tell someone about all the fucked-up, backass, conniving shit I've been doing! I finally spill my guts about everything, and not to mention pay your ass to let me do it, and this is what I get for my trouble? You telling me to keep doing it? What do you suggest? To maybe cut back to two sexual trysts a week instead of four? Let Quinton hit it on Mondays and Tyson on Wednesdays, and everybody's happy?"

Her hand started trembling while she attempted to light the cigarette with her silver-plated lighter. Her ass was just as nervous as I was, and she was supposed to be the expert. "No, not at all Zoe! I *am* going to help you! Just hear me out!"

I calmed down a little, plopped back down on the chaise, and stared at her.

She retook her seat across from me, inhaling like a mofo. "I have a friend who specializes in sexual addiction. He has a practice down in Florida, and I think he might be able to help you."

*"He?* Oh, hell no, this shit just gets thicker and thicker. I can't discuss this with a man. Men are the cause of all my fuckin' problems."

"I understand, but—"

I cut her ass off. "The main reason I came to you is because you're a female, and I thought, at the very least, you would be able to relate to my situation a little better. But a man can't begin to relate to the confusion going on in my mind."

"I understand what you are saying, but—"

"Besides, what am I supposed to do? Tell Jason I'm going down to Florida on a business trip while I go check into some clinic for nymphomaniacs? That shit is out of the damn question."

"Are you a nymphomaniac?" She asked the question as if she didn't already know the answer.

I got up and headed toward the door. "What the hell do you think?"

I was halfway to the elevator when she started tugging gently on my coat sleeve. "Zoe, come on back in the office so we can talk some more. Off the clock. We need to settle this. I don't want you leaving here so distraught. I really want to help you. Why can't you believe that?"

I tried to get my bearings and prevent my heart from pumping so fast. I sensed true sincerity in her voice as I pressed the call button for the elevator. The next words came out in a normal tone. "Look, Dr. Spencer—"

"Marcella," she corrected.

"Marcella, I really appreciate you listening to me and fitting me into your busy schedule. I'm truly sorry for snapping at you just now, but all the pressure and stress I've been under lately is destroying me." I started pressing the call button again.

"I can see that it's destroying you," she agreed, rubbing my arm. "That's why you have to let me help."

I gazed in her eyes, looking for some omen that she was my savior. "No, you can't help me. No one can. I got myself into this predicament, and I have to get myself out of it."

"That's where you're dead wrong." I noticed there were beads of sweat gathering on her brow. She was really stressing over my ass. "If you could get yourself out of this alone, you would have already. In fact, you never would have put yourself in this position in the first place if you had an option."

She had a point, but I still didn't believe she could improve anything. "The bottom line is this. After all the shit I've gone through with Quinton, I'm still fucking him. After all the shit with Tyson and that bitch of his vandalizing my car, I'm still fucking him. There's nothing that's going to make me stop, short of Jason finding out and wringing my neck. That's the truly pathetic part of all this."

The elevator doors parted. I got on and pressed the button for the lobby level. She prevented the door from shutting by leaning on it. "So what are you going to do now, Zoe? Just continue on your path of destruction?"

I threw my hands up in the air and then started grasping the chrome bar surrounding the inside of the elevator. "Gee, I don't know what I'm going to do now!" I fought back the tears, determined not to shed another tear in front of Marcella. "I love my husband to death, but maybe, instead of heading home, I'll go let one of my lovers have their way with me. Who knows?"

She sensed my sarcasm. "Actually, I do know what I'm going to do after I leave here," I continued. "I'm going to visit my best friend and make sure her ass is all right. I haven't seen Brina since I insisted on taking her to the emergency room last Saturday. And maybe, just maybe, if she's not in the middle of another crisis of her own, I'll ask her to let me cry on her shoulder for a change."

Marcella smiled at me. It was a weak, forced smile, but welcome just the same. She dropped her voice to almost a whisper. "Sounds like a good plan to me, Zoe. But listen—" She reached in the elevator and rubbed me on the shoulder. "If you ever want to talk again, I'll be right here. You can call me anytime, day or night. I can't make you continue therapy with me. I just want you to know I'm always willing. Always!"

"Thanks!" The smile I returned was genuine.

The elevator doors were halfway closed when she stuck her foot in. "Zoe, we never got a chance to discuss your third affair. You sure you don't want to stay for another hour so we can continue the conversation?"

I smirked, wondering how sick she would think I was if I told her the truth. Just threw the entire load of shit on her like I was tossing a penny in a wishing well. "Trust me, Doc. That's the last thing I need to talk about right now. In fact, that's probably something better off left alone, period."

She removed her foot. The last thing I saw as the elevator doors slammed was the perplexed expression on her face.

# chapter twenty-one

It was drizzling when I arrived at Brina's building. I didn't go in for a few minutes. I was still shook up over the unexpected altercation with Marcella. The last thing I was prepared for was her admitting she didn't have a clue what the fuck she was doing. She could've told me that from jump street.

I should've told Brina all of the drama from the get-go and saved all the dead presidents I was going to have to kick out on therapy. Not to mention the aggravation and humiliation I endured by telling a complete stranger all of my business. Still, I liked Marcella. I sensed something real about her. I only wished she could have helped.

I decided the heart-to-heart between Brina and I was long overdo. So what if she always viewed me as perfect? She understood the Zoe-Jason soap opera better than anyone. After all, she had a front-row seat to the whole thing. Gurlfriend was just going to have to get over the fact that her idol wasn't a lady, but a tramp. Brina and I went way back, and out of everyone, she wouldn't judge me. That much I knew for sure.

After making a mad dash to get in the carpeted hallway of her building, I folded the newspaper I had over my head to protect my hairdo and jiggled the dampness off my coat. I knocked on her door and didn't get an answer. Her car was parked out front, so I was surprised when she didn't come to the door. After all, she was the one who went on and on about how she just went to work and came straight home every day. I couldn't imagine her hanging out, and since it was raining, I knew she wasn't out walking anywhere.

I heard some music playing loudly and realized it was coming from her place. I figured she was probably in the shower or something and didn't hear the door. I contemplated waiting out in the hall for a few minutes and knocking again. I was used to just barging in with the hidden key but for some strange reason, I felt it would be obtrusive that day.

I decided to wait a few moments. I had no desire to go home and face Jason right then and running to one of my other lovers was out of the damn question. Besides, I wanted to check on Brina's bruises and see if she planned to take me up on my job offer. Most of all, I needed to confide in her in the worst way. Enough of the lies!

I swung around when I heard the door across the hall open abruptly. There was an old white woman standing there in a housecoat. She had a baseball bat in one hand and a demonic expression on her pale face. I immediately jumped back against the wall. An eighty-year-old white woman holding a bat and glaring didn't sit well with me.

She looked me up and down and lowered the bat, deciding I didn't look like a criminal.

"Something bad happened in there last night." She whispered the words, like she was afraid of being overheard even though I was the only person in the hallway.

I pointed at Brina's door, feeling my heart pounding in my chest. "In here? This apartment?"

She nodded her head. "Something *real* bad!"

With that, she slammed the door in my face. I stood there, paralyzed with fear. What the hell did she mean by that? I started banging on the old woman's door, but she didn't answer. "What do you mean, something bad? Ma'am? What are you talking about?"

My first instinct was to call Jason. I rummaged through my purse for my cell phone. After dialing the first five digits of our home number, I started laughing and turned the power off. This was ridiculous! That old woman was probably senile. For all I knew, she was making the whole thing up. Brina was just fine. She had to be. I'd just seen her ass the other day, after all.

I retrieved the extra key and stormed inside her apartment. Her living room was dark, but everything seemed intact. There was a light emitting from the cracked door of her bedroom. The music was coming from in there also. I'll never forget the song that was playing. It was Billie Holiday's version of "God Bless the Child."

I went into Brina's bedroom. I couldn't breathe. At first, my eyes refused to register what they were seeing. Ten seconds later, my screams began.

To this day, I'm still confused about the chain of events that happened next. It didn't really matter who ran in there, who called the police, who picked me up off the floor, who called Jason to tell him to come and get me, who did this and who did that. We were all too late. Brina was gone, and my life would never be the same.

I remember Jason rushing into the super's apartment, drenched with rain. At some point, the drizzling had turned into a full-fledged thunderstorm. The homicide detectives set up the super's place as their base of operations so the coroner's office and forensics team could do whatever it is they do when someone is brutally murdered in Brina's apartment without other people traipsing in and out. Jason joined me on the couch and almost had to slap me silly to get a response. I could only manage to wail, sink into his warm, muscular arms and pray for the whole nightmare to go away.

But it didn't go away. It seemed like we were there for hours while I answered all fifty million of their questions. Some of them I knew the answers to, and some I didn't. I told them they needed to go talk to that old heifer down the hall who didn't bother to call the police the night before when she heard something bad going on.

I described to them how I walked in the apartment and found Brina laid out in a funereal position on her bed, with her hands draped limply across her chest. All the bedding had been stripped away except the floral-patterned fitted sheet and mattress cover. I cringed at the thought of all the blood. There was blood everywhere. On the bed, on the carpet, even on the walls.

A forensics technician barged into the room to inform the detectives he'd counted eighty-seven stab wounds, as if he was proud to be able to count so high. Jason spoke the words I was thinking: "Why does Zoe have to hear this? Don't you guys have any compassion?"

One of the detectives obviously agreed. He took the insensitive bastard out in the hallway so he could finish relating his findings. I resumed giving my statement, what there was of it, telling them everything I knew—what Dempsey looked like, where Brina had met him, what I knew about the beatings, how I'd pulled my switchblade on him once to make him leave, and how I'd taken Brina to the hospital a few days before her death to get medical treatment.

After they were reasonably sure they'd gotten everything useful out of me, they told Jason he could take me home and assured me they would track that rabid dog down at all costs.

My mother was there with the kids when we got home. They were already snug in their beds. Thank goodness it was one of the regular nights she kept them. Jason was able to come to my rescue right away, and I was grateful for that. If I had to face all of that alone while he waited for someone to come over to baby-sit, I would've really been a basket case. Having my husband by my side during the ordeal was the only thing that kept me from slipping over the edge. Jason is my love, my life, my everything.


The next few days were pure hell. My mother practically moved in so she could treat me like a baby, bringing me mugs of warm milk, running my bathwater, and combing my hair like I was a complete invalid. Jason was a sweetheart. He took some time off from the office and handled Brina's funeral arrangements. Brina's mother was just as devastated as I was. She even sobered up for a few days to wallow in her grief. She couldn't deal with picking out caskets and a dress any more than I could. My baby did it all. He even arranged to pay for everything, since Brina had no insurance and her mother was barely making ends meet.

The weather was beautiful the day of the funeral. I was very thankful. Brina had very few friends and never stayed at a job long enough to make lifelong attachments with coworkers. For that reason, Jason arranged to have the funeral graveside. He'd selected a beautiful white coffin and a huge bed of pink roses to be laid over it. He held my hand and comforted me throughout the entire ordeal.

That's when I knew it was over. That's when I knew I could beat my sexual addiction. Jason was all I ever needed. If I had to live the rest of my life curbing my sexual desires in order to be with him, then so be it. That was one sacrifice I was more than willing to make.

While we were walking back to the black limousine provided by the funeral parlor, I stopped him in his tracks just to give him a hug and a passionate kiss. "I love you, Jason!"

"I love you too, Zoe, and this is forever!"

I managed a smile for the first time since Brina's death. "Always has been! Always will be!"

# chapter
## twenty-two

I didn't go back to work for another week after Brina's funeral. I just couldn't deal with making decisions. I delegated different tasks to several senior members of my staff and spent quality time with my husband and my kids instead. How foolish it had been of me to risk everything I had to sate my sexual urges. I'd lost so much valuable time screwing around, time I could've had with the love of my life and the beautiful little people we made together.

When I did finally return to the office, most of the business issues were cleared off of my desk, but I still had a huge pile of phone messages. I wasn't all that surprised. I knew the majority of them were from my lovers before I even read them. My secretary had been suspicious of my extramarital activities for a long time. I'm sure the three of them ringing the office phone off the hook during my absence had only cleared up any lingering doubts she may have been hanging on to. I didn't really care what she thought or knew. I already had enough people woven up in my web of deception.

I fingered through the messages and ended up ditching them all in the wastebasket beside my desk. It was time for all the bullshit, lies, and stress to be over, and there was no time like the present. I told my secretary I would be back later that day, after having spent only ten minutes in my office. I had been away from the office for over a week already. A few more hours wasn't going to make a drastic difference.

I got out on the sidewalk, took in a deep breath, and exhaled. I was ready to get the drama over with and my life back in order. I was going to end all three affairs in one damn day, go home, and make love to the one man who held the key to my heart. I knew it wasn't going to be easy, but never in a million years did I expect the shit to hit the fan as hard as it did.

I decided to go discuss matters with Tyson first because he was the most temperamental. I figured if I dealt with the worst of it and worked my way from there, I might end up with one hell of a migraine but with everything else intact. It was only about ten in the morning, so I had to go to the garage where he worked in order to talk. That was fine by me. Safety in numbers and all that jazz.

When I pulled up, I spotted his motorcycle parked on the side of the building. I found him inside one of the service bays working on an import. His head was up underneath the hood. He was surprised when he heard my voice. "Tyson, I need to talk to you."

He stood up, almost bumping his head on the underside of the hood. "Damn, you scared the shit out of me!" He grabbed a rag so he could wipe some of the oil and grease off his hands.

"Sorry, I didn't mean to take you off guard."

"Zoe, where have you been? I've been leaving messages for you at your office for almost two weeks."

I looked down at the concrete floor to avoid eye contact. "I've been busy. Something came up."

"Awwwwwwww, so in other words, you pushed my ass to the curb?" He walked over to a little cooler that was sitting beside one of the toolboxes on a workbench and got out an ice-cold soda. He held the can out toward me. "You want one?"

"No, thanks." I walked over toward him and leaned on the workbench. I needed some strength to come from somewhere and was hoping the bench would have some mystical powers and help a sistah out.

"So, what's up, Zoe? Must be mighty important for you to show up here out of the blue, *at my job*, after not even bothering to call for so long."

He was all eyes and ears. I was all nervous. Sex with Tyson had always been rough, and I had often wondered if that signified a violent streak in his nature. He had never hit me or anything, but there was a first time for everything. I was hoping I was dead wrong.

I cleared my throat and prayed he wouldn't haul off and punch me dead in the face. "Tyson, it's over."

He looked stunned at first, but the look was quickly replaced with one of anger. "What's over?"

He knew what the hell I meant. "You and I are over." I announced it like I was calling out the winning raffle ticket number at a bazaar. "I can't do this anymore."

"I see." Tyson was silent for a good two, three minutes and so was I. He didn't hit me, so things were looking up. "Zoe, I think you're just feeling stressed. Obviously something bad happened. You weren't even going to work or *anything*, so it must've been serious."

"Yes, something very bad did happen."

"Okay, and if you don't want to talk about it, that's cool too. But don't let this affect us, baby. We can get past this."

He was so sincere. I was seeing a side of Tyson I never even knew existed—a sensitive side. It almost made me want to keep him, but that was out of the question. "No, we can't get past this. I made a mistake, a terrible one, and this is all my fault. I take full responsibility for it. I played with other people's emotions to benefit myself, and I can't do it any longer. I have to burn the bridges with all of you and move on. My place is at home with my husband."

"Hold up, what do you mean by burn the bridges with all of you? *All of who?*"

Shit! I slipped! "It was just a figure of speech," I mumbled, trying to play it off. "I meant burn the bridges with you."

He looked puzzled. "Oh, I thought you meant something else."

I opted to play dumb. "Something like what?"

"Ummm, never mind. Let's get back to the matter at hand." He took me by the hand and started playing with my fingers, one by one. "I can understand if you need some time to yourself, but I don't want to lose you."

"Tyson—"

"Just hear me out. Please!"

"Okay." I agreed, even though I knew nothing he could possibly say would make a difference.

"If it's because I've been putting too much pressure on you, I'll back off. We can do this on your terms. I promise."

I was about to tell him that the situation was useless when all hell broke loose. I saw it and heard it at the same time. A rock hit my car, shattering the back window. *"What the fuck?"*

Tyson tried to prevent me from leaving the service bay. "Let me handle this, Zoe!"

*"Handle it? Fuck that!"* I pulled loose from him and went out into the sunlight to confront the bitch.

She was leaning on my car, smiling like she had just been crowned Miss America. "So, you're the tramp that's been fucking my man? Keep coming around him, trick! I just love fucking up your car!"

She was a big hoochie momma. Much bigger than me. She had to be at least five-nine and 185 pounds but I didn't give a shit. I caught her with a right hook as soon as I covered the ground between us.

After that, she and I started scrapping. She pulled a small clump of my hair out, and I scratched her jaw with my wedding ring. It went on from there. She ripped one of the buttons off my shirt. I retaliated and kicked her in the pussy. About that time was when Tyson pulled her off me.

"Dusty, get the fuck off her!" He grabbed her from behind and pulled her hands behind her back, holding them there.

I wasn't through with the amazon bitch though and kicked her again, in the stomach. "Dusty? You look like a dusty-ass bitch!"

"Fuck you, you trick!"

By this time, Tyson was becoming unglued. "Zoe, get in the car and leave! We'll talk later! I'll come by your office!"

"Tyson, my damn window is broke! This is the second time this bitch has fucked with my car!"

"Damn right, trick, and I will fuck with your car again if you ever come sniffin' around my man again!"

I couldn't believe she was still talking trash. Obviously, Tyson had heard enough of her ass too, because he pushed her down on the ground and kicked her. That's when I jumped on him because hitting a woman, even a bitch whose pussy is so dry the crabs have to carry canteens, isn't acceptable in my book. I pulled Tyson's arm and tried to get him away from her. "Tyson, leave her alone! She's a female!"

She looked up from the concrete with bloodshot eyes. "Trick, he don't give a shit about hittin' a woman! That's what got his ass locked up before!"

I looked at him, confused. "Locked up?"

"Zoe, do us all a favor, get in the car, and go back to your office! I will come for you!" He and I were staring at each other when Dusty took us both off guard by jumping up off the ground with the dexterity of a ninja and yanking Tyson's ear, pulling out the gold cross earring he wore in his one pierced ear. Blood started gushing everywhere, and she hauled ass. I would've too; from the look on his face he was ready to beat her to a pulp.

I wasn't waiting around to see whatever went down next. By the time he turned around again to check on me, all he caught was a glimpse of the exhaust from my muffler. I had accomplished what I went there to do, and that's all that mattered. I just prayed his ass wasn't serious about coming to my office, because I wanted the situation over and done with. The comment Dusty made about him being locked up threw me for a loop. I never thought I needed to run a criminal background check before I took on a lover. I began to wonder if he was a woman beater like Dempsey. The police had yet to track down Dempsey and they asked the Alabama State Police to keep a look out for him as well. I would've wished he was dead, but even death was too good for him after what he did to Brina. I wanted him to suffer in the worst way.

Driving back downtown, all sorts of confusion was going through my mind like a slideshow. I missed Brina, my head hurt, Tyson was a convicted criminal and I had no idea what crime he had committed, my window was busted out, my blouse was torn, my lip was bleeding, and I had one hell of a migraine. What worried me most was how I was going to explain any of it to Jason. He was all that mattered. Coming up with yet another lie about the car wasn't going to be that effortless. Not to mention the fact I looked like I had been in a street brawl, which I had. I would just have to come up with something to cover my ass. I always did.

The truly messed-up part was, the ordeal with Tyson only meant one down. I still had two more to go, and my sanity was slipping fast as I gripped the steering wheel with both hands on my way to my next and final destination.

# chapter
## twenty-three

       I got to Quinton's building about thirty minutes later and tried to make myself look presentable before I went up to the loft. I didn't care about the car window or any of that. I put some lipstick on, fingered my hair, and tucked my blouse into my skirt, trying to hide the fact it was missing a button. Why I was even going through that much trouble was beyond me. It wasn't like I was going on a date. I was going to end a mistake. Two of them.

  When I got off the elevator, I hesitated before deciding which way to go first. I knocked on Quinton's door. He answered right away. "What are you doing here, Zoe?"

  He stood in the doorway, blocking my entrance into his place. "Can I come in, Quinton?"

  "No!" I was wondering why he was being so foul toward me until it hit me that maybe he had already found out something I should've told him months before. "You can't come in!"

"Okay, fine. I'll say what I have to say right here and then leave." My legs started trembling, and for a brief second, I thought my knees were going to buckle underneath me. "Why are you being so nasty?"

"No reason!" He was snapping at me like a box turtle, and things were just not adding up.

"Quinton, I get back to work, and I have fifty messages from you asking me to get in touch with you. Then I come over here, and you won't even let me in the door. What's up with that?"

"What can I say, Zoe? Things change."

That's when I knew something *definitely* had happened I wasn't privy to. I was about to ask what it was when I heard the door to the stairwell creak. "Who's there?"

"Now you're imagining things, Zoe." I looked back at Quinton. I had never seen him leer at me that way. He had a look of hatred in his eyes. "I guess you would have reason to be paranoid, huh?"

"Quinton, I'm going to get straight to the point, since you seem to have a rock up your ass anyway." He rolled his eyes. "I can't see you anymore."

*He laughed at me!* Just stood there and laughed all up in my face. The same man that had begged me to leave my husband and move in with him a thousand times. "Oh, so now I'm a fuckin' joke, Quinton?"

His voice returned to normal, and his smile disappeared. "You've always been a joke, Zoe. I just never realized it until the other day."

"What other day? What in the hell are you talking about?" I was becoming irritated, and my head was still killing me.

"Guess what, Zoe?" He crossed his arms and relaxed on the doorframe like a man about to get some revenge on an archenemy.

"What?" I got the feeling it was going to be something I really didn't want to know but I asked anyway.

"I had a luncheon meeting the other day about a new
project I've been commissioned for."

"And? You lost me."

"And the project is painting a mural for the new civic
center currently under construction."

He grinned and sucked on his teeth, and I wanted to
die. "Please, no!"

"Oh, yeah. Now you're catching on. I always knew
you were smart. The same civic center your husband,
*Jason,* is the chief architect for."

*"Quinton, if you said something to him, I swear I'll
kill you!"*

"Relax, I didn't say anything to Mr. Jason Reynard of
Smith, Watson and Reynard over on Spring Street. You
want to see his business card so you know I'm not frontin'
about meeting him?"

*"No, fuck you!"*

"You already did that, Missy. Several times, as I recall."

I was in shock and couldn't utter a word. I just stood
there with my mouth hanging open, wishing all of it
would go away.

"Zoe, that man worships the ground you walk on. All
this time, you had me believing he was some punk ass
who doesn't pay you any attention and doesn't act like
you're alive. You're such a lying bitch!"

The *B* word brought me out of my trance. "I never
said that. I never said Jason was like that. All I ever said
about him was that he didn't want the same things sexually as I do. Jason loves me!"

"Yes, you're right. He does love you. Imagine how
stupid and shitty I felt sitting there at lunch, listening to

him tell everyone about his beautiful, perfect wife. How much he loves you, how the two of you first met and fell in love, how proud he is of you for starting your own business and standing by his side for always, how he built you a house so you could always see the stars, how—"

"He said all that?" I was overwhelmed because I never pictured Jason talking to business associates, or anyone else for that matter, about me like that.

"*Yes, he did say all that!*" Quinton was about to slam the door in my face, but I pressed my hand up against it to hold it open.

"Just promise me one thing. Give me your word you'll never tell him what happened between us. Please!" I was at his mercy, and I damn well knew it.

"Don't worry your little lying ass over it, Zoe. I would never tell that man about us for two reasons. First of all, I feel sorry for the poor bastard, and secondly because, as ridiculous as it is, I still love your scandalous ass. You need help, you really do, and not the kind of help you thought you could find in me. You need professional help."

I started crying. He was right. "Quinton, I tried to get professional help," I admitted. "She couldn't help me either."

"Well, I suggest you try harder." My cries went from sobs to straight-up wails. I could tell he wanted to hold me, but his common sense prevented him from doing so. I had hurt him enough. "Zoe, I'm not trying to be mean to you. That's the last thing I want to do, but if you're not strong enough to put a stop to this for once and for all, then I have to be man enough to do it."

"I understand!" Quinton was reading me like a book. Even though I came over there with the intention of breaking it off with him, more than likely we would've ended up in bed if he had let me in. Just like the many times before I declared I was never coming back but succumbed to my addiction in the long run. "I'm sorry, Quinton! I'm so sorry this had to happen!"

"I know you are, Boo." He reached out his thumb to wipe away some of the tears that were streaming down my cheek, and I savored the moment, for I knew it was the last and final intimate gesture between us.

It was then I heard another noise coming from the stairwell, but this time, I wasn't alone. Quinton yelled out, "Who's there?"

Tyson came barreling through the exit door with fire in his eyes. "You're fucking someone else too? You cheap tramp!"

"Zoe, who in the hell is this idiot?" Quinton demanded to know.

"Tyson, how did you find me?" I was freakin' the hell out. Being confronted by both of them at the same time was the last thing on my agenda.

"You wanna know how I found you?" It didn't really matter to me. Asking the question was a reflex. He was there, and I was in a shitload of trouble. Bottom line. "I was on my way to your office when I spotted your car and followed you here. My dumb ass was tracking you down to beg you to take me back."

"Hold the damn phone!" Quinton had gotten over his initial shock and rejoined the argument. "You're having an affair with his bitch ass too?"

I screamed at the top of my lungs, "It's over!"

Just then, Diamond, who would've had to have been plumb deaf not to hear all the shouting, opened her door and came out in the hall. "What the hell's going on here?"

Quinton was the first to respond. "Zoe's just out here trying to clear up all her loose ends with her lovers!"

"Lovers?"

"Yes, Diamond, lovers with an *s*! It seems Miss Zoe has been cheating on me while cheating on her husband, and lawd knows how many other poor bastards are caught up in this game!"

"You know what?" I was *tooooooo* through then and just wanted to leave. "I'm sick of this shit, and all I want is for everyone to leave me the fuck alone." I looked at each one of them individually and then repeated the request. *"All of you, leave me the fuck alone!"*

That's when Tyson called me a bitch and started strangling me. He was on top of me, his hands clasped around my neck like a vise. His anger was making his lips and cheeks shake. My airway was cut off, I was fading fast, and he would've killed me if Quinton hadn't pried his hands off my neck.

"Man, you can't hit a woman!" They struggled for a few moments while Diamond helped me get up off the floor. Quinton got a hold of Tyson long enough for him to calm down and realize he had almost committed homicide.

Tyson stormed off toward the exit door and paused just long enough to glare at me. "You're not fuckin' worth it! Not even a bitch like you is worth going back to jail for!"

He kicked the exit door open and disappeared. Diamond asked me, "Do you want to go in my apartment so we can talk?"

I broke away from her hold and screamed, "Hell no!"

She backed off, went back in her place, and shut the door while I pressed the call button for the elevator. When it arrived, I was still struggling to regain complete control over my breathing and didn't notice Quinton was still standing behind me until I got on and pulled the gate down. As I pressed the button for the garage, Quinton spoke his final words to me. "Zoe, get some help. If not for you or your husband, do it for your kids."

He went back into his loft and slammed the door. I went back to my office sick, hurt, and disgusted. At the same time, I was relieved it was all over. Facing off with all three of my lovers in the same hallway at the same time was pure hell, but it was over, and my life could finally get back to normal.

# chapter
# twenty-four

I sat in my office, looking at the hordes of people on their way to this place or that place on the city streets below. My eyes were bloodshot, my bottom lip was puffy, my shirt was torn, my nylons were ripped to shreds, and I had fingerprints on my neck, but all in all, it had been a good day. My secretary, as well as everyone else, gave me the what-the-hell-happened-to-you look as I made my way to my secluded office. I clicked on the intercom and asked her to come into my office. Shane came running in with a pen and steno pad, ready to take dictation, and was surprised when she found out all I really wanted was to bum a pack of cigarettes. She started trying to get into my business, and I told her to take the rest of the day off with pay. I suggested she go take in a movie or get her nails done—anything, as long as she got the fuck out of my face.

It had been ages since I took a drag off the legally manufactured cancer, but I was so stressed I needed

something to get me through the rest of the day. It was
only a little after noon, and all my walls had come tum-
bling down in the space of a morning. I called the auto
club and told them to tow the car to the garage near the
house. They asked a bunch of questions, since this was
the second vandalism in such a short time. I tried to explain at first, and then I simply cussed the old battle-ax
on the other end of the phone out. According to the contract, there was no limit to the number of times we could
use their services, so I told her to send the damn tow
truck and then slammed down the phone.

Getting the car taken care of was a start. However,
that wasn't going to help me explain the rest to Jason.
Specifically, why I looked like a female version of Rocky
after a championship belt fight. I had to make up the lie
of all mutha-fuckin' lies, and I had about five hours to
come up with it.

I thought about saying I was mugged in the parking
lot and blaming the broken car window on the assailant,
stating it all happened during the struggle. I quickly decided against that one since, it meant calling the police
and filing a false police report. It never could've worked.
There wouldn't be any broken glass on the ground
around the car in the parking garage of my office building, because all of it was in the parking lot at Tyson's
job. Besides, I was already involved with the police because of Brina's death, and I knew they would assume I
had been attacked by Dempsey if I professed I didn't get
a good look at my assailant. Horrible idea, so I scratched
it.

I thought about saying I got into a fight over a parking space on one of the downtown streets on my way to
a business meeting with a client. That wouldn't have
worked either; Jason would've insisted on knowing where

and with which client and then probably insist on asking them a bunch of questions. So that shit was out too.

There was always the truth of course, but my momma didn't raise no fool. I started chain smoking and choking, trying to get used to the nicotine in my system after all of those years. I spent a good hour trying to make up a lie and came to the conclusion I was basically ass out.

I stayed locked in my office for the next couple of hours and never did five seconds of actual work. Every time someone knocked on my door after realizing my secretary was gone from her desk, I told them I was in a meeting and to come back later. They bought into it, although I was alone. Even if they didn't buy it, their asses still weren't getting through the door.

By the time two o'clock rolled around, I was so overcome with worry about what I was going to tell Jason and stressed out about all the confrontations of the day, I felt like my world had come to an end. I got out the compact mirror from my purse and took a good look at myself. I looked like death warmed over. My cheeks were thinning, and I realized I had allowed my addiction to sex to take priority over every other aspect of my life, including my health.

Even though I couldn't imagine her ever forgiving me for the way I acted the last time we saw each other, I called Dr. Marcella Spencer's office and pleaded for an immediate appointment. Her secretary told me, in no uncertain terms, that the doctor was booked for the rest of the day and there was no way an exception could be made. I hung up and started sobbing. I had no clue what to do, and I felt so alone.

Less than fifteen minutes later, Dr. Spencer called me back and told me she had rearranged her schedule so she could see my pathetic ass right away. She sensed my nervousness over the phone and even offered to come to me. I told her I wouldn't be driving myself there and would prefer coming to her. We hung up, and I rushed past everyone in the outer offices before they could get a good look at me. I waved down a cab, and this man tried to playa hate me and jump in before I could. I told him to get the fuck out of my way and pushed him so I could get in. He had picked the wrong day to mess with me.

Dr. Spencer and I ran into each other as I was getting off the elevator on her floor. She was on her way back to her office from the ladies lounge. "Zoe, you got here quickly!"

She seemed more anxious to talk to me than I was to talk to her. The smile on her face changed to horror when she got a good look at me in the hallway lighting. "Oh, my goodness! What happened to you, Zoe?"

I couldn't say a word. I couldn't breathe. I just fell into her arms and started wailing. She put her arms around me and helped me make it into the confines and safety of her inner office. For once, she didn't have to suggest the chaise longue. I crawled up on it into a ball and let it all go.

For a good five minutes, we were both speechless. Marcella just kept handing me tissue after tissue until I had used up the remainder of the box. She broke the silence. "You want something to drink, Zoe? Some coffee? Hot tea? Water? Soft drink?"

I was beginning to wonder whether she was a therapist or a flight attendant and hoped she didn't ask me if I wanted some salted peanuts next. I just shook my head, letting her know all I wanted to do was lie there and drown in my own misery.

"Zoe, we have to talk about this. You're very upset, and you look like you may need medical attention. Do you need me to call an ambulance?"

She rubbed my back, and I could tell her concern for my welfare was genuine. "No, no ambulance. I'll be fine."

I turned over and lay on my back while she examined the marks on my neck with her hand. "Are those fingerprints on your neck? Did someone try to choke you, Zoe?"

I laughed—a man blind in one eye could tell that. "More like murder me. Tyson tried to kill me this morning."

"*What?*" She had been sitting on the edge of the chaise next to me but jumped up, headed for her desk, and picked up the phone.

"Marcella, what are you doing?" I sat all the way up. The way she jumped into action scared the living daylights out of me.

"I'm calling the police, Zoe. You need protection."

"*No!*" I sprang to my feet, and a sharp pain struck me in my side. "Put the phone down!"

"Zoe, you've got to go to the police. He tried to kill you. What makes you think he won't come after you again?"

I wrestled the phone from her hand and replaced it on the cradle. The irony of it all hit me. Less than three weeks before, Brina and I had the same argument, but she had been the one begging me not to call the police. Was I setting up my own untimely demise, just like she did?

"Please, Marcella. I really need to talk. After I've told you everything, if you still think I should call the police, I won't argue with you. Right now, I just really need a friend." I gazed into her eyes, hoping she would go along.

"Okay, Zoe." She got out her pad, pen, and tape recorder while I went and lay back down on the chaise. She sat down in the wing chair beside it. "Let's talk!"

I ended up doing all the talking. I spent the next hour telling her everything that had happened since I stormed out of her office. I told her about how I left with the intention of going to talk to Brina but found nothing except her body full of stab wounds and her blood splattered everywhere. I told her about Dempsey, how I pulled a switchblade on him that one time, and how the police had had no luck in tracking him down since the murder.

I told her how I had decided to go against her advice and try to end all the affairs at one time instead of gradually. I told her about all the shit I had endured since the sun came up that morning, and all the things I feared might happen before the sun went down that night. I told her about the confrontation with Tyson and Dusty and how a fight ensued between the two of us. I told her about my confrontation with Quinton and how he had shocked me by kicking me to the curb after he had a luncheon meeting with my husband. I told her about the confrontation between Quinton and Tyson after Tyson followed me there and tried to strangle me to death in the hallway.

I told her about the ultimate and last confrontation with all three of my lovers in the hallway. I told her about the sexual experiences I had with Diamond after her continual insistence that I try bumping coochies. I told her how I didn't like it at all and never even touched Diamond but just let her touch me. I told her how my need for affection had gone over the edge and that I regretted that situation most of all, because I was not and had never been attracted to women.

I told her that I would keep my eyes closed the majority of the time I was with any of them, imagining that their hands and tongues and dicks and other body parts really belonged to Jason, the only true love I had ever known.

Marcella listened intently and never interrupted me once. I felt much more relaxed after I let it all out and realized the explanation of what had been going on was more for my benefit than hers. As I listened to myself speak the words, it became all to clear to me what had to be done. So when she asked the question, I was quick with my reply.

She put her pad down, cut the recorder off, and then reached out to caress my hand. "Zoe, you do realize that if there is ever to be any happiness or hope for your marriage, you've got to tell your husband everything? You've got to tell Jason!"

I looked over at her and whispered, "I know."

Marcella lent me some clothes she kept in a duffel bag for working out at her gym three nights a week. The sweatpants were a size too big for me, and the T-shirt swallowed me up, but I didn't care. I simply couldn't face Jason with torn and battered clothing. I needed to maintain a slight air of dignity. Her tennis shoes were a perfect fit, though, so I didn't have to wear my heels with the sports clothing.

She was such a sweetheart, even trying to insist she go with me to hold my hand while I told him. I refused; it was something I had to do alone. We went to the ladies' lounge, where she helped me fix my hair and touch up my makeup, which was smeared all over my face. The marks on my neck were horrendous. She used some cake makeup to try to make them less startling.

I called Jason's office to tell him I was going to catch a cab over. I wanted to make sure I caught him before he headed home, so we could drive somewhere and talk without the kids being present. His secretary said he had someone in his office and was adamant about not being disturbed by anyone. I started to tell her I was the exception, which she should have already known, but elected to have her inform Jason not to leave until I got there.

The next call was to my mother, who was already at the house with the kids, having picked them up from school shortly after three. I asked her if she could stay late, because Jason and I had decided to have dinner in the city and possibly take in a movie, and she agreed. After I hung up the phone, I felt guilty about all of the lies I had told my mother. She was one of my many victims, along with my husband, my kids, and my lovers. I had no idea how I was going to admit all my appalling deeds to her—I would cross that bridge when I got to it.

Jason was the matter at hand, and one of two things would be the result of confessing all my sins. He would either believe I never meant to hurt him, realize I had an illness, and stick by my side throughout the recovery process, or he would leave, which was a fate worse than death to me.

Marcella called me a cab. While I was waiting, I asked if she was a religious woman. She smiled and told me how she had grown up in the church and was a true Christian. I told her I didn't have much experience with religion but did believe in God and asked if she would teach me how to pray. We both got on our knees, leaned our elbows on the chaise, clasped our fingers, and prayed for my salvation.

# chapter
## twenty-five

On the way to Jason's architectural firm, I stared out the window of the cab at all the people in a hurry to get the hell away from work. It was just after five, and the rush-hour pandemonium had begun. I asked the cabdriver if he could speed it up, because I was in a hurry. He cursed under his breath at me in some foreign language but did get a bit more aggressive with his driving.

After all the years of hiding things from him, going way back to our childhood, I was anxious to clear the air. Jason was the one person I should've revealed everything to from jump. If I had, none of the other events would have happened in the first place. There would've never been an affair, rather less affairs, and my marriage would never have been in jeopardy.

I was hoping Jason would understand. I believed in my heart he would, if I could only get him alone somewhere and explain it to him in my own way. Maybe I would take him back out to the observatory or the inn at the lake, since those were the sites of our most recent pleasant memories. No matter where I did it, it had to be done. I was prepared to face the consequences of my actions.

When we got about four blocks from Jason's office, I noticed the flashing police lights ahead and wondered what had happened. The cab driver was stuck in heavy traffic, so I decided to pay him and trek the rest of the way on foot. I walked toward the office, slowly at first, but broke into a run when I saw Jason being handcuffed. By the time I covered the three remaining blocks, they had already put Jason in a squad car and driven off. I was out of breath and in a state of panic.

I spotted Jason's secretary, Allison, standing on the steps and rushed up to her. "What happened? Where are they taking Jason?" She glared at me, gritting her teeth, and crossed her arms in front on her. "Why are you ignoring me? Where the hell are they taking my husband?"

"You know, you have a good man and don't know how to treat him." She rolled her eyes at me before continuing. "The rest of us spend our entire lives trying to find a good man. It's women like you that ruin it for the rest of us."

I wanted to slap the shit out of her but just got up in her face instead. "Listen, I don't know what you're talking about, nor do I give a shit. I asked you a question, and I would like a fuckin' answer. Now, what the hell happened here?"

"Fine, I'll tell you what happened. When you called earlier, and I told you Jason had someone in his office, that someone was your lover." My mouth fell open. She sucked her teeth and added, "You're such a tramp!"

I went ballistic, grabbed her by the shoulders, and started shaking her. "What lover? What the hell are you talking about?"

My immediate thought was that Quinton had changed his mind and broken his word to me about not telling Jason. I figured he told him out of anger or to protect him from my evil ways. It was apparent at the loft he felt more sorry for Jason than for me. I realized my mistake when Allison pointed to the other squad car that was still parked out front with the lights on. Tyson was seated in the back with handcuffs on.

I left Allison standing there along with other members of the staff, including one of Jason's partners, who was shaking his head in disgust at me, and walked slowly over to the police car, wondering how the hell Tyson knew where to find Jason in the first place. Then I recalled the creaking exit door at the beginning of my confrontation with Quinton and realized he must've heard Quinton talking about Jason, including the location of his office.

Tyson confronting my husband was the last thing I ever expected. I shuddered to think what he must've told him and the crass manner in which he did it. How embarrassing it must've been to Jason to be accosted in his own place of business and told what a sex fiend his wife really was.

Before I could get all the way to the car, a police officer grabbed me by the arm, instructing me to stand back. I informed him my husband had been taken away in the other car and asked where he was taken and why.

The officer informed me that Jason and Tyson had gotten into a physical altercation, and while no charges would probably be filed against Jason, since he was provoked into fighting at his own office, they had to take them both down to the station to get the mess sorted out.

"Officer, I can explain this whole thing. It's all my fault. My husband had nothing to do with it."

"Well, then, you definitely need to come down to the precinct and give a statement. Here's the address to the station. I'll put my name on the card as well." He scribbled his name on the little white generic card, on the blank line provided, and handed it to me. "Do you need a lift?"

I considered his offer, but only for a second. There was no way I was getting in the same car with Tyson, even if I was in the front and he was behind a barrier and handcuffed in the backseat. He had already tried to kill me and had apparently tried to kill my husband too. Getting in the car with him could only mean another ugly situation. "No thanks, officer. I have another way to get there."

"Okay, ma'am." He got into the driver's seat, and while he was pulling off, I stared at Tyson, who had a look in his eyes that could melt ice. His lips were trembling, and while not a professional lip reader, I recognized the all-too-familiar nickname for me when he mouthed, "Bitch!"


I kept a key to Jason's Land Rover on my ring, so I ran to the garage and found it parked in his assigned space. When I got to the precinct, it was pure madness. Those citizens who chose to cross the blue line of the law—from pimps and prostitutes to drunk drivers and drug dealers—and the ones paid to represent them were everywhere. They were all there. It was the one place Jason didn't belong.

The officer that gave me the card wasn't even there, having been sent back out on his beat. The female officer behind the booking desk told me to have a seat and wait for a senior officer to come and get me. I complied, even though I didn't want to. I wanted Jason out of jail right that second, but causing a scene and bumrushing the woman behind the desk would've only landed my ass in jail too. Then again, I was the one who really belonged there. I was the seedy element.

After about fifty minutes of pure hell, not knowing where my baby was, a man in a pair of gray slacks, white shirt, and paisley tie approached me with a shield hanging out of his shirt pocket. "Mrs. Reynard, I'm Detective Rinaldi. Please follow me."

He didn't shake my hand or anything. He just stood there while I gathered my belongings so I could follow him to a small, cramped room at the end of one of the several cluttered hallways. He was a big man; the floor seemed to shake underneath his feet as he walked. He was having trouble breathing, and it wouldn't have taken more than an educated guess to realize a heart attack was lurking in his near future.

Once we were in the room with the door closed, he asked, "Mrs. Reynard, I understand you think you can clear up the whole situation with your husband?"

"Yes, I can!" Twenty times a day, various people asked me would I like something to drink, and I always replied no. The one time I really was suffering from an extremely dry mouth, no one asked. I suppose making drink runs wasn't in the detective's job description. He was obviously a man on a mission, all about getting to the bottom of whatever dilemma faced him in the quickest manner possible. I decided not to waste his time.

I quickly related the whole sordid story—at least the part of it involving my extramarital affair with Tyson and the ultimate breakup. I told him Tyson couldn't deal with being dismissed from my life and decided to seek revenge by telling my husband. I conveniently omitted the attempted murder by strangulation and my other affairs. Things were complicated enough without bringing all of that into it. I knew that would only escalate matters and possibly hold up Jason's release.

Detective Rinaldi turned out to be a very nice man after all. He won brownie points for being one of the few people not to call me a bitch, ho, or tramp that day. He just calmly listened to what I had to say and informed me, "These types of situations happen every day."

That shouldn't have surprised me, considering all of the people who appear on talk shows fighting over their lovers, but his nonchalant approach took me off guard just the same. Scandalous affairs, dishonesty, violence, and things like that are supposed to happen to other people. Not to Jason and me.

"Wait here, Mrs. Reynard." With that, he left me in the room all alone for about ten minutes. It felt more like ten hours to me.

He came back in with a grin on his face. "Your husband will be released without any charges. His story matches yours, and in this country, self-defense isn't a crime."

I jumped up from the table and took his stubby hand, shaking it viciously whether he wanted to shake hands with me or not. "Thanks so much, Detective Rinaldi. I really appreciate this."

On my way out of the room, I hesitated. It shouldn't have mattered to me, but I had to find out. "Detective, what about Tyson? Will he be released too?"

He smirked, probably wondering why I gave a damn, since I claimed the affair was over. "Now that's a different matter. Mr. Chase violated his parole so the PO assigned to his jacket will have to deal with him."

In all that time, I never knew Tyson's last name. That made me feel even more like a whore. Jeopardizing my marriage for a man I knew on a first-name basis only. What

Dusty blurted out earlier ran through my mind. Gurlfriend had been telling the truth. "On parole for what?"

"I'm not supposed to divulge that information. Sorry."

"Please!"

"Sorry, no can do." He was ready to get rid of me and move on to the next case awaiting his attention. "You can have a seat out in the waiting area. He'll be coming out that way from the holding cell in a few moments."

"Thanks again, detective!" He didn't respond, so I closed the door and made my way back out near the booking area. The worst challenge of the horrid day was still in front of me. I only hoped I could make Jason see the light.

My optimism quickly faded the moment I saw Jason's face. I had known and loved the man all my life and had never seen him look so hurt, angry, and disappointed. He glanced at me, and when I headed toward him, he rapidly brushed past me, almost knocking me on my ass right there in the middle of the station. I followed him outside and caught up to him at the bottom of the station steps.

"Jason!" He just kept walking, headed in the opposite direction from the Rover, since he didn't know where it was parked anyway. He didn't care where he was headed. He just wanted to get the hell away from me. I was right on his heels. "Jason, you've got to talk to me!"

He stopped dead in his tracks, turned around, and glared at me. "Zoe, I don't have to do shit but stay black, pay taxes, and die! I don't have shit to say to you right now!"

He didn't say anything else, but he didn't walk away from me either. I took that as my cue to try to explain. Even though he claimed he didn't want to talk, I knew him like a book. He wanted me to make sense out of it to him, or at the very least make a sincere attempt. "I was going to tell you, Jason. I tried to tell you a thousand times, and after talking to Dr. Spencer today, I was on my way to tell you. I swear!"

He rolled his eyes and started walking around me like he was examining a piece of furniture. "Do you honestly expect me to believe you were going to tell me?"

He was right! There was no reason on earth he should believe me. I tried to touch his arm, but he pulled away from me. "Baby, can we please just go someplace quiet and talk? I asked Momma to stay late with the kids. I told her we were going to dinner and a movie."

"You lied to your mother?" Then as an afterthought, he added, "I guess you're an expert at lying though, aren't you?"

I could've denied it, but the lies were going to stop. Lying had done enough damage. "Yes, I'm an expert. Jason, I'm very sick, Boo."

"You've got that right! That's the one thing we can agree on, and who the fuck is Dr. Spencer?"

We were making some headway. We were having a conversation without raising our voices and I felt maybe there was a chance for us yet. "Dr. Marcella Spencer."

"What's wrong with you? What kind of doctor?"

"A therapist. The one I was telling you about. The one I met a while back." I diverted my eyes to the ground because I couldn't look him in the eyes and continue. "She's been counseling me about my addiction to sex."

"*What?*" So much for not yelling. "*Sexual addiction? What the fuck?*"

The poor baby was trying so hard to have some faith in me. He had loved me just as long as I had loved him, and I could tell he was trying to grasp on to whatever might be left. "The whole thing with Tyson was nothing. He means nothing to me. You're the only man I have ever loved, and you're the only man I will ever love. It's just that—"

"Just that what?" I stood there trying to figure out a way to tell him I sought things from others he would never give to me sexually. "Just that what, Zoe?"

I couldn't do it! I would have given anything for Marcella Spencer to be there. I would have given anything for my mother to be there. I would have given anything for Brina to be there. Anybody willing to hold me and tell me it would be alright.

"Jason, I love you, and you love me, and we'll work this out. I promise!"

"Zoe, are you even hearing the shit you're saying? That man barged into my office and told me you've been fucking him for months. What am I supposed to say now? Oh gee, it's no big deal?"

Jason sounded so sarcastic, his words cut through my heart like a knife. "Not at all. It's a big deal. It's a very big deal, and I understand that. All I'm saying is don't make a final decision to throw away everything we've built together until you hear me out."

*"YOU THREW IT AWAY!!!!!!!"* For a second, I thought he was going to hit me. "You threw our marriage and our life away for a piece of dick! Not me!"

"That's not the way it happened, Jason."

"I've loved you all my life, Zoe. I've tried to give you everything you ever wanted, everything you ever asked for. I have never, *ever* cheated on you. I've never even thought about it. Not once! Then you turn around and do this shit to me!"

"I know, Jason!"

"Do you have any idea how many women have tried to sleep with me? I have women trying to throw pussy at me every damn day, and I never cheated on you, because you were my life!"

"I'm still your life, and you're mine! Don't you see that? I just need to fix what's wrong with me, and we can go back to the way things were!"

He shook his head. "You don't even realize what you've done. You don't realize the damage you've caused. We have three kids, Zoe. Three beautiful kids. Did they ever once cross your mind when you were out in the streets acting like a whore?"

"All the time, baby. I never meant to hurt you. I never meant to hurt them. I never meant to hurt anyone, but I couldn't control it."

People were walking past us in both directions the entire time but we were lost in our own little world. "Jason, please. Let's go someplace where we can be alone and talk."

"I'm not sure I want to be alone with you! I'm not sure I want to be anywhere near you period!"

"Don't say that, Jason! Please don't do this to me!" I tried to touch him again.

"Don't fuckin' touch me!"

I started crying after managing to keep my tears under control up until that point. "I never loved them, Jason! Never! They meant nothing to me!"

*"They? They?"* I started backing away from him. I'd messed up big-time and I knew it. "What the fuck do you mean by *they?"*

"I can explain, Jason. Dr. Spencer will help me explain it to you. Let's go see her, and she can help us get over this."

"You're nothing but a tramp, a bitch, and a whore just like that mutha fucka said! Pure evil!"

"Please don't say that, Jason!"

He looked at me with pure disgust. "Why not? It's all

true, Zoe! It's all true! You're nothing but a manipulative, cheatin', bitch-ass whore! That's what you are, and that's all you're ever going to be!"

"Let's go home, Boo. Let's go home and play with our kids and get a good night's sleep. We'll talk about this in the morning when we both calm down."

"Hell no, I'm not going home with you! I'm not lying down with you! In fact, I'm going home alone, and if you try to show up there, I'll make sure you regret it!"

"You're not being rational. We have to go home at some point. What will my mother think if you go home without me?"

"She's going to think the truth, because I'm going to fuckin' tell her! I'm going to tell her all about her baby girl, and how she's nothing but a lyin' whore!"

He started walking away from me, and when I tried to grab his shirt, he swung around and hit me in the face. I fell on the ground but was determined to hang onto him. I grabbed hold of his pants leg but he kept walking, dragging me along the concrete until I couldn't hang on anymore.

*"JASON, NOOO!!!!! I can't live in a world without you!"*

He looked down at me, and I will never forget his words. "That's unfortunate, because as of this very moment, you're dead to me! Fuckin' dead! In fact, why don't you do everyone involved a favor and just fuckin' die!"

I got up from the concrete. He walked farther and farther away from me, and I realized he was right. I did deserve to die for what I did to him. "You want me to die, Jason?"

It was dark out, and the rush hour was over, so the speed of traffic had gotten back to normal. I repeated myself because I wanted him to see what I was about to do. I wanted him to see how much I truly loved him, how much he meant to me, and how my life meant nothing without him. "You want me to die, Jason?" He turned around and stared at me. "This one's for you, Boo!"

With that, I walked out into the middle of traffic and waited. Cars starting slamming on their brakes. All I could see were blinding headlights. I heard Jason scream, *"NOOOOO!"* and saw him running toward me as fast as he could. *He did love me! He did care!* I was about to run into his arms when I saw the lights fast approaching out of the corner of my eye. The guy in the floral delivery van tried to stop and turned the wheel, but the truck skidded toward me sideways. I took one last look at Jason, who was less than five yards away and closing. I felt the impact, and then there was darkness.

# chapter
## twenty-six

The dripping sound from my IV was the first thing I heard when I woke up. My eyes adjusted to the fluorescent lighting in the ceiling of my hospital room. At first I thought I was paralyzed, because I couldn't move my neck, but it moved a bit during my second attempt. I realized that it was just really stiff.

"Don't try to move, Zoe. I'll go get the doctor on call." I recognized Marcella Spencer's voice right off the bat, even though I couldn't adjust my neck to see her. I heard her heels clicking against the floor when she rushed out into the hallway to find someone to check me out.

Before I knew it, I was getting poked and prodded all over my body. The nurse took my temperature and blood pressure while the doctor, who had to be the resident on call because he looked like a teenager, examined me with his stethoscope and checked my ears, nose, and eyes. When he got to my mouth, it was so dry and brittle I could barely open it. "Mrs. Reynard, that's okay. I'll check your throat later. We've been feeding you intravenously for the past week, so a dry mouth is perfectly normal."

As much as it hurt, I had to speak. "Week?"

"Yes, you've been here in the University Hospital since last Friday. The night of your accident. Do you remember anything that happened?"

I blinked my eyes because they were watery and glanced over at Marcella, who was sitting in a pleather chair designated for visitors. "I remember everything."

The nurse returned with a small pitcher of water and a paper cup. I gulped the water down gratefully. The needle of the IV hurt my arm a little when I held the cup up to my mouth. The doctor was about to drill me with a bunch of questions. I immediately told him I was too tired and insisted on getting some rest. He agreed. "We'll talk later. It's the middle of the night, and it would probably be better if Dr. Ferguson, your regular physician, talked to you anyway. He'll be here first thing in the morning."

"Thanks."

Everyone cleared out of the room except Marcella. "How did you know I was here?"

"Your husband called me the night of the accident and told me."

I was extremely hoarse. "Jason called you?"

"Yes, he did. He told me about what happened and how you discussed the fact you had been seeing me with him." She moved the chair closer to the bed. "I must admit I was surprised you told him about the therapy. You seemed so ashamed about having to seek help for your addiction. I was even more shocked you would walk out in the middle of traffic and try to kill yourself."

A single tear flowed down my right cheek. "At the time, Marcella, I didn't think I had one reason to live."

She held my hand tightly. "In fact, I'm still not sure I have one."

"You have plenty of reasons to live. A lot has happened we need to talk about."

"Tyson told Jason about us, and now he hates me!"

"No, Jason doesn't hate you. He loves you very much. He and I have talked quite a bit this past week, and I can see why you adore him so. He's a very special man."

"Yes, he is." It suddenly hit me that Jason was nowhere in sight. I wondered why he wasn't by my side if he really loved me. "Where's Jason?"

"He's been here the entire time, Zoe. Your mother has been watching the kids most of the time, but Jason also hired a live-in sitter so she can come spend time with you at the hospital as well. I met your mother. She's a sweetheart."

I was so ashamed. "Does my mother know? About everything?"

"Yes, she does, and she loves you more now than ever." Marcella continued to grasp my hand and used her other hand to rub my arm. "Don't worry about a thing, Zoe. Everything is going to be fine. Jason wants to work out your marriage problems."

"He does? Are you serious?" Could it be my prayers had been answered?

"Yes, he does. I convinced him to go home for a little while and spend some time with the kids, since you were comatose anyway. I told him I would stay overnight with you. The hospital allows me visiting rights around the clock since I'm a doctor."

"I see. Thanks so much for everything, Marcella."

"No need for thanks, Zoe. You've become much more than a patient to me. I would like to think of us as friends."

I managed a weak smile. "I would like for us to become friends. I would like that very much."

"We're already friends, and friends we shall remain. Now get some sleep, and I'll be right here if you need anything. Jason will be back early in the morning. I'm sure seeing you with your eyes open will be a blessing to him."

I drifted back off to sleep, and for the first time in a long, long time, I fell asleep not dreading what would happen when the sun came up. Marcella said Jason still loved me and wanted to save our marriage. Thank goodness my accident wasn't fatal. Thank goodness I had a second chance with the love of my life.

I slept like a baby for the remainder of the night. Just like Marcella promised, Jason was there when I opened my eyes the next morning. I was so relieved to see him. I was on my side, and he was behind me on the bed, also asleep, with his arm draped over my waist.

I wanted to let him sleep, but I was anxious to talk to him. Having his arm around me was extremely comforting. At least I knew he didn't find the thought of touching me repulsive. "Jason."

I tried to turn over to face him but had a hard time maneuvering with the IV in my arm. My movements jolted him awake. He opened his eyes. I had made it as far as getting on my back so I could look at him. "Hey, Jason," I whispered.

"Hey, Boo." I took a survey of my hospital room and noticed the drastic yet pleasant change from the night before. There were helium balloons, cards, and flowers everywhere, and a huge red balloon with the words *I LOVE YOU ALWAYS* was tied to one of the safety handles of the bed.

I started blushing. "Jason, did you do all of this since I went to sleep last night?"

He brushed his hand across my cheek. "Yes—Marcella called me to tell me you came out of your coma, and I rushed over here. She told me to wait until this morning, but I couldn't, so while you were sleeping, I raided the all-night drugstore down the street. It was after hours for the gift shop here in the hospital."

"You're so sweet! Thanks!"

"No, thank you for being alive and coming back to me. I was so afraid you were going to die when I saw that van hit you. I didn't get there in time to stop it. It was all my fault you were out there in the middle of the traffic in the first place."

"Jason, none of this is your fault. I'm the one who fucked up, just like you said. I can't believe you're even here with me after all the things I did. I deserve to lose everything, and I'll understand if you want to end the marriage. I don't want you to stay just because of the kids."

He took my hand, spread my fingers open, and kissed them one at a time. "Zoe, I want you to listen to me very carefully, okay, and don't interrupt, because I might lose my nerve and never get all the words out."

I turned a little bit more toward him so I could rest my hand on his thigh. "Okay, I'm listening."

"Before there were any kids, before there was any house or any business, there was me and you. As much as we hated each other the first time we met—and by the way, I still swear up and down you are exaggerating about kicking my ass." We both giggled. "Anyway, as much as we despised each other at first, what eventually grew out of that was love, *real love*, and it's the kind of love that never dies."

I bit my bottom lip to make sure I wasn't dreaming. I knew that if I felt the pain, then I wasn't imagining Jason's words. My lip *did* begin to ache, and I was grateful for the pain. "I love you, Zoe. That's why it hurt so bad when Tyson came storming into my office telling me not only things about you that I never knew, but also things I could never imagine you doing."

Tears starting running down my cheeks, and I wanted to tell him I never meant to hurt him. I wanted to tell him so many things, but he had asked me not to say a word, so I just listened. "Looking back on it now, all the signs were there. You did try to talk to me on countless occasions, and I always snapped at you. I can see that now. Dr. Spencer told me how you related everything to her about how we met, how we fell in love, and how things got complicated. She even told me you thought I looked sexy riding my dad's old lawn mower with no shirt on. I never knew that."

He made me laugh again, and hearing the old version of Jason again was heartwarming, to say the least. "You see, the only side of this whole story I've ever been able to relate to is my own. I never knew your side of the story. I never knew the things that went on in your mind. Not until now.

"Somewhere along the way, we lost something, and I think that something is communication. I promise you that you'll never have to look for love and attention from anywhere else. Not ever again. You can talk to me about anything, and I won't snap at you. I won't say it's immoral or disgusting. I promise!"

He took his hand and gently started caressing my stomach. "As far as the affairs you had, I was very upset and disappointed. I have to be honest and tell you it may take a while for me to truly get over it, but I will. We can get past this because I realize you didn't do it to hurt me, you didn't do it because you didn't love me, and I *know* you never loved any of them. When you told me you were sick that night, I didn't believe you. Now, after talking to the doctor, I do think you did all of those things for reasons beyond your control."

Jason kissed me gently on my lips. "We're going to get through this, and we're going to save our marriage—no matter what it takes, no matter how long it takes. Dr. Spencer's going to help us, and she has a friend down in Florida who's willing to come up here and help us overcome our sexual issues. I love you, Zoe, and this is forever."

He got quiet so I added, "Always has been! Always will be!"

We lay there, holding each other in silence, and something Jason had mentioned began to worry me. "Jason?"

"Yes, baby?"

"What did you mean when you said Dr. Spencer and her friend are going to help us deal with our sexual issues?"

"Huh?" He had a perplexed look on his face.

"You said our sexual issues, not just mine."

He stared at me, and his eyes got watery. "Yes, I did say that."

"What did you mean by that?" My heart started thumping loudly in my chest.

"There are some things I need to tell you also, Zoe. There are reasons why it's always been difficult for me to make love to you completely. Just know that it was never anything about you. It was never anything about your appearance, like you apparently thought. You've always been and will always be the most beautiful and amazing woman in the entire world to me."

I tried to prop myself up on a pillow using my elbows, but I was too weak. "Are you saying you cheated on me too, Jason?"

"No, I told you I never cheated on you, and I haven't. I've never even thought about it. I promise you that."

"Then what is it, Jason?" I wanted him to explain what he meant, because he was scaring the hell out of me.

"Zoe, let's just get some rest. I'm so tired. Running back and forth from the hospital and trying to keep up with everything else has drained me this past week. I'm just glad you didn't fool around and die on me. After we get some rest and the doctors get here, we'll get this all cleared up for once and for all."

He didn't say anything else, and I didn't bother him. I let him fall asleep with his head on my chest. I wanted to know what he meant, but decided to wait until the doctors got there, as he requested. All that time, I thought I was the only one with the sexual issues. While I knew Jason was not willing to experiment in bed, I never thought he had any *real* problems except for lack of creativity. Obviously I was wrong, and the road to recovery was going to have more twists and turns than I had ever imagined. We loved each other though, and our love was strong. If it could survive all the shit I had dealt it, then it could survive anything about Jason that might surface. As I drifted off to sleep, I whispered aloud to no one in particular, "I've survived my cheating. I've survived getting hit by a freakin' van, and I *will* survive this too, so bring it on!"

# chapter
## twenty-seven

Dr. Leonard Graham was a very handsome older man. He was full of energy, even after his flight in from Florida and fighting his way through the crowds and congestion at the airport. He looked to be about six feet even, with a bit of a tummy, nothing fifteen minutes on a Stairmaster for a couple of weeks couldn't cure. He was caramel, with droopy yet sincere dark brown eyes, and his perfectly capped teeth gave him character. All in all, I liked him right off the bat. I got the feeling Jason did too. It would make it a lot easier for us to talk to him, since we thought he was cool. If some uppity, thinking-he-knew-it-all nucca had shown up instead, I would've had to tell Marcella all bets were off, friend of hers or not.

A couple of days had passed since I first woke up from my coma. I spent them trying to recover from my injuries, which thankfully didn't amount to much more than a few bruised ribs and a big-ass lump on the head. There's a lot to be said for being knocked out for a whole week. Because I didn't know what was going on, I missed out on the worst of the pain and had been so drugged up by the IV when I woke up, I didn't have to deal with all of that. Whatever pain I missed, I'm quite sure it was nothing like labor. Jason had the nerve to suggest another baby. I told him his ass had better be joking—if I went through labor one more time, both of us were coming out of the delivery room on a stretcher.

Jason was there around the clock, except for going home to shower and change. Dr. Ferguson, my physician, wouldn't let the kids come visit, but Jason took instant photos of them every day so I could see their smiling faces. How foolish of me to try to kill myself and leave them behind! Jason's partners were handling the firm, and as for my business, the same executives who covered for my ass after Brina's death willingly stepped up to bat once again. I made a mental note to make sure to give them all a raise and extra vacation time with pay, once everything was back to normal. They more than deserved it.

Jason and I never talked about whatever was lurking in his past again. We decided the best thing would be to wait on the actual therapy sessions. I was just glad he loved me, and I was beginning to understand the reasons why he didn't just haul off and hit my ass or leave me. Somehow, Jason was able to relate to my illness, and it would all come out in the wash. The chickens always come home to roost.

Well, the time had finally arrived. Dr. Leonard Graham, our savior dressed in a leisure suit and sporting a toupee, had arrived to mend the situation. Marcella was there in my room, along with Jason and my mother. Dr. Graham could only stay one day, so it was agreed that no matter how many hours it took, everything, and I do mean *everything*, was coming out.

I knew I could handle it. After dealing with all my lovers, Marcella, Jason, and getting hit by a van all in one day, lying in one position on a bed all day was going to be a breeze. I was concerned about Jason, though. He seemed extremely uncomfortable, and I can't say I blamed him. Most of the conversation would be about my sexual escapades with other people and the reasons behind them. My mother, I didn't want there at all, but she insisted, and even though I'm an adult, disrespecting her wishes was not an option.

So there we were, packed into my hospital room. Dr. Ferguson came in and gave me a once-over to make sure I could physically handle whatever stress might arise and one of the nurses brought in some extra chairs, a couple of pots of coffee, and a pitcher of ice water. I felt like a prisoner in the infirmary of a penitentiary about to give a deposition for a Mafia murder case. All we needed was a court stenographer and someone wearing a black jurist robe. The doctors had several memo pads with them, and tape recorders. When I saw the stack of notepads, I wondered who in the hell was going to be saying enough shit to fill them all up.

Dr. Graham took the lead. "Now that we're all gathered together here today, shall we begin?"

I was expecting him to say, "Shall we pray?" He reminded me of an evangelist I used to trip off of on a local cable channel who claimed he could heal people. Once the one who was healed had thrown his crutches away or announced he could see again, the minister would quickly pass the collection plates.

I had Jason sitting on the bed right next to me for moral support. It was more than likely we were both going to need each other to lean on throughout the ordeal. He held my hand, kissed me on the cheek, and attempted to reassure me. "Everything's going to be okay, Boo. I promise!"

"Zoe!" Dr. Graham blurted out my name, and all of a sudden I felt all eyes on me. "Marcella has filled me in on the majority of your case. I've also listened to the audiotapes and read her notes. She and I have had several phone conversations as well. She sent copies of everything to my office in Florida overnight express so I would be all caught up when I arrived."

I glanced over at my mother, who looked like she might need a straitjacket before the end of the day. Her hands were trembling and she had terrible bags underneath her eyes, which probably could've been attributed to spending many sleepless nights worrying about me. She noticed my stares and managed a slight grin, which I returned.

"However, there are some things only you can clear up for me, Zoe. As Marcella has probably mentioned, I'm quite experienced in the area of sexual addiction, and if you let me, I can more than likely help you tremendously."

"I would appreciate that very much, Dr. Graham."

Jason seconded the motion. "We would both appreciate it, Doctor."

"You're extremely lucky for a lot of different reasons, Zoe. Your suicide attempt failed, your mother loves you, your kids love you, and your husband loves you. I hope you'll think about them if thoughts of suicide should ever arise again."

I cut him off because I wanted them all to know. "That won't happen. No matter what, I'm in this for the long run. No more trying to take the cowardly way out."

"That's good, Zoe. That's real good."

Marcella was sitting in the chair beside him, looking

like a college student trying to keep up with a professor. She was taking notes. I guess she was attempting to gain some worthwhile knowledge about an area she knew nothing about—sexual addiction. That made two of us.

Dr. Graham took a sip of his black coffee and cleared his throat. "There's something that's been bothering me about this whole thing, Zoe."

"What's that?" I asked, even though the whole damn situation was bothering me.

"You talked to Dr. Spencer about a lot of things dating back to childhood, such as sexual feelings and masturbation at a considerably young age."

I looked down at the blanket covering my legs. I was totally embarrassed. "I realize now that it wasn't normal."

"No, it wasn't, but what bothers me is *why* it happened. Do you have any thoughts on that subject?"

"No, none. Maybe I was just born that way."

"Anything's possible, Zoe, but I don't really think that's the case. I think something occurred in your childhood that started the whole chain of cause and effect."

I started laughing; he couldn't have been further off base. "That's ridiculous. Something like what?"

"Something traumatic maybe? Possible something that was sexually related? Something . . ."

I preempted the rest of his commentary. "Ummm, Dr. Graham, far be it from me to criticize you, but nothing like that ever happened to me. I had a very normal childhood, a childhood I remember extremely well."

"Are you sure about that, Zoe?"

"*I am positive!* The most traumatic thing that ever happened to me when I was young was the death of my father. I was in junior high, and I remember it like it was yesterday." Jason grasped my hand tighter; he knew talking about my father's death was very painful for me.

"Hmm, I see. Well, maybe something occurred that you don't even remember, Zoe. That does happen, you know."

"Not to me, Doc. Nothing happened, and I would most definitely remember if it did!" I was getting mad offended. He was insinuating I was too dumb to recall my own childhood. Plus, I didn't like what he was implying. I wondered if he was trying to say I was abused by my parents or something of that nature and hoped he wasn't. I would've hated to get up off the hospital bed and give him a beatdown.

Then Marcella jumped into it. "Zoe, are you really sure?"

"I'm *very* sure! What the hell is this? What are you two trying to insinuate?"

Marcella replied, "Zoe, to be honest, I was thinking the same thing before Leonard even brought it up. Why do you think you were so obsessed with sex at such a young age?"

"Hell if I know!"

Jason sensed I was about to go off the deep end. "Zoe, calm down, Boo. It's all good, and everything's going to be fine." I clenched my teeth and listened to my husband.

Dr. Graham took the conversation back over. "Zoe, have you ever considered being hypnotized?"

That's when I broke out in hysterical laughter. I stopped when I realized no one else found it funny. "No, never thought about it and would never do something so silly. There's no point to it, because *nothing happened!*"

My mother started squirming in her seat and then raised her hand as if she needed permission to speak. "Momma, you don't have to raise your hand. What is it?"

Everyone's attention turned toward her. "Are you

doctors saying that everything my baby has done might be attributed to something horrible from her childhood?"

I didn't even let them answer. "Momma, that's what they're saying, but it's all bull. You and I both know nothing ever happened to me as a child that could even halfway be considered sexually traumatic."

Marcella got up, went over to my mother, and sat on the wooden armrest of her chair. "Well, is Zoe right? Was her childhood free of such incidents?"

My mother stared at me and whispered, "Not exactly." Then her tears began to flow.

# chapter
## twenty-eight

Never in my life had I cursed my mother, but there's a first time for everything. "What the fuck are you talking about, Momma?"

She just kept crying, and Marcella was rubbing her back, so I turned toward Jason. "What the fuck is she talking about, Jason?"

He looked as dumbfounded as I did. "I have no idea, Boo!"

I wanted somebody, *anybody*, to make sense out of what I just heard. Confusion turned to terror as all kinds of shit starting running through my mind. Was I molested by my father as a baby? Another relative? "What the fuck is going on here?" I asked.

Dr. Graham swung into action, realizing he was about to lose control of the situation before anything could be resolved. He came over to the opposite side of the bed from where Jason was lying and patted me on my shoulder. "Calm down, Zoe. Just calm down, take a few deep breaths, and relax. It's all going to be alright."

I took my free hand and knocked his hand off my shoulder. "No, it's not going to be alright, because I don't know what the hell is going on! This shit isn't making any sense! How the hell could something have happened to me, and I don't even fuckin' remember it?"

"Zoe, maybe if you let me hypnotize you, we can all find out the answers."

I turned back to Jason, who looked more lost than I was. "Jason, I'm scared." He released my hand, put his arm around me, and held me tight.

Marcella was bent over my mother's chair, whispering in her ear, and I didn't appreciate the hush-hush going on over there at all. Enough of the secrets and lies! "Momma?"

Silence befell the room, and I could hear Marcella whisper the words, "Tell her."

"Yes, Momma, tell me!" Half of me wanted to know, and the other half wanted to crawl up in a hole somewhere with a pair of earplugs so I wouldn't find out a damn thing. Whatever it was had my mother crying, and it was obvious I wasn't going to like it.

She got up from her chair and came over to the bed. I reached out for her hand. She sat down on the edge of the bed so her hips were touching mine.

"Zoe, something did happen when you were younger. I don't know all of the details because you never really told me. Not me or your daddy. All I know is it happened."

She rubbed my hand rapidly like a mother trying to warm her toddler up outside in the dead cold of winter. "All what details, Momma? I'm so lost! So completely lost!"

"I know you are, darling. Something happened, and somehow you managed to bury it deep inside you. It was the reason we really moved to Atlanta from Dallas in the first place."

"Momma, you aren't making any sense." I kept looking from her to Jason and back, wishing someone would throw me a life jacket because I was sinking fast.

"You remember how we moved in the middle of the year and you were a transfer student and all of that?"

"Yes, of course I remember. Daddy got a job in Atlanta, and we had to move right away."

"Actually, your father accepted the job because we *needed* to move right away. We *needed* to get out of Dallas." She broke out into wails, but I couldn't cry. I was petrified.

"What happened to me in Dallas, Momma?" I sat up further on the bed, let go of her hand, and started shaking her. Not because I was angry with her, but because I wanted her to tell me the freakin' truth. "Momma, look at me. What happened to me in Dallas?"

Jason and the two doctors weren't saying a word. Then again, I guess there wasn't anything for them to say. They were just as confused as I was. "Zoe, baby, I don't know exactly what happened, but—"

"Yes?" I let go of her shoulders and clasped her hand. I started rubbing her hand like she was the toddler. "Go on, Momma!"

"One day, about a month into your fifth-grade year, you came running in the house crying, and your clothes were torn." My eyes bulged out of my head, and Jason put his arms around my waist to try to brace me for whatever was about to come. "You were late coming home from school, and I was worried. I called your father at work, but he told me to calm down. He figured since you walked home from school everyday, you probably just stopped over a friend's house for a little while, lost track of time, and forgot to call."

I didn't remember any of the things she was talking about, and that made me ten times more scared than I was before. "What happened to me on my way home from school, Momma?"

She grabbed both of my cheeks in her frail hands and pulled my face all the way up to hers until our noses were touching. Her tears were rolling down both of our cheeks, not just her own. "I don't know, baby! You would never tell me. You would never tell your daddy or anyone else. All I know is I felt so bad that I didn't call the police or try to look for you, even if you were only an hour late. I should've realized you wouldn't go someplace and not call. I should've realized something was wrong, and I've lived with this guilt ever since."

I threw my arms around her, almost yanking the IV needle clear out of my arm to do it. "It's not your fault, Momma. It's not your fault!"

Jason gathered both of us in his arms. "It's going to be okay."

My tears started flowing, and I wasn't sure they would ever stop. Never had I been so utterly confused. I thought the whole situation with Quinton, Tyson, and Diamond was fucked up. Now, I come to find out something happened to me when I was just a child that was the underlying cause of it all. "I had to have told you something. What did I say?"

She started shaking her head, and Marcella came over with a tissue for her to blow her nose out. Once she completed the task and wiped some of the tears from her face, she replied to my question. "Zoe, the only thing you ever said to us was, 'Why did they hurt me?' "

"Why did who hurt me?"

*"I DON'T KNOW!"* She was screaming, and Dr. Ferguson bumrushed into the room to make sure everything was under control. Dr. Graham politely showed him to the door and assured him things were fine. He reluctantly departed.

"You came home crying with your clothes ripped, and I called your father back immediately, telling him to get off work and come home. You kept saying, 'Why did they hurt me?' over and over again, but you wouldn't say anything else. It was like you were in a trance or something. My immediate thought was that you'd been raped, but you wouldn't even let me touch you down there. Every time I tried, you pushed my hands away violently, so we took you to the emergency room. They had to strap you down to examine you. You put up one hell of a fight, kicking and screaming and—"

"And? Was I raped?" I clamped my eyes shut and waited for her to reply, hoping the answer would be one I could live with. Jason was crying too by that point, but they were silent tears. No noise was coming out with them.

"According to the doctors, you were *not* raped. They did say you were bruised down there and red. No penetration though. They were very definite about that point."

Dr. Graham jumped in and asked, "So Zoe was the victim of some type of sexual trauma other than rape?"

"Yes, Doctor, she was." For the next few minutes, my mother and I were tightly intertwined in a bear hug, consumed in wails. All of those years, she'd blamed herself for something beyond her control. "Doctor, I wish I could be of more help, but after a couple of weeks, Zoe started acting real strange. She acted like nothing even happened, and when my husband and I broached the subject, she gave us the impression she didn't remember. He and I decided the best thing was to just move away and leave it all behind—especially since we never discovered who harmed her. In our eyes, that meant they could do it again. We didn't trust anyone after that. Everyone was suspect."

Jason, who loves my mother almost as much as he loves me and wanted to comfort her, told her, "It's not your fault. Zoe's going to get through this. We're all going to get through this together."

My mother glanced up at Jason. "She almost lost you because of this. She almost lost everything. My baby even tried to kill herself, and all these years I thought she was faking about not remembering. I thought she pretended not to know just so she wouldn't have to talk about it. When she fell in love with you, I was so happy, because I was scared she would never lead a normal life and find someone who truly loved her."

"I do love Zoe. You know that more than anyone."

"Yes, I do know that, and I'm so very grateful that she has you, Jason."

I was totally unnerved. "For the life of me, I don't remember any of this."

Marcella walked closer to the bed, looking wearier than I had ever seen her. I guess we were all emotionally drained. "There is a way you can bring it all back, Zoe. There is a way to find out what really happened to you that day. Let Leonard hypnotize you. We'll all be here for you, and when you wake up, this entire nightmare will be over."

"Will it be over, or will it be worse?" I pondered out loud.

"Let him do it, Zoe." My mother made her request. "I

wish I could fill in all the missing pieces, but I can't. You have to do it."

Finally, I looked at Jason to get his opinion. He kissed me on the forehead and then whispered in my ear, "I love you, and this is forever."

Dr. Graham was standing at the end of the bed, waiting for my decision. "Well, Doc, I guess if I ever want this to end, I have no choice. So, bring it on."

It all happened so quickly. I remember his pocket watch swinging back and forth in his hand like a pendulum, and I remember him softly speaking some words to me. He didn't say the comical shit I was expecting like, "You're getting very, very sleepy!"

Whatever he did say worked like a charm, because the next thing I knew, I was ass out.

# chapter twenty-nine

I have no idea how long I was in a hypnotic trance, but after I woke up and took a quick survey of everyone's face, I wanted to be put the hell back out. Dr. Graham looked as if he had just been on the receiving end of an enema. Marcella looked as if she'd just found out she had fibroids the size of grapefruits. My mother looked like hell froze the fuck over, and poor Jason looked like someone had just chopped his dick clear off. All of them had their mouths hanging wide open, and if a bumblebee had been in the room, it could've stung each and every one of them on the tongue before they even saw it coming.

I couldn't decide which one of them to ask, so I directed it to the love of my life. "Jason, is it that bad?"

He broke out of his own hypnotic trance, pressed his thumb under my chin, and gave me a kiss on the lips. "It's bad, Zoe, but nothing we can't fix together."

I didn't say another word. You could have heard a pin

drop until Dr. Graham broke the silence in the room. "Umm, Zoe, the reason we're all shocked is, as it turns out, there wasn't just one incident in your past that came out during hypnosis. There were two."

*"Two? What the hell?"* I looked at my mother, but she could be of absolutely no help to me. She was too busy fighting demons of her own, thinking I was perpetrating a fraud all of those years by pretending nothing happened when the entire time to me it never did happen. All of it had been suppressed somewhere in the deep, dark crevices of my mind.

Marcella finally spoke up. "Zoe, the best way to clear all this up is by letting you hear it in your own words." She pressed the rewind button on her mini cassette recorder and asked, "Ready?"

Jason still had his arm around me, and I laid my head on his chest, hoping I would still have an ounce of sanity left after I listened to the tape. "Ready!"

When the tape first began playing, it was about what I expected. Dr. Graham was asking me a bunch of questions about my life, gradually working his way back to my childhood. We got back to when I first moved to Atlanta, across the street from Jason, and of course I mentioned the ass-whupping I gave him, since it was one of my most shining moments.

Then he asked me about Dallas, and with the mere mention of the city's name, my voice on the tape changed to one even I would've been hard pressed to recognize if I didn't already know it was me. As an adult, if you were to tape record yourself and then play it back, you would probably wonder to yourself, "Is that me?"

That was the case. It was me—the younger version of

Zoe, who had disappeared once puberty set in. I hadn't heard the voice in almost two decades. My mother and Jason recognized the voice of my youth. I heard my mother on the tape, sounding frantic. "Zoe? Doctor, what's happening? That's what she sounded like when she was a little girl!"

Dr. Graham responded, "I'm sure it is, but please calm down. That's the Zoe we need to talk to."

I heard Jason jump in, yelling at the top of his lungs, "Dr. Graham, if this is something that's going to damage my wife in any way, I want this shit to stop right now!"

"Jason, it won't harm her. It'll make her better. She has to get the secrets out, or they'll destroy her, like they almost did this past year."

Jason's voice lowered, but I could hear him breathing heavily, and I could sense the fear. "Okay, Doctor. As long as you understand I don't want my wife harmed."

"I understand, Jason, and I promise you that won't happen."

Everyone fell silent, allowing Dr. Graham to continue. He asked me several questions about my early childhood. I was amazed, listening to the tape, that I even knew the answers to half of them. We all sat there while the little Zoe described her first day at kindergarten and how she won the biggest smile contest in the schoolyard, how most of the other kids had cried when their mothers left them there but not her, and that's why she won the lollipop. Then, little Zoe talked about how much she liked finger-painting and playing ring-around-the-rosy, she talked about the various dolls she had as a child, including the black Barbie I still have stowed in the attic to give Kayla Michelle once she's old enough to appreciate it. She talked about how she used to make new dresses for it from old pieces of clothing around the house and how she always wanted to be an official member of the Mickey Mouse Club. She talked about the piggyback rides her daddy used to give to her and how he used to sit her on his lap in his recliner and read Dr. Seuss books to her. Little Zoe talked about how much she used to hate carrots and how she would sneakily feed them to her dog, Spot, underneath the dining room table, and how he got ran over by a car when she was in the third grade.

Then, the first incident came to light. Since the incidents seemed to be running in chronological order from kindergarten on up, it appeared to have happened sometime during my third-grade year—an incident my parents obviously never knew about, one that preceded the incident in the fifth grade that ultimately made my parents relocate to another state.

I still had my head resting on Jason's chest. I tried to let his heartbeat comfort me while I listened to the little Zoe on the tape begin to recall the story. "It was a holiday. I'm not sure which one, but it was one where everyone has cookouts and get-togethers at someone's house so all the kids can play. Momma and Daddy took me to one of Momma's friends' houses from college. Her name was Lisa or Laura or something else with an *L*."

I heard my mother call out, "It was Laura! Oh my goodness, did Laura do something to her?"

Marcella said, "Shhhhhhh!"

Little Zoe continued. "All of the kids were out in the street playing when Momma's friend came out and told her daughter to walk down the street to get her son from his girlfriend's house because it was time to eat. She told her daughter to take me with her so I could go for a walk too, since we were about the same age."

My mother interrupted again. "Laura did have two

kids. A daughter, Monique, who was about a year older than Zoe, and a son who was in his teens."

Dr. Graham told my mother to calm down. "That's great, but let her finish, and then you can fill in the blank spots, okay? We've got to let her tell it in her own way!"

"When we got down to the other house, there were a bunch of teenagers hanging around outside. When we went indoors to get him, there were people everywhere, and music was playing. I don't think any adults were home, and they were having a party. The girl I went down there with asked where her brother was, and some boy told her he was upstairs in the bedroom."

"She led me by the hand up the stairs. There were a bunch of teenagers in the hallway up there too. One of the doors was open, and everyone was standing around laughing and saying things I knew they shouldn't be saying because they were all *very bad* things. We went into the bedroom, and her brother was on the bed doing all sorts of things with this girl. His girlfriend, I guess."

I heard my mother scream out on the tape, *"Oh, God no!"* Marcella asked her if she wanted to leave the room and wait out in the hall, but she refused and got quiet again so I could move on.

"They were both naked, and he had his mouth on one of her breastesses." I sat there, shaking my head at the words I was hearing, but it couldn't be more realistic. When I was little, I mispronounced several words, and *breasts* was one of them. I distinctly remember calling them *breastesses* instead. "He was on top of her and he had his dang-a-lang inside her coochie-coo. When his sister told him to stop, he wouldn't. He yelled at us to go away. Everyone started laughing and knocking us around."

I took a deep, restorative breath on the tape. It was

almost as if I feared what I was about to say next. "I ran
out the room and left the little girl there I had come with,
but when I got to the bottom of the stairs, there was this
boy there, an older boy, and he smelled like liquor. He
wouldn't let me get past him, and he pushed me down on
the steps and starting putting his hands all over me. I was
so scared."

My mother's sobs were easily recognizable on the
tape, but she didn't say anything else. "He put his hand
underneath my T-shirt and started squeezing me, and it
hurt. He tried to pull my shorts off, but I started kicking
and screaming just like Daddy told me to do if someone
ever tried to hurt me. All of the other kids were standing
there laughing, but then one boy helped me. He pulled
the bad boy off me, and then he hit him.

"They started fighting right there in the living room,
and everyone was yelling and screaming at them. I ran
out of the front door and down the street to find Momma
and Daddy. I got back down to the house, and when
Momma asked me why I was crying, I made up a lie because I didn't want to tell her the bad thing I had done. I
told her the little girl had been mean to me and told me to
go back to her house because she didn't want to play with
me anymore."

My mother spoke up then, happy she could actually
finally be of some help. "It was Memorial Day! Laura and
her husband had a cookout, and she did send them to go
get her son because the food was ready. When Zoe came
back alone, she was crying, but she didn't tell me what
really happened. I just thought she and the little girl had
gotten into a petty spat because neither of them had
taken a nap and it was late in the afternoon. The other
kids returned to the house about fifteen minutes after
Zoe, but no one said anything. They were all acting nor-

mal by then, and Zoe and the little girl started playing together again."

Dr. Graham reassured Momma that she was tremendously helpful and then told her we were going to move
on. "Zoe, let's jump ahead a bit. Do you remember your
fifth-grade year? The beginning of the year, when you
were still in school in Dallas?"

"Yes, I do remember it!" My voice instantly changed
on the tape. It was still one of my youth, but it was somehow more mature than the previous one. It also seemed
more tense and uneasy than its predecessor. "I remember
everything, including the day they hurt me."

Jason yelled out, "Who hurt you?"

"Jason," Marcella jumped in. "Calm down. I know
this is hard on you."

"Hell, yeah, this is hard on me! My wife was molested, and you all are sitting around here acting like she's
talking about a ballerina recital or something!"

"Jason, we're all just trying to get to the bottom of
this, but we can't do that if you're going to overreact
throughout the whole process." As an afterthought, she
asked, "Do you want to go out in the hallway? I'll go with
you."

"Hell no, I'm not going out in the hallway! I'm sitting
right here on this bed with my arms around my wife!"

"Okay, Jason, that's your prerogative."

"Damn right, it is!"

My mother asked him to please calm down. Dr. Graham
then asked me, "What happened the day they hurt you,
Zoe? What happened on your way home from school?"

"I was supposed to walk home from school with Dena
and Kelly, but I had to stay behind for a few minutes to
complete a science worksheet I forgot to do for homework
the night before. When Mrs. Thompson finally let me

leave, Dena and Kelly were both gone, and so was everybody else. The schoolyard was completely deserted, so I started to walk home alone. I was angry they didn't wait for me, but I knew they were trying to rush home to see *Fat Albert and the Kids*, our favorite cartoon. Besides, it wasn't their fault I forgot about my homework.

"I got to the walkway at the edge of the playground that led out to the street and noticed there was a group of boys standing at the end of it. The walkway was surrounded by woods, and I was scared to walk down it because one of the boys, Chucky, had teased me earlier that day at school. He said I had big breastesses for a girl my age and asked could he feel them. I told him no.

"The only other way for me to get home was to take the long way around, and I knew Momma would be worried if I did that because I was already late. I walked down the wooded path, and when I got closer to them, they all started whispering and laughing. It was Chucky and his younger brother, Steven, and some other boys I'd seen around school, but I didn't know their names.

"They started pushing me back and forth between them and calling me bad names. Suddenly, Chucky and Steven dragged me into the woods. I dropped my bookbag on the walkway and tried to yell out, but one of them, I can't remember which one, put his hand over my mouth so I couldn't. They told me they would kill my momma and daddy if I didn't do what they said.

"They did some really bad things to me. They pulled my panties off from under my skirt and yanked my shirt up over my head so I couldn't see. Then Chucky pulled his pants down and was rubbing his private part up against mine. It hurt me, and the rocks and branches underneath me hurt. I felt his tongue on my chest, and he bit me on my breastesses, and it was very painful!

"Chucky got angry at me about something. He kept yelling, 'I can't get it in!' He picked up a stick and started hitting me all over, like it was all my fault. He hit me in my privates, and I started screaming. That's when I heard a woman's voice call out, 'Who's over there?'

"Chucky and Steven jumped up off the ground and ran away. So did the other boys. Somehow, I managed to stand up. I was crying and covered with their sweat and spit. I pulled my shirt down and put my panties back on. I had cuts and bruises all over my body. Then, this lady came running into the woods. I'd never seen her before. She asked me was I alright. I just cried and ran away. I found my bookbag and ran home to Momma, but I couldn't tell her what happened. I thought it was my fault. After all, I had done a bad thing by not doing my homework."

There was a brief moment of silence and then I started screaming, "Why did they hurt me? Why did they hurt me, Momma? Why did they hurt me?"

That's when Dr. Graham clapped and woke me up out of the trance, only to see them all sitting around with their mouths hung open. After I heard the tape, my mouth was the one hanging open and waiting for the imaginary bee to strike.

"Dr. Graham, I don't remember any of that! None of it whatsoever! Was it real?"

"Yes, Zoe, it was very real. That was you—well, the younger version of you—relating the whole thing."

I knew he was right, but I still didn't want to face the facts. I just laid my head back on Jason's chest and wished none of it was happening. Marcella was full of energy and appeared to have gotten a second wind from somewhere. "This is a great start, Zoe! At least now we know what the underlying reasons are for your behavior and attitude toward sex!"

I looked at her in amazement. "Have you lost your fuckin' mind? What does any of that have to do with me cheating on Jason?"

I felt bad as soon as the words left my lips. It was bad enough everyone in the room knew I cheated on him without me making public announcements. "It has everything to do with it. Dr. Graham and I will explain it all to you a little later. But first—"

"First what?" I noticed her eyes were not on me. They were directed toward Jason.

"Jason, listening to Zoe throughout our therapy sessions and hearing about your apparent fear of sexual openness has caused me a great deal of concern. Dr. Graham and I discussed it, and he tends to agree with me."

Dr. Graham was standing there, nodding his assent. Marcella continued, "Do you think if we hypnotized you, we might be able to figure out why that is?"

Jason gasped, and I sat up to stare him in the eyes. He looked back at me with his beautiful hazel eyes before he whispered, "That won't be necessary, Marcella. I already know why."

# chapter
## thirty

"Could you all please leave Zoe and me alone for a few minutes?" Jason was on the edge, and I was falling over the cliff with him. I wasn't sure I could handle everything in one day after all. I would've preferred another day of everyone kicking my ass and getting hit by a delivery van.

"Jason—" Marcella looked almost as worried as I did. "It would really be better if this all came out with Dr. Graham and I present."

Jason snapped back, "*NO!* I need to talk to Zoe alone. At least at first, and then you can all come back in here. Once she knows everything, I don't give a damn who finds out!"

I convinced them to go get something to eat, since lunchtime had rolled around. If Jason didn't want them there, that's the way it was going to be. They all filed out of the room, headed to see what nasty yet nutritional food the hospital cafeteria was dishing up that day. My mother, being her typical indulgent self, asked Jason and I if we wanted her to bring us something to eat, but we refused. The last thing either one of us needed was heartburn or a gas attack on top of everything else.

Jason and I were left in the room alone. I wasn't about to pressure him or rush him to tell me, so I ran my fingers through his hair and waited. "Zoe."

"Yes, baby?"

"Let me say straight up this has nothing to do with cheating. I already told you I would never do that to you, and I haven't!"

"I know you wouldn't, baby. I believe you." I gave him a kiss on his forehead and then raised his hand up to my lips so I could kiss it too. Then I asked him what I'm sure was on everyone's mind. "Were you sexually abused when we were kids, Jason?"

He jumped up off the hospital bad. "No, hell no! I was never sexually abused or molested!"

I turned on my side to face him while he stood by the window, looking out. "Then what is it, baby? You know you can tell me anything."

"Zoe, I don't know how to say this, so I'm just going to come on out with it full force. Willard and Lorraine Reynard are not my real parents."

He kept looking at the window, at nothing in particular. I started feenin' for some Prozac or something. "Ummm, Jason, what do you mean, they're not your real parents?"

He glanced at me and then walked back over to the bed. He didn't lie back down beside me, but pulled up one of the chairs and sat down in it. "I should've told you all this a long time ago. You had a right to know. After all, you're my wife, Zoe."

"I had a right to know?"

He took a deep breath. "I'm going to make a long story short. I was adopted when I was six. Before then, I lived in an orphanage and was a ward of the state."

I couldn't talk, so I just reached for his hand and held it tight. "My mother, the real one, was a prostitute. I remember her clearly. She left me on the stoop of the orphanage when I was only four, telling me she couldn't take care of me anymore and had to go away."

He started crying. I reached over on the metal table beside the bed and retrieved one of the rough, generic-brand tissues the hospital provided. I dried his tears for him. "Did something happen to you in the orphanage, Jason?"

"No, Zoe! Actually, the nuns at the orphanage were very nice. That's why I believe in Catholicism, even though we don't attend church that often." I made a mental note to myself to start taking my kids to church—we all needed some religion. "I'm not an expert on orphanages, but I've heard horrible stories about some of them. The one I lived in was nothing like that."

"Okay, I believe you. Did the Reynards do something to you?" I was sitting there calling my in-laws the Reynards like they were strangers instead of my husband's parents. Every thing was getting weirder by the minute. "Did they hurt you, baby?"

"No! Of course, there were times when they would get angry at me and throw it up in my face. Telling me I should be thankful they even took me in when they could've just left me there. They didn't really mean any of those things, though. It was all said out of anger and frustration."

I was missing something! "Baby, if you weren't abused and nothing happened at the orphanage, then why are you so afraid to touch me?"

He hesitated, and there was no sound in the room for a few minutes. "Like I said, my real mother was a prostitute. Her name was Delilah. At least, that's what she called herself."

"Did Delilah hurt you?"

"Not physically!"

"Then what?"

"She used to leave me alone in this nasty, dank, rat-infested motel room for hours at a time. One time, she left me alone for several days. I lost count after the fifth one, and I was so scared she wasn't ever coming back."

He started sobbing uncontrollably. I pulled him back on the bed with me, whether he wanted me to or not. I pushed his head down on my chest, hoping my heartbeat would somehow comfort him for a change. "She would go out and sell her ass to support her heroin addiction. She spent all of her money on drugs and hardly ever bought me anything to eat. I was so skinny and frail, my ribs were showing and my cheeks were sunken in.

"I would have to watch her shoot the poison into her arms and legs, and sometimes, when she didn't have anyplace else to take them, she would bring her tricks back to the motel with her. She would make me sit in a corner and watch when she was high and thought it was funny, or tell me to go sleep in the bathtub while they were there."

"Oh, baby! I'm so sorry!" I just kept kissing his forehead over and over again because I didn't know what else to do.

"Looking back on it now, I realize Delilah did me a favor by abandoning me outside that orphanage. I was real sick when the nuns found me. I had pneumonia and an extremely high fever. While I was upset my mother would leave me like that, she actually saved my life, because I was literally hours away from dying. The nuns rushed me to the emergency room, and they were able to pack me in ice and bring down the fever before I had a seizure."

He slid up more on the bed so that we were face-to-face and kissed me gently on the lips. "Besides, if she hadn't left me there, Willard and Lorraine never could've adopted me, and I never would've found you!"

"Well, you did find me. Somehow, in this big old fucked-up world, we found each other."

"Yes, we did, Boo!"

"This is meant to be, Jason, and we *are* going to get through all of this. Together!"

He grinned at me. "Like the lemon to the lime! Like the bumble to the bee!"

# chapter thirty-one

About an hour later, Marcella, Dr. Graham, and Momma all came traipsing back into the room. It couldn't have possibly taken them that long to eat that nasty hospital food. I pictured them sitting around a table in the cafeteria, downing coffee like springwater and worrying about what the hell Jason and I were upstairs talking about. I was glad they took so long because it gave me a chance to calm Jason down some.

He was having trouble telling them all the things about his past, so I did it for him. It was like shock therapy, part two: they were all once again sitting there with their mouths hanging wide open. When I finished, I added my whole take on the situation, trying to add a little humor. "Pretty wild, huh? Two fucked-up-in-the-head people end up married with children? You think they'll make a TV sitcom about us? *The Crazy Bunch?*"

"Zoe, that's not funny!" Obviously, my mother was not in a humorous mood.

Dr. Graham decided he couldn't possibly do anything to rectify the situation in the span of one day and left the room to call his office from the nurses' station. Upon his return, he informed us he would be staying for an additional three days. Marcella was happier about his extended stay than anyone. She thought she was going to be left to sort out the entire mess alone.

"Dr. Graham, Jason's tired, and so am I. Since you're staying, could we possibly continue this tomorrow?" I looked at Jason, who was half asleep. "We're both emotionally drained, and it would be great if we got a fresh start in the morning!"

Much to my surprise, he agreed. "I'm kind of emotionally drained myself. I think we all are, and besides, Marcella and I really need to put our heads together to figure out the best way to go about treatment."

"Sounds like a winner, Doc!"

I bid Dr. Graham and Marcella adieu, and they went off to rack their brains. "Momma, please drive Jason home."

Jason sat up, acting offended I would even make such a suggestion. "Zoe, I'm not leaving. I'm not going anywhere."

"Yes, you are. You're going to go home, kiss our kids goodnight for me, and take instant photos of them for me to add to my collection tomorrow."

"But your mother can handle the kids. Plus, the sitter is there."

"Not the point." Jason was tired and stressed, and I didn't want him spending the night in the hospital with me. I knew the kids stood a better chance of cheering him up, and I really needed some time alone to sort through all the secrets revealed from my own past, as well as his. "Do it for me, Boo. Please!"

After throwing a bit of a temper tantrum, he finally agreed to leave with my mother, making me promise to take my ass straight to sleep. I assured him that wouldn't be a problem at all.


Sure enough, I fell into a deep sleep and would've slept most of the evening if I didn't sense someone standing over me. I woke up, and when I opened my eyes, Diamond was hovering over me, gripping a pillow in both hands.

I was taken completely aback. "What the hell are you doing?"

She sat the pillow down on the end of the bed by my feet. "You were sleeping so peacefully. I was just going to put another pillow underneath your head because you looked like your neck was twisted."

"Oh!" I rubbed my eyes. I still wasn't fully awake, and they were sore from all of the crying. "Diamond, what are you doing here?"

She plopped down in one of the chairs. "I called your office and told your secretary I was an old college buddy of yours. After a little prodding, she told me about the accident and where I could find you."

I rolled my eyes; I couldn't believe Shane would be stupid enough to give out information like that. Not to mention that I never went to college. Her doofus behind should've known better. "Well, what do you want?"

"I wanted to check on you and make sure you're alright. What else? By the way, I didn't tell Quinton you were in the hospital. He would've asked me a bunch of questions about how I knew so much. I figured you wouldn't want that." She sucked her teeth, taking advantage of the fact she had something to throw up in my face at will. Even though Jason knew I had experimented with a female, I would've been totally ashamed if Quinton ever found out about Diamond. She damn well knew it too.

"You figured right!" She was irritating me, and it was beginning to show in my voice.

"Why are you being so nasty with me?" She was about to go into a bitch mode. It was a scene I wasn't even trying to have.

"No reason. Sorry if I snapped at you." I wasn't sorry. I just wanted her to hurry up and leave.

"I came here to see you, out of the goodness of my heart, and this is the shit I get?"

She went there! "Look, I never asked you to come see me. I never asked you for jack shit, and I would appreciate it if you would get the hell out so I can get some rest."

"You weren't saying that shit when I was sucking on your pussy!" She smirked, realizing that statement would piss me off.

"I never asked you to do that either! You insisted, and it's not like I returned the favor!"

She got up from the chair, fired up. "You're right! I did insist, as you put it, but the bottom line is you let me do it, and you would probably let me do it again!"

"Don't flatter yourself, trick! I let you do it because, at the time, I didn't give a shit who was sucking on this pussy as long as it was getting sucked! I don't want you! I'm not attracted to you! I don't even fuckin' like you!"

"You're such a bitch!"

"Oooooooh, that really hurts," I chided. "Bitch is my middle name. Haven't you heard? I've been called that so many times lately, having your little scrawny ass call me that doesn't even faze me!"

"Well, everyone can't be wrong! Maybe you should try to figure out why you're getting called out of your name, Zoe!"

"Maybe you should drop dead! You're a waste of fuckin' oxygen anyway!"

"I should've—" Diamond looked away from me and started eyeing the pillow at the end of the bed.

"You should've what?" She didn't say anything, and I was looking around the room for something to clock her with. I picked up the hard metal telephone and flung it at her. She managed to duck, but not before it caught her in the shoulder blade. She yelped out in pain.

The nurse came flying into the room. "What's going on in here? Mrs. Reynard, are you okay?"

"I'm fine, but could you call hospital security and tell them to get this skank ho out of my room!"

"Don't worry, bitch! I'm leaving!" She headed for the door.

"Good! Don't let the door hit you in the ass on the way out!"

Diamond left, and the nurse was standing there, looking silly. "Umm, could you hand the phone back over here, please?"

She picked it up, handed it to me, and uttered, "Sure."

"Thanks." She was still standing there and didn't look like she had any immediate plans to vacate. "If you don't mind, I'd like to get some rest now."

"Okay, just let us know if you need anything." She forced a smile and then made a quick exit, probably hoping the crazed bitch in Room 301 would hurry up and get her release papers.

Before I drifted back to sleep, I looked at the crumpled pillow at the foot of the bed and wondered if Diamond was really demented enough to try to smother me. In my mind echoed the word, "Naw!"

●   ●   ●

As promised, Dr. Graham and Marcella got down to business. For the next few days they counseled Jason and I together and apart. They made us read several books. I thought I was back in high school for a minute—homework assignments and shit—but it was all worth it.

Jason and I spent hours on end talking about everything that had happened throughout our years together—what went right and what went wrong, where we wanted our marriage to go in the future.

Jason learned to deal with his mother's prostitution and the things he witnessed and was subjected to at such a young, vulnerable age. Marcella made us do touching experiments, which made Jason understand that there was nothing nasty or vulgar about having oral sex with his own wife. He confessed that he had always wanted to try it but could never bring himself to let me. As it turns out, while I was hiding sex toys all over the house, Jason was hiding porn flicks that he watched on a regular basis when no one was around. He said he mostly watched them on the TV/VCR combination in his drawing room, and a lot of times when I thought he was down there sweating over blueprints, he was watching the movies and jacking off. I was stunned—I couldn't even picture Jason jacking off. I wondered was he better at masturbating than me because lawd knows, I thought I was a pro.

His main fear about letting go sexually was allowing me to take control of the situation. We talked it over, and I promised him I would never do anything to make him feel uncomfortable. We could do it at his own pace, gradually adding new things and positions as time went on.

As for me, that was another story altogether. Dr. Graham requested I make arrangements to come down to his clinic in Florida for a couple of weeks. I told him I would, but not right away. I had been away from my home and my kids for too long. Being back there was the best therapy for me at the time. Marcella agreed to work with me three times a week. I told them that just knowing what happened to me when I was younger had helped me tremendously. All along, I never understood why I became so obsessed with sex at a young age. I felt I could put those incidents behind me and move on. As long as I had Jason, I could move mountains.

Jason and I wouldn't be able to recover from everything overnight, because it didn't happen overnight. We made a pact that whatever it took and no matter how long it took, we were both in it to win. Everyone seemed satisfied with the results of the first three days of therapy, and Dr. Graham headed back to Florida, making sure Jason and I had both his home and office telephone numbers.

That night, I called Dr. Ferguson at home. I looked his digits up in the phone book and told him if he didn't let my ass out the hospital the next day, I would become the patient from hell, screaming all day and all night disrupting the other patients. He laughed, even though I don't think he found my intrusion into his quality time at home humorous, and agreed to release me the next day.

# chapter thirty-two

The next afternoon Dr. Ferguson finally released me with a clean bill of health. I was so excited about going back home, I didn't know what I wanted to do first when I got there. Well, second, because kissing and hugging the hell out of my kids was definitely the first thing on my agenda. Taking a long, hot bubble bath and raiding the fridge for some decent food were tied for second place.

Jason arrived at exactly two to pick me up. While they wheeled me down to the nurses' station to get my release papers, I got suspicious about why Jason was smiling so damn much, so I asked him why.

He laughed and told me, "No reason! Just happy my Boo is coming home. Things haven't been the same without you."

I lifted one of my feet up off the slat on the wheelchair and kicked him lightly in the shin. "Things better not be the same. I'm not easily replaceable, you know?"

He knelt down and kissed me. "You could never be replaced."

Once we were in the car headed home, we talked about what the children did and did not know about the recent turn of events. The twins were too young to understand anything more than the mere fact I had been away for a couple of weeks. Peter, on the other hand, was another matter altogether. Jason comforted me and assured me Peter didn't know anything except I had been involved in some sort of automobile accident and had to stay in the hospital until I got better.

I was relieved. Jason held my hand the rest of the way home, telling me all the wonderful things he had planned out for our future, including buying some land up in the mountains, designing and building us a summer home. That brought a smile to my face; a summer home had always been a big dream of mine. It wasn't that we couldn't afford it. It was just the lack of free time that had held us back. Jason told me he was willing to talk to his partners and make the time to do it if I was willing to do the same. I quickly replied, "Not a problem, Boo. Now's the time to do everything we've ever dreamed of. Life is too short not to."

When we walked in the front door, I was taken aback when I saw the Welcome Home banner, flowers, and balloons everywhere. Momma was standing there in the middle of the great room and had all three kids dressed alike in stonewashed jeans and red T-shirts. Kayla had an abundance of red ribbons in her hair. She reminded me of a picture of me when I was a little girl in a similar outfit.

Peter was kneeling on the floor, and he had his arms around a Dalmatian puppy with a huge red ribbon attached to his flea collar. "Mommy, this is Spot! Daddy bought him for you!"

I rushed over and hugged all my kids and even the

dog. Jason had gone out and found me a dog just like the one that I used to feed my vegetables to under the dining room table as a child, who had been hit by a car. He obviously had a little help from my mother: the puppy was the spitting image of the original Spot and could've passed for his grandchild.

Peter helped Jason fire up the gas grill on the patio while I played some board games with the twins. They showed me some of the new toys their grandmother had gotten them while I was away. My mother loved to spoil her grandkids and went overboard in my absence, knowing I couldn't object.

The phone rang. I yelled out to Jason, "I'll get it!" I picked up the cordless and said, "Hello." There was no answer, but I could hear someone breathing heavily on the other end. "Hello? Who's there?" Still nothing but the breathing, and then the line went dead.

Jason came into the house to retrieve the steaks and chicken breasts for the grill. "Who was it, baby?"

I shrugged my shoulders and whispered, "Wrong number, I guess."

We had a lovely picnic on the screened-in porch. Afterward, my mother went home to spend some time with her husband, who I'm sure felt mad neglected by that time. Jason decided to keep the live-in sitter a while longer. He had given her two weeks' notice, figuring that would be enough time for me to get readjusted to family life.

The sitter's name was Angelique, and she was a college student, working on her undergraduate degree in business administration. She lived in a dorm on campus but took on the live-in position eagerly when she saw the ad on the bulletin board in the student union. She was a sweet girl and talked me half to death when she showed up at the house after her afternoon classes. She told me all about growing up in Maryland and how she chose to go to college in Atlanta because she wanted a change of pace and a break from her overbearing parents.

At about seven, I asked Angelique to start getting the kids ready for bed. I went up to the master bathroom to drown myself in a hot bath, since that was the only thing left to do after hugging my kids and feeding my face with some real food.

Jason joined me a few minutes later, locking the bedroom door and putting on some jazz before stripping down and getting in the tub. Something about the way he held me confirmed what I had hoped. The therapy sessions were working, and things would be way different.

He got behind me in the tub and kissed my ears and neck while he took a loofah sponge and squeezed warm water all over my shoulders and breasts. He put the sponge down and grabbed them, one in each hand, rubbing his thumbs over my erect nipples.

I turned to the side so that I was sitting on his thigh in the tub, instead of between his legs, and we started tongue-kissing. He grabbed me by the back of the neck and pulled my mouth closer into his so that his tongue could go deeper into my mouth. I broke the kiss just long enough to turn completely around and straddle my legs over his thighs. I locked my arms around his neck, and our kissing continued for several moments.

Jason caressed my ass cheeks, one in each hand, and I started to grind my pussy onto his dick in the warm water, letting the shaft of it rub between my thighs. He let go of one of my ass cheeks and cupped one of my breasts in his hand, bringing it up to his mouth and sucking on my nipple. I reached into the water and held his dick steady so I could climb on top of it. I sat down on it slowly. My ribs were still a bit sore from the accident, but there was no way I was missing out on the opportunity to *really* make love to Jason. I had wanted to for so long, he was finally receptive to my advances, and I was in heaven.

Jason let me ride his dick. For the first time, he let me be in the position of control—the one thing he had feared all those years—and from what I could tell and the sweet things he whispered to me, he loved every minute of it. We stayed in the tub until the water was almost freezing, and then he got out to get some towels. We dried each other off, and he carried me to our bed, where we made love again—another first. In all our years together, Jason had never been with me intimately more than once a night. He was no longer a two-minute brother either. In fact, he made love to me longer and harder than anyone. He surprised the hell out of me when he told me to turn over and then entered me from behind. I came all over the place, and he came all up in me.

I chided him, "Damn, Jason! I hope you didn't get me pregnant!"

He chuckled. "Well, don't worry about it if I did. I still have the umpire mask in the garage."

We were about to drift off to sleep, with smiles on both of our faces, when the phone rang. I glanced over at the clock and realized it was well after midnight. I reached for the phone, since it was on my side of the bed. "Hello."

Nothing. "Hello!"

All I got back in reply was a single word. The caller's voice was being distorted by a rag or something held over the phone. The single word was "Bitch!"

They hung up, and so did I. Jason sat up in the bed, "Who was that calling here so late?"

"I don't know, baby. Let's just get some sleep." He lay back down, and I sought comfort by laying my head on his chest and listening to his heartbeat like I always did when I was scared. I had trouble falling asleep, wondering who the hell it could've been and if it was the same person who'd called earlier, breathing heavily on the phone. I came to the conclusion it could have only been one of two people; Dempsey or Tyson. Both of their whereabouts were still a mystery. I made a mental note to myself to make a stop on my way home from work the next day. I would go buy me a freakin' gun.

As planned, I returned to work the very next day after my release from the hospital. It was very important for me to try to pick up all of the pieces of my life and move on. The last thing Marcella told me before my release was, "Always remember the past is a guiding post and not a hitching post. You must learn from your mistakes and keep on going."

She was right, and that was exactly what I intended to do. Everyone was very pleasant to me upon my return to the office, and most had the common sense and decency not to pry into my personal life. A couple of the water-cooler gossipmongers tried to get in my business, but I set them straight fast. I brazenly reminded them I was the head of the company; they were employees and needed to remember where their bread and butter came from. After that, they didn't have a damn thing to say and expeditiously returned to work.

I called Jason at his office to see if he wanted to have lunch with me. His secretary, Allison, got bitchy with me on the phone. She had been cool with me until she called me a tramp that day, and I wasn't about to forget that. I wanted her ass gone, and after a few conversations with

Jason, I was sure she would be, if for no other reason than to make me happy. She was probably one of the women that had been throwing pussy at him all along. The hoochie had to go—no if, ands, or buts. I wasn't about to be subjected to her attitude every time I called or went by my husband's firm.

I was disappointed when Jason told me he couldn't make lunch due to a business appointment, but I fully understood. He had missed a lot of time at work and needed to play catch-up too. I bought a sub, some chips, and a bottled soda and ended up having lunch on a bench in front of the mural Quinton painted at the MARTA station. I missed Quinton, but not in a sexual way. He had always been kind to me, and I missed his friendship—a friendship we could never have because of the sexual nature of our relationship. His loft was directly across the street. I glanced up at it a few times while I picked at my food. I ended up feeding most of it to the birds that gathered around once they picked up on the scent of the turkey breast and cheese on the freshly baked sub roll.

When I got up to head back to the office, I almost strayed over to his building, but I caught myself. I didn't want to run the risk of bumping into Diamond, the anorexic beanpole bitch who had the audacity to come up in my hospital room with all her drama. Besides, even with Diamond out of the mix, I still couldn't see Quinton. Not then. Not ever again. Quinton had lived through too many people walking out of his life already. Since I knew I couldn't walk back into it for good, I decided to leave well enough alone. I already realized I would have to make up one last lie once the Civic Center had its grand opening. I couldn't possibly attend, even though Jason was the head architect. While Jason knew about the affairs, he didn't know Quinton was one of them, and I wanted to keep it that way. There was no way I would disrespect Jason like that, letting him find out he had actually had lunch with my lover, and there was no way I could handle it. It was bad enough he had to confront Tyson. He didn't need an altercation with Quinton. In another lifetime, Quinton and I could have been the best of friends, but not in this one.

Ironically, I now understood why Quinton's mother killed herself. It took me trying to do the same thing to comprehend it. When I thought I had lost Jason, my life was over, and I didn't want to go on. I guess she felt the same way when her husband left her and the kids for a white woman. Luckily, my attempt had failed and I had been given a second chance. I wasn't about to mess it up. I had a renewed desire and appreciation of life. I also had a new Jason.

"Goodnight, everyone! Have a good evening and see you tomorrow!" I rushed through the outer offices and pressed the button for the elevator to go down to the garage. I was in a hurry, since I was trying to make it to the gun shop about ten blocks away before they closed up for the day.

I didn't tell Jason about being called a bitch on the phone the night before. I was determined not to let anything upset our happy home. I didn't want to get the police involved either. They were already looking for both Tyson and Dempsey, so there was really nothing more for them to do. On the flip side of the coin, I wasn't a fucking fool either. I realized getting a gun was not a bad idea, just in case. I would have to take special precautions to make sure it was never left anywhere one of the children could get hold of it.

When I got off the elevator, I spotted my Mercedes,

twice vandalized but still hanging in there with me, parked in my assigned space at the far end of the row. There was a security guard stationed in the garage twenty-four hours a day, seven days a week. I didn't see him anywhere, but that was no big surprise, since they only had one guard to patrol all three levels.

I got about halfway to my car when I heard some footsteps echoing from somewhere in the garage; I couldn't pin down the exact location. I don't know what made me call out—it was almost rush hour, and it could easily have been another building occupant on their way to their car or the guard. I had a very uneasy feeling, though, so I called out, "Who's there?"

There was no response, and I suddenly realized I had stopped walking and was just standing there, frozen like a sitting duck. If there was indeed a maniac lurking in the garage, the last thing I needed to be doing was waiting for him to attack. I made a mad rush for my car, searching through my purse for my keys along the way. I had seen fifty million tapes on safety and yet didn't have my keys out before I entered the garage. I guess it's true what they say about leading a horse to water but not being able to make it drink.

I got to my car and still couldn't find my damn keys underneath all the other junk in my bag. I sat my brief-case down on the ground and put my purse up on the roof of the car so I could go through it at eye level. I finally found them and unlocked the door, flinging my purse onto the leather passenger seat. I turned around to get my briefcase, which was behind me on the ground, and came face to face with Dempsey.

"You looking for this, bitch?" He had my briefcase in his hands. Before my reflexes could spring into action, he hit me square in the face with it, knocking me back against the open driver's-side door. The door caught me in the ribs, and I bent over in pain. He threw the briefcase on the ground. "Now, what you got to say, bitch? Where's your fucking switchblade this time?"

He hit me across the face with his fist, and I could see my blood splatter on my light gray business suit. The left side of my face went numb. I wanted to scream, but no sounds would come out. "You told the fucking police about me, and now your ass is going to pay!"

Dempsey grabbed me around the neck, and that's when I decided to fight back. I remembered how Tyson had choked me and knew if I didn't do something fast, he would cut off my airway and I wouldn't have a prayer. I pulled every ounce of strength left in me together and kneed him in the groin. He squealed out in pain and let go of my neck so he could hold onto his privates.

My first instinct was to get in the car and drive off, run over his crazed ass if need be, but then I realized he had knocked the keys out my hand at some point during the struggle. I did a quick search and couldn't find them; they must have landed somewhere underneath my car or the one parked beside it. Before Dempsey could fully regain his composure, I took his head in both my hands and kneed him in the face while he was still bent over. I had seen that move in dozens of karate flicks, and I must have administered it right because he started yelping like a dog.

I hauled ass, and my vocal cords finally kicked back in as the polluted city air pumped in and out of my lungs. I had lost one shoe already and paused long enough to pull the other leather pump off. I ran uphill, to the next level of the garage, which was also the entry level, hoping to locate the guard in his booth. I could hear Dempsey yelling out behind me, but if he was running, he didn't seem to be closing in on me and I was sure as shit happy about that. I reached the guard booth, screaming, "Help me!"

To my dismay, it was empty. I turned around, getting ready to keep hauling ass out onto the busy street to seek help from one of the many strangers on the sidewalk. Instead, I ran straight into the guard, who was coming out the small, and probably filthy, bathroom hidden behind a steel door marked for employees only. He was zipping up his fly when I started screaming at him to call the police. He radioed for help right away, but by the time the police arrived and cornered off the building and garage, Dempsey was nowhere to be found.

# chapter
## thirty-three

                     By the time Jason arrived, my nerves were completely shot. I couldn't believe, after all the other shit I had been through, I now had to deal with Dempsey stalking my ass. I began to wonder if the madness would ever end. The homicide detectives assigned to Brina's murder case were called to the scene, and I finally learned their names—Wilson and Reed. They told me their names and gave me their cards the night of the murder, of course, but I was too out of it and upset to even care.

    I told them about the two phone calls from the previous day. Jason looked at me with stunned disbelief that I had yet again not been completely truthful. I explained to him that I didn't want to ruin my first day back from the hospital and my first night with him since we started therapy, and told him I was on the way to the gun shop when the attack happened. He didn't appear satisfied with my explanation but didn't sweat the issue. He was just glad I was alive.

They already had an all-points bulletin out on Dempsey, so there wasn't much more they could do except offer me around-the-clock protection. After two near-death experiences from strangulation, once by Tyson and now by Dempsey, I gratefully accepted. My lips were swollen, and so was one of my eyes from the hits I took from the briefcase and Dempsey's fist. I absolutely refused to go to the hospital—I had just got out of that bitch, and there was no way I was going back. They handed me some pain medication, gave my ribs the once-over, and told Jason he could take me home as long as I promised to get plenty of rest and not overexert myself.

That night I told Jason about Tyson's attempt on my life. He said the doctors at the hospital asked him about some marks on my neck, but he assumed they were somehow from the accident. We mutually decided to stop talking about negative things. Two police officers were stationed out front in a patrol car, and the alarm system was on, so I felt perfectly safe.

I wanted to make love again more than anything in the world, but Jason was quick to inform me, "That would be considered overexerting yourself."

I was hoping he wasn't retreating back into his shell after the hellified night of sex we had the night before. I wasn't about to let that shit happen, beaten up and bruised or not. He didn't keep me guessing long. "Making love would *definitely* be too physically straining. However, there is something I can do to you that wouldn't fall into that category. Yet it would bring about the same end result."

I started laughing, and it made my ribs hurt for a moment. "Jason, what the hell are you talking about?"

"Hmmmm, I can show you better than I can tell you." And that's exactly what he did. My previously shy, sexually repressed husband got up from the bed to lock the door, even though the kids had been asleep for hours, and then wasted no time getting my black lace panties off.

"I thought you said we can't have sex, Boo?"

"We're not going to have sex. At least, not sexual intercourse." He started grinning, and I was still lost as a virgin in a whorehouse.

That is, until he spread my legs open and started sucking on my pussy. I was likely to faint. Jason was eating my pussy, and I couldn't hold in my surprise. "Jason, you're eating my pussy!"

He paused long enough to say, "Uh-huh, yes I am eating your pussy, and it's good too!"

He started eating me with more and more intensity. I think the mere thought of him going down on me made me cum the first two or three times, but it didn't stop there. My baby ate me like I was an all-you-can-eat-buffet, and I had orgasm on top of orgasm. He must have been trying to make up for lost time. At one point, I had to grab a hold of the headboard just to be able to hang in there with his tongue action.

I wanted to suck his dick so bad, and he told me it wouldn't have been a problem if my lips weren't so damn swollen and sore. I was madder at Dempsey for keeping me from sucking Jason's dick than trying to kill me. We fell asleep about 1 A.M. but a couple of hours later, a noise startled me awake. At first, I thought it might have been Angelique up late studying for some exams or something like that. I decided to play things safe and walked to the window facing the street to make sure the police were still out front. They were.

Since I was already up and about, I decided to go downstairs and make a pot of blackberry tea, another one of my favorites I missed while I was in the hospital. I loved to make a pot of tea, take it out on the screened-in porch on the back of the house, and listen to the birds and other animals rustling about. I made my tea and headed outside onto the porch. As soon as I opened the patio door, I smelled something cooking and wondered who the hell would be crazy enough to be grilling at that time of the morning.

That's when I noticed the smoke escaping from the air holes of our gas grill. *Something was cooking in my own backyard!* It was pure stupidity not to go get the cops or call for Jason, but I had to see for myself. Once I unlocked the porch door leading out into the yard itself, I noticed Spot was not on his chain, and his dog house was empty. I ran barefoot over the cobblestone patio and threw the hood of the grill up. Two seconds later, my screams woke up the whole damn neighborhood.


That shit did it! I told my mother to come get the kids and take them back to her house. I also asked Angelique to stay over at my mother's to help Momma and Aubrey out. She was a sweetheart and quickly agreed. Besides, I don't think she was too thrilled about staying at a house where people trespass in the backyard and grill the family pet anyway.

Jason and I refused to leave our home, especially not for the likes of Dempsey's bitch ass. I had one of the police officers escort me to a gun shop, where I purchased a .45-caliber handgun. They couldn't really take issue with it in light of the fact that the officers positioned out front had done absolutely nothing to prevent what happened to Spot.

We stayed in the house most of the time for the next few days. Since Jason had a drawing room, keeping up with his work was not that big of a deal. Allison came over with some papers he needed to sign, and the bitch had the nerve to come up in my house with an attitude. While she was waiting for Jason to come downstairs to the great room, I made it perfectly clear all of the commotion had nothing to do with an affair but with the murder of my best friend. She looked at me, rolled her eyes, and muttered, "Oh!"

I went the hell off. "You know what? I don't owe you an explanation in the first damn place, so just do your job, let Jason sign the papers, and then get the hell out my house!"

"Fine, then! I'll do that!" I wasn't going to say another word, but she went there. "One of these days, he's going to wise up and get him a *real* woman!"

"Bitch, please!" I got loud with her ass. "Let's get something straight! I've been with Jason since eighth grade and have known him even longer than that! His ass is not going anywhere! Don't believe me? Just ask him!"

She never got the opportunity, because he caught the tail end of our conversation and confirmed it. "Definitely not going anywhere!"

He got to the bottom of the steps, put his arm around my waist, and gave me a big, juicy kiss. Even with all the things stressing us, we were acting like newlyweds again. "Allison, where are the papers I need to sign?"

She handed him a manila folder. "Right here." He took them, signed them, and handed them back to her. About to leave, she muttered, "Good-bye."

"One more thing, Allison." She was almost to the door when she turned around to face Jason.

"Yes, Mr. Reynard?"

"Don't ever talk to my wife like that again, or you will have to find employment someplace else." He paused and then decided to drive the knife in deeper. "Without a recommendation from me, at that. Addressing Zoe in such a fashion is not professional, and it won't be tolerated. You understand?"

"Yes, I understand." She looked like she was about to cry when she went out of the door. I giggled with delight; that's what the bitch deserved.

I had my secretary bring all the important papers that couldn't wait over to the house for me as well. Fortunately, Shane and I had no beef, so her visits were pleasant. If anything, she was too concerned about my health and welfare. I appreciated it and gave her a bonus for working overtime and making the runs back and forth to the house.

The sex between Jason and I was nothing short of the bomb! The kids were gone, we were there in the house together around the clock, and we made good use of the time alone. Once the swelling went down around my mouth, I wasted no time putting my lips to his dick and going to work. In fact, you might say I got a bit obsessed. Jason had to almost put my ass on a dick-feeding schedule just so he could get any work done.

However, he loved performing oral sex just as much as I did. He became a little *over*attentive to exploring my pussy with his mouth. It was all good though! We took advantage of every possible moment. We fucked all over the house, like teenagers. We did all the freaky shit we didn't have the nerve to do when we were younger. We utilized everything from his drafting table and the kitchen countertop to the hearth of the fireplace and the top of the washing machine during the rinse cycle.

I was lying between Jason's legs on the couch and sucking his dick while he was watching the late, late news about a week after Dempsey's attack on my life when the top news report caught my attention. I heard the newscaster mention a shoot-out at a nightclub called the Zoo and stopped sucking Jason's dick so I could pay attention to the rest of the story. Apparently a scuffle had broken out over a woman, and a gun battle had ensued. "Jason, that's the club where Brina met Dempsey!" I exclaimed.

He whispered, "Really?" and tried to maneuver my head back down toward his dick so I could finish what I started. Shootings were so common that one at a club didn't impress him much.

I went back to sucking his dick and caught a rhythm, but I was still listening to the news. The reporter that was covering the scene live informed us that the police had confirmed three dead and seven injured. I thought to myself that one of the dead might be Dempsey, but decided I couldn't be that lucky; he wouldn't be stupid enough to go back there after I specifically told the police he hung out there.

Jason had just cum in my mouth when the phone rang. He answered and kept saying, "Yes!" over and over again. I looked up at him, with his juices still trickling down my chin and tried to judge what the call might be about from the expression on his face.

He replaced the phone back on the cradle. "That was Detective Wilson." I closed my eyes and prayed Jason was about to say what he ultimately did. "It's all over, Zoe! Dempsey's dead!"

# chapter thirty-four

It was such a relief to have it all behind us. I'm not the type to wish death on anyone, but I have to admit I wasn't the least bit upset when Dempsey was shot and killed at the Zoo. Personally, I felt a quick death, albeit a violent one, was too good for him after what he did to Brina. My only regret was that two other people died along with him, and one girl who was too young to be in the club in the first place, an innocent bystander who was shot in the spine, would never be able to walk again. I found out her name from Detective Wilson and which hospital she had been taken to. I went to visit her, since I could move about freely again. The police protection had been pulled, and it was great to be out and about, even if it meant getting thrown a bit off my dick-feeding schedule.

I took the girl, who was named Octavia, a dozen roses and a card. Her sister was there with her, and we all sat and talked like old friends for about an hour before I brought up the reason I was really there. I was hoping she wouldn't take it the wrong way. "Octavia, I know your health insurance covers all of your medical expenses, but I thought you might want someone to talk to about coping with your handicap."

Her voice was very weak, and her skin was flaccid and pale. "Someone like who?"

"I have a friend. Her name is Dr. Marcella Spencer, and she's a wonderful psychiatrist. I think she might be able to help you tremendously."

Her sister put her two cents in. I noticed she had quite a southern drawl. "We can't afford no head doctor."

"I would be willing to cover the costs." Both of them were shocked, and their mouths were hanging wide open. I guess good Samaritans went out with bell bottoms and the Afro.

Octavia cleared her throat. "Why would you be willing to do something like that for me? You don't even know me."

"The man who hurt you . . . well, one of them at least, also hurt me as well as my best friend. In fact, he killed her and ultimately tried to kill me."

They were utterly speechless. "Helping you would make me feel like I have undone some of the things he did wrong. Does that make any sense? Probably not."

I was on the brink of tears. So much had happened over the past few months that crying had become almost second nature to me. "Yes, it makes sense to me, and thanks, lady."

"The name is Zoe. Zoe Reynard, and thank you for accepting the help. Dr. Spencer helped me overcome something once, and she's still helping me. I'm sure she will help you too." I held the door open briefly as I was leaving, taking one last look at the young girl who would never walk, run, dance, drive a car, or make love again. "I'll have Dr. Spencer stop by tomorrow to set up a schedule with you."

She smiled at me, and I headed for my office to play catch-up.

For the next two months everything ran smoothly with my marriage, my business, and my relationship with my kids and my mother. Things had never been better. My business picked up considerably, probably because the CEO of the company was finally content with her own life and able to run everything in a more pleasant and efficient manner.

Angelique was back in her dorm, but still watched the kids for us when Jason and I went out on dates twice a week. We made that promise to one another and held to it faithfully. We spent two romantic evenings a week alone together away from the kids and household. It was during one of those romantic evenings that Jason surprised me with his master plan.

We were having dinner at a soul food restaurant when he told me he had rented a log cabin up in the mountains for us to have a weekend getaway. He suggested we drive up that Friday, which was three days away, and spend all day Saturday looking at land for sale to build our summer home. I told him it was on and then got up from my chair, sat on his lap and starting tonguing the hell out of him. The woman that owned the place came over and asked us to stop because there were children present. I replied, "Oops, my bad!" She had no idea what the hell that meant but was clearly relieved when I returned to my seat.

I dropped the kids off at Momma's house that Friday

afternoon. Jason had the Land Rover packed and ready to roll when I pulled up at home. We had a great drive up. It took us about two hours to get to the cabin, and I fell in love with it at first sight. It was nestled deep in the woods, a split-level with three bedrooms and two full baths. What I loved most was the huge fireplace. Jason headed right outside to get some wood so a fire would be up and going for dinnertime.

We had plenty of groceries. I went shopping the night before and purchased everything we would need for our romantic weekend getaway. I made baked chicken breasts with rice, green beans, and rolls for dinner. We ate on the bearskin rug by the fireplace. After we washed the dishes, we returned to the rug and made love for the remainder of the night.

Jason got up before me the next morning and prepared a huge breakfast. I didn't even know his ass could cook like that. My baby was just full of surprises! First, eating the pussy day in and day out and then, cooking me an actual meal.

We spent most of the daylight hours riding around in a Jeep Wrangler with Roscoe Carter, the one and only local real estate agent. He showed us every section of land up for sale in the county. Jason and I were both worn out by the time he dropped us back off at the cabin. I tried to call my mother to check on the kids but got the machine and left the number where we were, just in case she had misplaced it. I figured she and Aubrey had decided to take the kids to a late matinee or out for pizza.

"Boo!" Jason crept up behind me and grabbed me around the waist.

I pretended I was mad but loved his touches any way I could get them. "Jason, you scared the hell out of me! My nerves are wracked enough as it is!"

"Oh, come on, Zoe. We're here all alone. Who else would be grabbing you?"

"That's not the point!" I started to walk away, but he grabbed me and plopped down on the couch, pulling me down with him.

"You're still jumpy, aren't you?" He started kissing and sucking on my neck.

"Yes, I'm still a little perturbed by all of this."

"Well, don't be." He started unbuttoning my flannel shirt. "We're safe now, and the kids are safe. It's all over, baby!"

"If you say so."

"I *do* say so! Now, give me my tatas!"

I started giggling while he unfastened my bra and popped a breast in his mouth. After a few more moments of foreplay, all my fears disappeared and my sexual desires took their place.

We were in the bed, even though it was only about ten o'clock, when we heard a loud rapping at the door. Jason threw on a robe and went down stairs to see what the ruckus was about. "Who is it?"

"It's the county sheriff! Mr. Reynard?"

Jason opened the door. By that time, I was at the top of the steps wearing one of Jason's undershirts and a pair of panties. The sheriff came into the living room with one of his deputies right on his heels. "What's wrong, sheriff? What's this all about?"

"Mr. Reynard, we tried to call, but your phone seems to be off the hook." I looked around and saw that the phone on the end table beside the couch had been knocked over. I probably hit it with my foot accidentally when Jason picked me up and carried me off to bed.

"There's been some trouble back in Atlanta, and a detective—" He pulled out a small notepad and flipped the cover open. "Detective Wilson asked me to drive up here and inform you about what happened."

I came down the steps in a state of panic. "What happened? Did something happen to the kids? My mother? Were they in an accident?"

"No, ma'am. Nothing like that. In fact, he wanted me to tell you that your mother, stepfather, and the kids are all in protective custody and have been transported to a safe house. Your mother is the one who told us how to find you."

Jason yelled it out before I could. *"A safe house?"*

"Yes, sir. Do you know an Allison Morton?"

"Yes, I know Allison. She's my personal secretary at my architectural firm."

"Well—" He took off his hat, scratched his head, and then replaced it. "Not anymore, she isn't." The deputy walked around the couch, sat the phone back upright, and made sure it was operational.

"What do you mean, not anymore?"

"She was found murdered a couple of hours ago in her apartment in southwest Atlanta."

"Murdered?" I went running up to him. I had called Allison a bitch, told her to get the hell out my house, threatened to have Jason fire her, and now she was dead. One thing I knew for sure, and that was her death was somehow attributed to me, or the sheriff wouldn't have been there, and my kids wouldn't have been in protective custody. "What happened to her?"

"From what I understand, she was severely mutilated, ma'am. Look here, here's the number to the station house back in Atlanta." He ripped the piece of paper out of his pad and handed it to me. "The best thing would be for you to call Detective Wilson. He's waiting to hear from either you or me anyway. He can clear this whole thing up a whole lot better than I can."

The sheriff was obviously a man who didn't want such evil in his county. A couple of good ole boys driving drunk or getting in a bar brawl seemed more his speed. Even *talking* about murder made the hairs on his neck stand up.

I called Detective Wilson. He yanked the phone up on the first ring after I was connected to his desk. "Mrs. Reynard, I have some extremely disturbing news for you."

Jason was sitting beside me on the couch and holding my hand while the sheriff and his deputy paced back and forth, seemingly more nervous than anyone else. "So I heard, Detective. What exactly happened to Allison, and what does this have to do with me?"

"Ms. Morton was discovered by her boyfriend a few hours ago. He went over there and used his key to gain entry when she failed to show up for a date. He found her hanging from the piping in her basement apartment." He paused before adding, "She'd been gutted like a pig."

"*WHAT?*" I started trembling, and Jason kept asking me what the detective was saying. I told him I would fill him in when I got off the phone. "Detective, that's horrible, but her death might not have anything to do with me at all! Dempsey's dead, remember?"

"Yes, I remember. I identified that bastard's body at the crime scene myself."

"So what makes you think this involves me?" I was on the edge of my seat, nervously awaiting his answer.

"Hmm, I guess you could say the writing on the wall was a dead giveaway."

"What writing on the wall?" There was a silence on the other end of the phone. "Detective?"

"It was written in Ms. Morton's blood on her bedroom wall."

"What was?"

"Zoe is one dead bitch!"

# chapter
## thirty-five

I dropped the phone into Jason's lap and froze in place. "Zoe, what's wrong with you? You look as pale as a ghost!"

I wouldn't answer him! I couldn't answer! I was in the middle of having a fucking heart attack! "Detective Wilson, this is Jason Reynard. What happened to my secretary?"

Jason listened intently while the detective repeated everything he had just told me, adding he thought the most likely motive for the murder was gaining information about our whereabouts. Apparently, whoever killed Allison tortured her first and didn't put her out of her misery until she told them what they wanted to know. That explained a hell of a lot and made my guilt grow ten times over. Someone was after me, and poor Allison had died because of it. She was tortured because she tried to protect Jason and me. Her death on my hands was something I would have to deal with for years to come—if I lived that long.

I was in a trance until I heard Jason, still on the phone, blurt out, "A gold earring? What about it?"

I yanked the phone out of his hand. "Detective, what about a gold earring?"

"It just seemed out of place. It was found on top of the comforter on her bed, but she wasn't wearing the match. We couldn't find the other one in her jewelry box or anywhere else in the apartment. It may show up after forensics goes through the place more carefully, but the way it was positioned, I figured the assailant may have lost it during a struggle." He paused and then added, "It's probably nothing. Just a hunch."

I could have just asked him what type of gold earring it was, but I decided to play a hunch of my own. "Detective, was the earring a gold cross?"

I could hear his breathing become exasperated over the phone. "How did you know it was a gold cross?" I didn't answer him. My mind was playing back memories in my mind. "Mrs. Reynard?"

"Tyson wears a gold cross earring in his left ear!"


Unfuckenbelievable! How could everyone I ever ran across in my entire life turn out to be a loony? Dempsey, Diamond, Tyson—all fucking crazy. I began to wonder if the old saying, "You are what you attract," was written specifically for me. Maybe I was the maniac, and all the others were just following my lead.

All that time the police had assumed Tyson had fled jurisdiction to another state to avoid doing time for his parole violation, and I figured the same. When he tried to strangle me that day in Quinton's hallway, I figured it to be a one-shot deal, caused by a fleeting moment of anger.

I had chalked the incident with him and Jason up to the same. Never in a million years would I have thought Tyson was capable of such madness.

The sheriff informed us we had two choices. There was really no place for us to go stay that side of the county line at that time of night, so we could either stay where we were and have him and his deputy keep watch outside or we could bunker down for the night at the Sheriff's Department. I opted for the first choice, and so did Jason. No way was I trying to spend the night sleeping on a hard cot in a cell.

The two officers, who I affectionately nicknamed Andy and Barney, took up a post out in their car in front of the cabin about midnight. I refilled both of their thermoses with hot coffee, and they took turns relieving themselves in the downstairs bathroom before heading out into the cool March night air.

Jason and I took our asses to bed, and for the first time since my release from the hospital, nothing sexual happened before we drifted off to sleep. We were both stressed the hell out and worried about our kids being in a safe house that sounded like something for people in the witness protection program. I didn't like it, any of it, and I desperately wanted it to all end. So many times I thought the shit was over, but each problem resolved seemed to bring about an even bigger one. Now Tyson was after my ass. Shame on it all!

I fell asleep thinking about the fight between Dusty and me that day in the parking lot of the garage where Tyson worked, and how she ripped the gold cross earring out of his ear, causing it to bleed, when he pulled her off me. The same earring I used to take into my mouth and suck on, along with his earlobe, while he was fucking the

ZANE

shit out of me in his apartment, and the same earring they had found in Allison's apartment after he "gutted her like a pig," to quote Detective Wilson.

Jason and I were both in a deep sleep when glass shattered somewhere downstairs. We both jumped up. I picked up the phone beside the bed, but the line was dead. Jason covered my mouth, muffling my screams, and whispered in my ear, "Zoe, don't say a word. Just listen to me and do exactly what I say."

I nodded and listened while he instructed me on what to do. Jason helped me climb out the top-floor window, and I jumped down onto the ground below. My ribs, still damaged from the accident and Dempsey slamming them up against the car door, hurt like all hell when I landed, but at that point, I really didn't give a damn about the pain. I had to make it to the police car to let them know Tyson was in the house.

I was about five yards from the sheriff's car when I realized something was terribly wrong—deadly wrong. The sheriff's arm was hanging limply out of the driver's-side window. When I got closer, I saw his eyes in the moonlight, and I knew right off the bat they were the eyes of a dead man. There was a small bullet hole in his forehead, and his deputy had his head on the senior officer's shoulder. If I didn't know any better, I would have thought he was napping. Andy and Barney were both dead, and Jason was alone in the house with Tyson—Tyson, who had a gun and was blowing people away with it.

I opened the driver's-side door, and the sheriff fell halfway out the car. I reached over him and yanked on the part of the police radio you speak into. It came to me too easily, and once I had it in my hand, I discovered why.

The cord had been cut. Calling for help on the radio was out of the question. I felt all over for the guns they both wore on their hips earlier that evening. They were nowhere in sight. They could have been anywhere—tossed in the bushes, or taken by Tyson. I didn't have time to search, and my stupid ass had left my gun at my office, figuring the whole ordeal was over and done with. I had to get to Jason! I had to save my baby! Too many people had paid the ultimate price, and my husband wasn't going to be one of them. Even if it meant laying down my own life to save his.

I snuck around to the back so I could look in through the rear windows of the cabin. I couldn't see anything at first, but then I spotted Jason sprawled on the kitchen floor, unconscious. There was no blood, so I didn't think he had been shot. I had to find out.

The patio door was ajar and missing a pane. That was obviously the glass we heard breaking. For once in my life, I wasn't afraid. I was sick of all the bullshit; if Tyson wanted to kill me, he was going to have a hell of a time doing it, because I had no intention of going out without a struggle. I went in and looked around the downstairs living area. It was dark in the living room. I didn't sense or hear any movement. I made my way over to Jason and tried to wake him up to no avail. He had a nasty knot on the back of his head, and I figured Tyson must have cold-cocked him with the butt of the gun. For the life of me, I couldn't figure out why he hadn't killed Jason like the cops, but I was happy as all hell he didn't.

Suddenly I heard some footsteps coming down the stairs. I let Jason's head down gently before sneaking off to conceal myself in the darkness of the living room.

"Where's that bitch wife of yours?" Jason started to regain consciousness. A swift kick to the chest cavity made him wake all the way up. "Where is she?"

Jason didn't answer. He just looked up off the floor with fear and pain in his eyes.

"Come on out, Zoe, my love! Snookums! I have something I want to give to you, a present!"

Jason started to blurt out a question. "Aren't you—?"

"Yes, I am. I'm also the man who's been fucking the shit out of your wife. Well, at least one of the men she's been fucking."

Jason muttered the word, "Bastard." All he got in return was another violent kick, but this time to the leg. I wanted to rush over to him, but I needed to think things through clearly. I simply couldn't believe my eyes.

"Zoe's such a whore, Jason. Don't you realize that?"

Jason spit on his assailant's shoes, and I noticed blood coming out along with his saliva.

"I thought for sure you would leave her. Kick her ass out of the house. That way she could have been with me. We could have been together forever, Jason."

Jason's temper started to flare up. "If Zoe's such a whore, as you put it, why would you even want to be with her?"

"Don't get smart with me, Jason!" Another kick to his chest. "Don't *ever* take that tone with me! The only reason you're still breathing is because I need you to get to her! I know the skank bitch won't show her face unless it's to save your pathetic ass!"

"Zoe loves me and only me!" Jason exclaimed. "She always has!"

"How sweet! Not that it's going to matter much a few minutes from now."

I saw Jason about to get kicked again, and I couldn't

maintain my composure one more second. I screamed out, "Quinton!"

Quinton swung around to face the living room. I could see him squinting to make out my shadow. "Zoe, my love!" He reached out his arms. "Come to Poppa, baby!"

"What are you doing here, Quinton?" I asked as I walked into their view. Jason was frantically trying to wave me away, silently telling me to run. There wasn't a chance in hell of me doing that. I looked back at Quinton. "You killed Allison, didn't you?"

Quinton grinned at me like he thought the question was humorous. "A man's gotta do what a man's gotta do!"

I was dazed and confused. Part of me still didn't want to deal with what was going on. I was prepared to face off with Tyson, but not Quinton.

"But, but, but why?" I stuttered. "Why are you doing this?"

Quinton held up his gun and scratched his temple. "Gee, I dunno, Zoe. Maybe something just snapped."

I noticed the gun had a silencer on it. No wonder Jason and I didn't hear the gunshots when Andy and Barney were killed.

"Yeah, that's it," he continued. "Temporary insanity brought on by falling in love with a trifling-ass bitch!"

I struggled to find some words. "But, but we thought Tyson—"

He interrupted me before I could finish. "Ingenious, wasn't it?" he boasted, waving the gun around in the air. "Planting the earring and everything? I knew the police would pick up on that, and if they didn't, you would."

He gave me a devilish grin. "Setting up Tyson as the fall guy was perfect. Not that he gives a shit!"

"How did you—?" I hesitated and thought back to

the confrontation in Quinton's hallway. I clearly remembered that Tyson wasn't wearing the earring because Dusty had ripped it out in the parking lot. "The day Tyson came to your place, he wasn't wearing it."

"Uh-uh-uh-uh-uh," Quinton chuckled, shaking the index finger of his free hand like he was scolding a toddler. "Correction! The *first* time he came to my place he wasn't wearing it."

"What do you mean by that?"

Quinton ignored my question. "Now that I've had a couple of months to reflect back on it, Zoe, I really should have let him kill your bitch ass then. The stupidest thing I've ever done was prying his fingers off your neck."

Now I was starting to get pissed. How dare he come off at me like that? I realized I needed to stay calm because Quinton was there for one reason and one reason only—to kill me. However, when he made his last statement, I threw tact out the damn window. I walked within two feet of him and slapped him in the face. "Then why didn't you, you bastard? You fuckin' piece of shit!"

Quinton rubbed his cheek. I started to try to grab the gun, but I didn't want to risk Jason getting shot. I didn't care what happened to me at that point. I probably deserved it anyway.

"Aw, come on, Zoe," Quinton chided. "No need to be rude. Let's not make this situation any uglier than it already is." He pushed me down on the floor next to Jason. "Why don't you just have a seat down there with your man? Cool your heels off."

Quinton was really sick! I thought back to all the passionate afternoons and evenings we spent together. He was so romantic, so giving of himself. To think, all along he was a psychopath.

"As I was saying before you so rudely interrupted me,

Zoe. Tyson didn't have on the cross earring the first time, but he did the second."

I glared up at him, trying to make some sense out of what he was saying. "The second?"

"Can you believe that piece of shit came banging on my door, demanding I leave you alone?" Quinton asked, enraged.

I was beginning to get a sick feeling in the pit of my stomach. If Quinton was crazy enough to kill Allison and two police officers, what would keep him from killing Tyson? "And what did you say to him?"

"Aw, nothing much," Quinton quickly replied. "I sat there for a few minutes, listening to him profess his undying love for you. I told him he really needed to be telling all of his bullshit to Jason. He said he already had and told me about their punk-ass fight."

Jason yelled out, "You're the punk, mutha fucka!"

Before I could stop him, Quinton kicked Jason in the head. "I beg to differ with you, Jason! You're the biggest punk of all! You married the queen bitch and bred babies with her!"

I cradled Jason's head in my lap and looked around for a weapon, anything I could use to defend us. I was willing to die, and I would have begged Quinton to get it over with if Jason was safe and in the clear. I couldn't let Jason pay the ultimate price for my sins. I just couldn't. Our kids needed at least one of us to survive.

Quinton was pointing the gun at Jason's head. I desperately needed to change the subject, so I asked him, "What did you do to Tyson?"

Quinton started laughing, guffawing even. He went over and leaned on the counter in hysterics. I was just glad he stopped pointing the gun. "You want to know what I did to him? I'll be glad to tell you. I killed his ass!"

I prayed the whole nightmare would go away.

"I killed his ass and buried him in the train yard right along with my brother, my sister, and Diamond!"

"Train yard? Diamond?" I just knew I had to be hearing things.

"Yes, Zoe." Quinton came back over and knelt down in front of us. "You remember the first time I fucked you, Zoe? In the train yard? Guess what? We did it right on top of the graves I dug for my brother and sister fifteen years ago."

I was in shock. "You killed your brother and sister?"

"Among other people," he answered calmly. "As for Diamond, I know what you did with her, Zoe." I looked away in shame. "I know what you did, and she paid the ultimate price for your pussy too. Just like Tyson."

He ran his fingers through my hair, grabbed my face, and tried to force his tongue in my mouth. I refused it.

He stood back up. "I hate to borrow that old cliché, but if I can't have you, nobody will."

Jason tried to push his way up off the floor, using his hand to no avail. His eyelids were fluttering and he was barely conscious.

"Enough of this!" Quinton exclaimed. "Come to me, Zoe!"

I hated to let go of Jason but I had to try something, and there was nothing on the floor that would help out my cause. I placed Jason's head on the floor and slowly got up. "Quinton, I have an idea. If you really want us to be together, why don't we just leave? I'll go anywhere you want to go. Just don't hurt Jason, okay?"

"How admirable, Zoe." He looked me up and down like he was pondering my offer. "However, I don't believe shit you're saying."

"I'm telling the truth."

"Truth?" He started laughing again. "You don't know the meaning of the damn word."

Quinton suddenly grabbed my arm and flung me against the kitchen counter, making me hit my ribs against the overhang. I screamed out in pain. He walked up behind me and pressed himself up against my back. "Oh, did I hurt you?" he asked, pulling back the hair out of my face so he could see my profile. "I didn't mean to hurt you, baby."

I asked a logical question. "If you don't want to hurt me, why are you here?"

He took a deep sigh. "Because I'm confused, Zoe. Part of me wants to wring your little neck, but the other part of me wants to carry you away someplace and *make* you love me."

I didn't reply. I just stood frozen in place while he started licking all over the back of my neck.

"Maybe if I fuck you right here, right now, in front of Jason, I might be able to figure out the solution to my bitch problem. You think?"

"You're sick," I blurted out, searching the countertop for something to hit him with. Since the cabin was a rental, most of the countertop was cleared off.

He swung me around to face him. "I'm sick? What about you?"

"Okay, we're both sick," I readily admitted. "But Jason has nothing to do with this. Let him go," I pleaded. "For the sake of my kids."

For a brief second, I thought I saw a tear forming in Quinton's left eye.

"Please, Quinton! You remember what it was like to grow up in a home without parents! Look at what it did to you!"

"Shut up, Zoe!" Quinton punched me in the face. "Shut the fuck up!"

Before I could react to the punch, he started ripping off my clothes. He lifted me up on the counter and hit me again in the face until I had no choice but to succumb to his advances.

I shut my eyes because I didn't want to see what I knew would be next. I heard him unzipping his pants, and then he entered me roughly. I laid there in fear while he had his way with me. The mere fact that he was fucking me with Jason in the room made me want to crawl up in a hole and die. I just wanted the whole thing to be over with. I began to think about all the things I would never get to do, including watching my kids grow up.

I opened my eyes when Quinton dropped the gun on the counter so he could grab my hips and push himself deeper into me. I tried to gauge whether it was within my reach and stretched my fingers out in a useless effort.

Quinton noticed what I was doing and chuckled, "Forget it! Not a chance! Just fuck me, Zoe! Fuck me hard!"

I wouldn't move my hips, and that made him even more irate. "Fuck me, dammit!"

I clamped my eyes shut again and prayed for it to end. That's when I heard the crack, like a walnut being opened with a nutcracker.

Before I could see what was happening, Quinton was suddenly no longer inside me.

"Who's the punk now? Who's the punk now, you fuckin' bastard?" Jason exclaimed, beating Quinton on the head ferociously with the butt of the gun.

By the time I managed to get down off the counter, Jason was on top of Quinton on the floor, still beating the shit out of him. A handful of Quinton's teeth were scattered on the floor, and his face was so bloody it was almost unrecognizable.

I tried to pull Jason off him. "Jason, that's enough!" He kept beating him, and I was afraid he would kill him. "That's enough, Jason!" I reiterated, pleading with him not to take a life. "Death is too good for him! Let the police handle him!"

Jason finally stopped hitting him and tossed the gun aside. I got down on my knees and hugged him tightly. He started crying and he wasn't alone.

I kissed him all over the face. "I love you, Jason!"

"I love you too, Zoe," he whispered. "This is forever."

"Always has been! Always will be!"

# epilogue

They found more than a dozen bodies buried in shallow graves in the train yard where Quinton painted his first mural—the mural of the perfect family he wished he had.

Along with Tyson and Diamond, they also identified the bodies of Quinton's brother and sister using dental records they obtained from a court order. Two additional bodies are believed to be those of his father and stepmother. Quinton admitted to killing them on the one-year anniversary of his mother's suicide.

Quinton is permanently confined in the criminally insane ward of St. Elizabeth's Hospital. They are still trying to get him to reveal the identities of his other victims, but he refuses. However, all of the remaining victims are believed to have been young females.

"My name is Zoe, and I am addicted to sex!"

I was attending my first Sexual Addiction meeting,

and I decided to waste no time telling the whole room my dilemma. Marcella told me I could just sit back, watch, and observe the first few times until I felt comfortable enough to speak. I jumped right in with my testimonial, though. Hiding things and keeping secrets had caused enough damage in my life, and never again would I allow them to overpower me.

Marcella had located the addiction group through a local Atlanta hospital. I still planned to spend a couple of weeks in Florida with Dr. Graham in the summer, but attending local meetings with other people suffering from the same illness as myself was a start. Surveying the room, I was surprised to see so many faces. Even stranger was how normal they all appeared to be. They came from all walks of life—from accountants and housewives to lawyers and college students. While I was not happy to find out so many others shared the same problem, it felt good to know I was not alone.

Jason was outside in the waiting area with Marcella. He was dying to come in with me, but I reassured him I could handle it alone. Things between him and I were improving every day, and our lovemaking was nothing short of awesome. I always knew he was the man for me, and my love for him had never been, and will never be, more profound.

I gave my testimonial to the group. I told them how my life had been turned upside down because of incidents in my childhood. I explained that nothing and no one had been what they seemed. I told them my life had transformed into a web of lies and deceit filled with people who all had their own secrets and mental issues to deal with. I described how I was stalked and almost murdered. Finally, I explained how it all came to a horrible end in the mountains a week before the meeting.

I made it through the session and listened to a few of the others relate their depressing stories and enlightening recovery experiences. Then I went back out in the hall and kissed Marcella good-bye, promising her we would do that gurl thing real soon—go shopping or take in dinner and a play together, just like Brina and I used to do. Jason reached out for my hand, and we headed out the hospital exit, on our way to rebuild our lives together free of chaos and lies.